Smoke and Steel

Benton Security Services, Volume 2

Christine D. Shuck

Published by Christine D. Shuck, 2021.

SMOKE AND STEEL

First edition. April 15, 2021.

Written by Christine D. Shuck.

A Voice from the Past

Present Day...

"I love you, Jack." The feel of her body nestled in the crook of his arm; her soft lips captured in his was so real. Then the ratchet of a nail gun in the distance jarred him from his sleep. His dream evaporated, leaving behind an emptiness that compressed his heart. It had been five years, plenty of time to get over her, but the dream brought her back as if it were yesterday.

The sun barely lit the horizon, creating a hazy, indistinct glow through the large picture window on the far side of the room. The latest wildfire, now contained, had trapped pockets of haze in the valley. A decent wind and heavy rain would deal with that, but Mother Nature seemed loathe to cooperate. The air quality remained poor, and it had forced Jack to take his daily run on the treadmill inside of the house, where the air filters cleaned the quality of the air and smoke didn't burn his throat or redden his eyes.

He sighed, stretched, and glanced over at the other side of the bed. He didn't miss Tiana, and he certainly wasn't dreaming about her. A few months of fun, but not worth the pettiness or bullshit mind games. He wanted something more than just a pretty body by his side. He rubbed his hand through his hair, thinking of Kaylee. The softness of her skin, how she had felt in his arms; it hung in the air, an echo maybe of what he had, what he still wanted.

Maybe I want too much.

In all of his life, only one woman had captured his heart. And she was half a continent away and likely had forgotten all about him.

1

Jack sat up, tossed the covers off, and stood. The haze was driving him nuts, the traffic and plastic people in L.A. were driving him even more so. He wanted to leave, escape somewhere, anywhere, and get away for a while. This was a thought that was quickly discarded as more basic needs made themselves known.

In the opulent marble bathroom filled with stark colors of black, white, and gray, he stood in front of the mirror, inspecting his reflection. His hair was no longer black, streaked with just a little gray. It was now predominantly gray, with only a few jet-black strands remaining. His father had been the same. The color gone by the age of forty, even if his face had remained youthful. He wondered briefly how Dad would have looked today, would the gray have turned white?

Jack ran his hand over his stubble and then slipped on his running shorts. He'd get in a run, then shower and shave before Azule showed up. He shook his head thinking about his assistant; she had been worrying over some investments that had tanked and wanted to talk to him first thing about Benton Security Services. Azule's mind was a formidable weapon, one she wielded daily. He wasn't sure what she was going to say, but he knew something was bothering her. It had been for weeks, and he dreaded the conversation they would have in a few hours.

He left his suite and made his way down the curving staircase to the main level. He pressed a panel in the wall and walked through it to another set of stairs leading down to the basement. The door closed, soft and silent behind him. The basement comprised a completely self-sufficient living space which included three bedrooms, each with their own bathroom, that shared a kitchenette, and a large living area. They had converted one bedroom into a workout room, moving it from its original location in the living area. There were no windows, nothing to even show that the house above had a basement. And it had served its purpose well a time or two in the past. It was literally a panic *suite*, rather than a panic room.

Malcolm was still asleep, not that he expected anything different. His baby brother rarely varied from his routine, and that meant that he had at least an hour before Malcolm would emerge from the furthest bedroom and head upstairs. Plenty of time for him to get a workout in.

Jack stretched first. He could feel the muscles tighten around the scar that ran along his abdomen, a curve of silvery scar tissue that wrapped around from the left of his belly button into a long, upward curve towards his back. No matter how many years had passed, or how much he had continued to work his muscles or tone his body, the scar tissue still gave him twinges. It was a permanent reminder of his failure to keep the woman he loved safe.

As he reached for the weights and ran through his reps, toning each muscle, slow and steady, he could think of nothing else. It was the dream that had started it. It had certainly set the tone for his morning.

Jack shook his head, wishing he could shake out his thoughts of her. It did no good to think about it, no good to miss her.

He stepped onto one of the two treadmills and pressed the preset for a punishing five-mile trek, his feet stretching as the treadmill rose in height. It wasn't the same as being outdoors, pounding down a trail outside, but he also wouldn't be gasping like an asthmatic in less than ten minutes. The air quality remained poor, thanks to the wildfires and haze that filled the air.

Two hours later, Jack sat in his office across from Azule and wished he had followed that brief, waking desire to flee Los Angeles.

"Benton Security Services is over budget by nearly one hundred thousand dollars in the past six months," the large, buxom woman declared, her full lips pressed tight, disapproval written all over her smooth brown face. "It doesn't make good business sense."

Jack leaned back and folded his arms against his chest, unconsciously mimicking the woman across from him. "I understand that, Az, but..."

"But nothing, Boss. You can't run things at a loss, not in this economy, and not if you want to stay rich. Benton Security Services is hemorrhaging money and your other investments aren't keeping up."

Jack hid a smile. Azule was a financial wizard, among other business-centric talents, but she was rather one-minded. To her, if the money wasn't growing, then it was in danger of heading the other way. As it was, he could overspend twice as much as he had, twice a year for the rest of his life and still never see a significant decrease in his overall worth. No one, not even Azule, was privy to all of his financial dealings. That it bothered her, however, was exactly the reason he kept her on. Azule looked after his interests and he paid her 50% above the average salary for the area.

"This is a project I'm willing to take a loss on."

Azule scowled at him, her rich dark skin showing frown lines around the eyes as she contemplated what to say next, whether to argue further, before shaking her head and rolling her eyes. Was she appealing to the heavens to save her from the clutches of a mad white man with far too much money and not enough sense? Jack wasn't sure, but he couldn't help but grin when she threw her hands up in disgust.

"Have it your way, Jack." Her eyes narrowed. "Where's the mantiquer? I haven't seen her in days."

"Mantiquer?" Jack asked, laughing.

"You know who I'm talking about."

"Tiana?"

"Right, her."

Jack couldn't stop laughing. "Why did you call her a mantiquer?"

Azule sighed, rolling her eyes so hard he saw the color disappear into white. "Women like that don't want you, they just want your bank account. Guaranteed she was with a couple more on the side. Hope you wore your pelvic poncho when you tapped that."

Jack threw back his head and guffawed. The sound filled the room as he rolled the words around in his head.

Guaranteed, "pelvic poncho" is a term I won't be forgetting soon.

The phone rang then. Not the one on the desk that Azule insisted on answering, but his private cell, which only a handful of people knew of. Jack reached into his pocket and pulled it out, his eyebrows rising as he saw the 816 area code. He didn't recognize the number, but there was only one person he could think of who lived in flyover country, and he was the one who had helped get her there.

He pictured her face as he stared at the phone. It rang again, insistent.

Azule looked at him curiously, but said nothing, her eyebrows raised.

How long had it been? Four years? Going on five? Not a single call, no emails, nothing. The silence had been complete. It had felt like a death. It still did.

The phone rang a third time, and he pressed the green button, bringing it up to his ear. "Jack speaking."

"Hi, Jack." Her voice was the same, unmistakable, and one that he couldn't forget. His heart beat faster, and he could feel a warmth spreading through him. It was as if she were here, standing next to him, and her unique scent of honey and vanilla filled his nose.

"Kaylee." He breathed her name out, his mind a whirlwind of emotion, and Azule's eyes crinkled around a smile, one that looked almost victorious. She nodded at Jack, and then stood, stepping out of the room and closing the door firmly behind her.

"I'm sorry to call you like this, but..." There was silence and he could picture her nibbling on her lower lip, a habit she had tried hard to eradicate but one that was intrinsic to who she was. "I need your help, Jack. It's for a friend."

"Five years." The words escaped his lips. "It's been five years."

"I know." She sighed then. He could see her face, imagine just how she looked. Eyes closed, her face a mixture of sadness and regret. "I thought it would be best. For both of us. For Malcolm. I just wanted to forget my life from before and concentrate on starting over again."

Jack wanted to be angry. He had been. But now? He knew how afraid she had been, that the shadow of her family's deaths, and of the darker force of the people behind those killings, two forces that seemed too large, were too overwhelming for them to fight. It was why she had been in danger. The people who had killed her family had taken everything from her, had broken her, and she watched everyone she loved die. She had left in order to protect him, even if he hadn't needed protection. If he didn't handle it right, she would rabbit again, and Jack wasn't ready for that.

"I understand." Saying those words felt like he was chewing on sharp glass. It was a lie. He didn't understand, couldn't.

"I'm calling for a friend," she continued. "Someone in need of protection. I think her life is in danger."

How long had he hoped for her call? And even if it wasn't to have her return to him, he couldn't help but take this small opportunity and run with it.

"Tell me more," he said, his voice all business. "I'll be happy to help."

Jack listened as she described the situation. Her voice sounded stronger, more self-assured, and he had so many questions. But they would wait. He listed off the main phone number, the one that would route through Azule and set a bodyguard detail into motion. The property there in Kansas City, Kansas, would do as a safe house. It was well-stocked and prepared. He had made sure of that when he knew Kaylee would end up living in the area. From the sound of it, Kaylee's friend direly needed it.

"Don't worry, I'll make sure she's safe," he promised.

The relief in her voice was unmistakable. "Thank you, Jack." She paused, then whispered, "For everything."

There was a click, the rapid triple pulse that showed the caller had hung up on the other end, then nothing. Jack stared at the dark screen. That was it?

Azule was waiting for him to reemerge, her long, ornate fingernails tapping away at the computer. She looked up, gave him an assessing stare, and stopped typing.

"Well?"

"Benton Security Services will receive a call from a Lila Benoit in Kansas City," he said. "Put Jesse on it. He just moved to the area last month to work for the KCPD, but he might have time."

Azule shook her head, "He's out until the end of the week. He had that family emergency, a sick sister."

Jack groaned, "Shoot, I forgot all about that." He thought for a moment, "What about Ellis?"

Azule nodded, "I'll call him and arrange for the flight," she said, scribbling the details onto a notepad. Then she stared back at him expectantly.

He shrugged, turned on his heel, and returned to his office. As the door closed behind him, his steps slowed and he stared out at the thicket of trees outside his window. Like the rest of the L.A. hills, they looked dry, desiccated. There had been too much heat and not enough rain. El Niño was in full force.

Five years.

Just hearing her voice had brought it all back. His entire body was reacting. Even after all of this time, all that Jack wanted was to wrap his arms around her, press his nose into her hair, and feel her body against his. His reaction shocked him, but the thrill of connecting with her again helped him realize that there was a reason no other woman had stayed in his life longer than a few months. This time, he was going to do something about it.

This time? I'm not going to just stand there and watch her walk away.

Nowhere to Hide

Five years earlier...

There was no use fighting the restraints. She couldn't get out of them. Sure, she had tried at first, and realized that she would be better off trying to bend steel bars. She was lucky the older man hadn't tied them tighter and cut off the blood flow. Perhaps he had done that on purpose. Perhaps it would make it easier to administer the drugs.

Adrienne watched as the older man slid out of his coat, the blue shirt underneath clearly displaying an LAPD badge. Him not caring that she knew he was a police officer was terrifying. It meant that, whenever they decided she had no more useful information, that would be it, lights out. She thought of Rainier, Lincoln, and the blood that had pooled beneath their bodies. These men didn't care if she knew they were cops because the only way this would end was with her buried in a shallow ditch.

The tray had a bottle on it, but she couldn't read the label. It was too small, too far away, despite her excellent eyesight. Her stomach plummeted as she watched the man insert a needle into the tiny bottle and fill the slender syringe with the colorless liquid.

"Tie off her arm...I don't want to miss the vein," he said, and the younger man wrapped a length of tubing around her arm, snugging it tight.

Adrienne could feel her heart pounding, her entire body shaking with fear. The gag in her mouth prevented her from speaking, arguing, even pleading with them. She could feel beads of sweat forming on her forehead, despite the cool dampness of the warehouse. One foot twisted against its bindings.

It didn't matter what she did. She was tied tight, completely at these two men's mercy, and mercy wasn't something either seemed capable of.

She tried to catch the younger man's eyes, to plead her case, desperate to find some way to stop them from injecting her with that needle. Whatever was in it, it would either kill her or subdue her.

The older man removed the needle from the bottle and gave a tiny squeeze. The arc of tiny droplets spun through the air, vanishing. He looked up at her impassively and she shook her head slowly, wishing she had the power to stop him, to talk him out of what came next. The corners of his mouth quirked up in a small smile as he closed the distance between the tray and Adrienne's chair.

She moaned in fear, the sound low, primal. The younger man turned away.

"Please hold still," the man said, his tone indifferent. "This won't kill you, simply loosen your tongue, but if I waste the injection and miss the vein, the second dose almost certainly will do damage. An overdose could stop your heart. So be a good girl and hold still."

It took seconds for the needle to slide into place, yet it felt like forever as she watched him slowly press the plunger down. She could feel the coldness spreading, mingling with her blood, then racing through her body with each beat of her heart.

He spoke again, but this time he directed it towards the younger man.

"Remove her gag and leave it off unless she does something stupid like scream. The drug can cause nausea and I wouldn't want her choking on her own vomit." He had turned away from Adrienne and set the syringe down on the small tray before reaching for his coat that hung a few feet away on a nail.

"I've been up thirty-two hours straight and I need caffeine. You?"

The younger man nodded. "Uh yeah, grab me a Red Bull, would you? There was a convenience store about two miles down the outer road."

The older man nodded, and to Adrienne he suddenly looked hazy, almost blurry. "Perfect. It'll take a few minutes for the drugs to take effect and then we'll get started."

He slid his coat on, reached in a pocket, and jingled his keys in his hand. It seemed like such a normal gesture. Like something Rainier would do before heading out to meet his friends. But there was nothing normal about this. Adrienne could feel tears tracking down her cheeks. Rainier was dead. Lincoln was dead. Her father was dead. There was no one left to trust, and nowhere that she was safe anymore.

My fault, my fault, my fault.

She watched as the older man walked away, out the far door, into the rain and wind. A few seconds later, she heard a familiar car engine start up and gravel spit under the tires. She had spent most of a day locked in the trunk of that car; she was overly familiar with the sound of its engine.

The young man had turned back towards her when the other man put the needle down. He didn't like needles, and that was the only thing she had learned so far.

Then again, he looked at my breasts a little longer than a second. Which is far better than how the older man had stared at me like I was already dead. I might as well be a piece of furniture as far as that guy is concerned.

He leaned over and removed her gag, fishing the rough cloth out of her mouth before setting it on the rough-hewn table next to the tray. She coughed a little, and licked her dry, cracked lips.

"Please," she asked, "a little water?" She could feel the beginning of a headache, one that thudded in time with her heart. She felt nauseated, as well. Whether it was from the drugs or the constant state of fear she had found herself in for the past twenty-four hours, she wasn't sure, but it felt as if it were increasing by the minute.

The younger man mumbled something and walked away. A moment later, he returned with a cup and placed it roughly against her lips. His eyes slid away from hers.

He doesn't like this. He doesn't want to hurt me. I can work with that. I just need to get him to let me go.

"Thank you for the water."

He didn't respond.

"My name is Adrienne."

No response.

Adrienne searched for what to say next. Every word mattered. She remembered the instructor telling her to choose her words carefully.

Keep it simple. Have your captor connect with you as a person. Tell them your name. They might already know it, but that doesn't matter. What matters is that you establish a connection, one in which they see you as more than a dollar sign or something to abuse and kill.

The instructor's words had stayed with her, even though over three years had passed since taking the training.

Somehow, she had to get him to look at her differently.

"Please, I..." Adrienne did her best to look embarrassed. "I need to pee something awful."

"Hold it." He said it and stared away from her towards the far end of the warehouse. Adrienne wondered how long she had before the older man would be back.

"I have been holding it since I was in the trunk. I'm going to burst. Please." Her voice dropped to a whisper. "I don't want to go in this chair but if I don't go soon, I..." She let her voice trail off and she looked down, hoping her expression matched her words, and that it would convince him enough to release her bonds.

She could feel him staring at her. A moment ticked by. How much time did she have left? The younger guy had said the convenience store was two miles away on an outer road. Two miles, at forty miles per hour, plus at least three to five minutes in the store itself, meant, what, seven, maybe eight minutes at a minimum. At least two had passed since then. She had to get out of her restraints, disable her captor, find keys, and escape before the older man returned.

"Oh God," she sobbed, "please don't make me soil myself, please. I just, of all the..." Real tears ran down her cheeks and she clenched her legs together. "Please."

"Fuck. Okay, fine. But don't you try anything. I swear, if you do, I'll fucking kill you myself."

He reached for the first restraint and she curved her body inwards, cowering, hoping against hope that all he saw was weakness and fear. The drug, whatever it was, made everything feel weird, hazy. She waited until he removed each of the restraints, eyes down, shoulders slumped. He stood back.

"Get up, then," he said, gesturing at her, confused. "The bathroom is behind you."

"I, I can't. I'm dizzy and nauseous, and I don't know if I can stand on my own."

She needed him close. Really close.

"Christ." He threw up his hands. "Just don't throw up on me, or piss right here. Damn it. I should wait for Ro..." He stopped before he said the man's full name. "Never mind, just, here, lean against me."

Adrienne let him slide his arm around her and lift her from the chair. She was shaking, whether from nerves or the drugs or the actual fear she would fail and die here, she wasn't sure. But she used it, turned the shaking to her advantage just like she had learned in the class with Rainier and two others, twins, whose family had owned a lion's share of stock in Berkshire Hathaway. All of them rich, all vulnerable to kidnapping.

She placed her left hand on the side of his jacket. She had inches to go. Did he remember what was there? Had he ever even used one?

He didn't respond, and she moved slowly, shakily, as if on uncertain, half-numbed legs, and calculated how long she had until he remembered or she lost the chance.

No time like the present.

She jerked, as if stumbling, and his hands briefly were off of her, long enough for her to reach for it, and twist away, her instructor's words ingrained in her memory just as the movements themselves were.

Step, rake your heel down along the instep, then twist away from them.

It was a textbook move, and as he reacted, she stepped away from him and jabbed the taser in her hand into his side, pressing down hard on the side buttons. The taser leads imbedded into his chest and he stiffened, hands falling from her, a stuttering howl erupting from his mouth. She pressed the buttons again, holding her fingers in place.

He screamed and flailed his limbs, pinwheeling as if they had a mind of their own. It nearly knocked the taser out of her hand. He fell to the floor, his head smacking hard against the concrete.

Adrienne knew better than to stop. How many times had she forgotten and been dragged back by the instructor? Too many to count until she had learned her lesson. She pulled her leg back, then swung it as ferociously as possible into his groin. His body shuddered and lay still. Whether it was from the force of his head hitting the concrete or her testicle-destroying kick, Adrienne wasn't sure, but she was sure he was unconscious.

She reached for the bulge of keys in his front pocket, fingers shaking, heart racing. He had to have driven here separately, because he had been here, outside next to the car when it had rolled to a stop on the gravel. She had heard him walk over to the vehicle before the older man had even gotten out of the car.

She ran for the door, her stomach heaving, the headache having wrapped its tentacles around her brain and squeezed, sweat trickling down her forehead and in the small of her back. She had no time, no time to get out of here, but she was going to try.

It had been near dusk when she first arrived, trussed up like a Christmas turkey, ready for slaughter. A light rain had been falling then, but now it was a downpour, heavy, relentless, and she could barely make out the outline of a beaten-down Civic. She stared at the keys in her hand. Did they belong to the Civic? Adrienne wasn't sure. She ran for the vehicle and the door opened at her touch, unlocked. She scanned the horizon. There was nothing in sight past this long, low-slung warehouse. No lights, no trees, no buildings, and just one road in and out. Her one shot to get out. Here it was.

Adrienne slid into the seat, closed the door, and jammed the larger key into the ignition. It fit. She was about to turn it when she saw a set of lights flicker on the horizon. The road here had felt like a series of low hills, the car tilting up and down with each hill they crossed. Adrienne watched as the headlights disappeared and the incoming vehicle dipped down out of sight.

Adrienne turned the key in the ignition, which was rewarded with a slow rumble. She pulled her seatbelt on, fingers shaking, and glanced over to see if the door to the warehouse was closed. It was. Time to go. If she dared to drive past the oncoming car, it was still a distance away. She could see the headlights come into view and then disappear again.

It's now or never.

She put the car in gear and pressed down on the accelerator, a shower of gravel spewing as the tires spun and then caught and the vehicle careened out of the small parking area and towards the road, towards the oncoming car.

In seconds, she could see it flying towards her, and then she was past it and moving past, accelerating as much as she could without the risk of going airborne, as she navigated the wet macadam in the dark. Occasionally she glanced behind her. Sure, the car would have turned around, recognizing her. But it didn't.

And just when she was sure she had escaped, she saw the railroad crossing ahead. The arms were down, the train already blocking the road, and nowhere to go. Nothing to do but to stop and wait. Moments ticked by. The train rumbled, the rain pounded, and Adrienne's fear ratcheted up by the second. She had to get out of there before the older man got to the warehouse, realized she had fled, and caught up to her.

Her eyes continued to dart from the train to her rearview mirror. Were those headlights she just saw? She turned to look through the rapidly fogging back window and sucked in a sharp breath when a brief flash of headlights appeared, then disappeared down the hill. They were three, maybe four hills away.

Adrienne turned back to the train. She could see it now, the end of it was in view, a short caboose on the back in the distance, coming closer.

Her stomach roiled again, and she felt the burn of stomach acid in her throat. She stared back at the rearview mirror. The headlights were closer. Once again, they disappeared from view.

"Come on, come on, come on!"

The train rumbled on, oblivious, set in its ways and indifferent to the danger. The caboose was closer, nearly there.

The headlights flashed again. One, maybe two hills away.

The caboose clacked by but the crossing arms didn't move, wouldn't move, not until the train was thoroughly past and long gone.

Adrienne yanked the wheel to the left and stomped on the gas. The Civic jumped forward, narrowly missing one arm, and snapping the end off of the second as she floored the pedal and sped through the train crossing. The ground was more level here, and her eyes flicked to the rearview mirror and saw the headlights appear and disappear one last time.

Heart racing, mouth dry, she drove faster than was safe. In the distance, she saw the headlights crest the last hill and now hold steady in her rearview mirror.

The miles flew by and she finally saw the signs for Highway 101, turned onto it, and increased her speed until the aged Civic shuddered in protest. She raced past cars, some honked at her, but the highway was clear, thanks to the downpour.

Once, twice, she felt the little car hydroplane, and she slowed enough to regain control before accelerating again. As the lights of Los Angeles appeared in the distance, she knew she had to get off of the highway. It wasn't safe to stay on it, not with traffic ahead slowing and knotting, as she drew closer to the city.

I need to ditch this car, find another.

The thought of trusting the police again made her shudder. The police had taken the lives of her brother and his friend. She could never trust them again.

The drugs the man had injected her with, combined with sleep-deprivation, wore at the edges of her consciousness. Adrienne yanked on the wheel, taking the next exit without reading the sign. She needed to get somewhere safe.

There's nowhere that's safe. There's nowhere to hide.

The car was shaking now, a yellow warning symbol flashing, and Adrienne slowed the car. The rain had slackened somewhat, and the road she had chosen was dark, empty. A two-lane road stretched and wiggled before her, lined by trees, nothing else. She drove down it, noticing a slight rise in elevation, and driveways at long intervals, curving away from the road and out of sight, likely large, private estates.

If I drive down any of these and ask for help, they will just call the police. And the police are in these guys' pockets. Come on, Adrienne, think!

Thinking, however, was something better done with a well-rested and drug-free mind, neither of which she possessed.

Driveway after driveway passed, and occasionally a flash of lightning lit up the sky above, which was mostly hidden by the thick overgrowth of trees. Once, an oncoming set of headlights had her holding her breath, her heart rate once again ratcheting up, until Adrienne reminded herself that they would come from behind, not ahead. Behind her, the road remained empty of everything except rain and leaves.

It was one of those moments of staring into the rearview mirror, terrified of what might come for her, that took her attention away at a crucial moment. Just a half second, really, and that was all that was necessary. In the dark of night, the denizens of the forest traveled, whether it was raining or not. And the family of raccoons, a group of perhaps three adults and half a dozen juveniles, were lit up in the Civic's headlights, a wash of yellow that caused them to stop in their tracks in the middle of the road.

Adrienne stomped on the brakes and felt them lock up as the steering wheel went rigid in her hands. The car fishtailed back and forth, enough to break the raccoons loose from their headlight-induced trance. They scurried out of the way, as Adrienne fought to regain control. The car spun, out of control, and she felt the tires bite into the edge of the tarmac, then slide over the edge, down the embankment, in free fall.

The last thing that Adrienne saw before everything went dark was an enormous boulder caught in the headlights.

It was the rain pelting her that woke her first, wet and cold, falling through the shattered remains of the driver's side window. Adrienne lifted her head and instantly regretted it. Her neck and back were in agony, and her face ached where it had slammed into the airbag, the remnants of which surrounded her. She reached with her right hand and felt for the seatbelt latch. The car was silent. Adrienne looked around in the dim interior.

How long was I out?

There was no clock to inform her, and her captors had taken her cell phone. The dash of the Civic was dark, unresponsive, and she slowly looked over the car, her head muddled. Whether it was from the drugs or the impact, she did not know. She felt, rather than saw, the dried, crusted blood on her mouth. A tooth felt loose. After a moment of fumbling, she finally found the button for the seatbelt and unlatched herself, thankful she had been wearing it on impact. The car was on a steep incline and her body fell forward without the belt holding her in place. Everything hurt and Adrienne groaned.

Her hair was soaked. Her dress was as well.

How long was I sitting here?

She walked the fingers of her left hand over to the door, finally finding the latch. She pulled it, but the door didn't move. No amount of yanking made the difference, and moving hurt. There were no broken bones, but she still could feel a dozen different pain points.

If I get out of this, I'm going to be all kinds of colors.

There was no other option. She was going to have to climb out of the window. She moved slowly, hurting, thoughts muddied, and slowly levered her way out of the crumpled car. The boulder was within arm's reach, dark and gray, lined with lichen and moss. The window's safety glass had already shattered into hundreds, no, thousands, of square pieces that poked at her uncomfortably as she half crawled, half slid out of the car.

She could hear the rushing of water nearby, a low roar that distinguished itself from the downpour of rain.

There was little in the way of light, the distant glow of the vast city the only aid to her making her way through the darkness. If it hadn't been raining, she would have been able to see enough to walk, but the rain and the cloud cover combined to consume the forest and trees into a thick gloom that had her stumbling as she tried to make her way towards the sound of the water.

A few minutes later, now scratched and bleeding from falling, one ankle aching after she slid a few feet in the mud, Adrienne had found the source of the water. On a normal day, it was likely nothing more than a gurgling creek with plenty of boulders to balance on when crossing. Now, however, it was a raging torrent of ice-cold water, tumbling and roaring along. There was no crossing it. Not unless she wanted to drown.

Adrienne tried making her way first upstream, then doubled back and heading downstream. It made no difference; it was completely impassible. At the furthest point downstream, she had discovered a wooden footbridge, the ends of which were poking out by less than a foot. The rest of it disappeared beneath the torrent of tumbling, frothing, growling water.

She had no choice; she would have to climb up the hill, back towards the road. The idea of it frightened her. What if they were there, searching for her? What if she couldn't find a place to shelter?

Adrienne could feel the difference between the rain and her tears. Her tears were warm, and they quickly washed away in the cold. Her teeth chattered, and she was so tired. She thought briefly of returning to the car, taking shelter in its battered remains, and then shook her head.

That's the first place they would look if they found the tracks off of the road.

She had to keep moving. Slowly, exhaustion seeping into her tired and aching body, she slogged her way up the steep embankment, towards the road, towards civilization or shelter.

All You Have is Each Other

I t felt like forever. Adrienne's limbs moved slower and slower, and dragging herself up the steep embankment took forever. The car had come a long way before stopping at the bottom. Her eyelids were heavy, the adrenaline that had served her so well to escape her captors now wearing off. Whatever was in the needle the older man had injected into her, combined with a lack of sleep over the past three days, it wore at her. She clawed her way up the hill, inching her way toward the same road she had come from. She had to find help, or a place to shelter. Every piece of her ached.

Near a tree, she stopped, her foot tangled in the roots that protruded from the ground. It stood at a slant, desperate to keep its place despite the sharp angle of ground, determined to survive. That wasn't so different from what she felt like. Adrienne stopped then and rested, her heart hammering in her chest. She was cold, her fingers stiff, coated with mud and leaves, her dress torn. She leaned against the base of the tree, her eyelids drooping. The rain slackened and Adrienne caved to the exhaustion clawing at her.

Her eyes closed, and she fell into a memory of childhood, of her mother. The rain and dark replaced with the memory of warmth on a humid New Orleans summer morning.

Adrienne stood by the side of her mother's bed and waited for her to open her eyes. It didn't take long...it rarely did. Mom always seemed to know when her daughter needed her.

Colette's eyes flew open, and a smile appeared seconds later. Her skin was ashen, and the only spots of color were the dark gray shadows under her eyes.

"Good morning, Bumblebee," she whispered.

When Adrienne didn't smile, a look of concern appeared. "What's wrong?"

"Rainier told me to go away. He says I'm a pest."

"Oh dear, what made him say that?"

"I wanted to play Mario Kart with him, but he won't let me. He only has one friend visiting, and there's four controllers, so he should let me play too!"

"Rainier has a friend over, darling. You remember how it feels when you have Sydney over. All you want to do is spend time with her. Not us, not Rainier or his friends."

"But..." Adrienne stopped, frowned, and stared at the ground. She knew Mom was right, and she couldn't come up with any good argument. Sydney was away at camp, and every day since she left Adrienne had been bored to tears. Normally Rainier would have let her play with him and his friend, but since last year, when he turned thirteen, her brother was different, less kind, more impatient with her. He no longer wanted to spend time with his nine-year-old sister.

Colette sighed. "Bumblebee, you and your brother need to work this out. Sometimes, Rainier needs to be by himself and other times it is important for him to spend time with you. There needs to be a balance, my love."

Adrienne's bottom lip pushed out. "There's no balance. None!" She would have run out of the room if it hadn't had been for her mother's hand on her sleeve.

"Adrienne, my love, all you have is each other." Her mother's eyes glistened with unshed tears. "How I wish I had had more children so that you had others to play with. But we live with the life we have been dealt, my darling."

Adrienne had snuggled up to her mother in bed and watched cartoons for hours until Mom was strong enough to get up, the dark circles under her eyes just one of the many signs that Mom wasn't okay. Adrienne watched as her mother slowly slid clothes on, her body pale, thin.

"Mom?"

"Yes, Bumblebee?"

"Will the surgery make you better?"

Her mother smiled at her, bright white, a stark contrast to the weary lines on her face. "Oh yes, I hope it will."

"And you are going to have a hyster...hyster..."

"Hysterectomy."

"Right." Adrienne slipped into the bunny slippers she had left by the side of the bed. "Rainier says that it means you won't be able to have babies anymore."

"No, I mean, yes, that is what that means. No more babies." Adrienne could hear the sadness in her mother's voice.

Colette sat down on the edge of the bed. "There are other ways to have children, Bumblebee. And once I have the surgery, and have time to recover, I'll feel better, stronger, not so tired all the time." She ran a hand through Adrienne's hair, kissed her forehead, and smiled. "We can go to Disney World, visit New York for New Year's Eve, or so many other places, once I am better. Would you like that?"

"What other ways, Mom?" Adrienne's curiosity whetted.

"Well, there's fostering, adoption." Colette's smile broadened. "Why? Would you like another brother or sister?"

"A sister, but not a brother. I think brothers are too much of a pain," Adrienne answered, her eyes shining with excitement.

Colette laughed. "Well, it's a long way off. And your father and I haven't even discussed it, but I'll keep your request in mind." She stood up, reaching for the bedpost to steady herself as she swayed in place. "Now for some very important decisions, Bumblebee." The edges of her *mouth quirked up in a conspiratorial grin. "Crepes at Muriel's or Eggs Hussarde at Brennan's?"*

Adrienne jumped up and down. "Just the two of us?"

"Of course, Bumblebee. Besides, Rainier and Jesse have eaten a metric ton of Eggo waffles by now, if I know those two. Just you and me."

"Crepes! Crepes!" Adrienne jumped up and down in excitement, and her mother laughed. "Can we go to the park afterwards and feed the ravens?" Adrienne loved the ravens who flocked to Louis Armstrong Park, a few blocks away from the restaurant. She had sat patiently, a seed in her hand, until one had approached her and took it from her fingers. After that, it had become something they just did each time they visited the restaurant.

Mom smiled at her. "We might need to drive to the park instead of walking."

Adrienne whooped in happiness. "I'll go get my shoes on now!"

Her mother laughed and called to Adrienne as she ran out of the bedroom, "Change out of your pajamas as well!"

The brunch had been marvelous, but they cut their adventure short as they left the restaurant, Colette shaky, her skin pale and clammy to the touch.

"Bumblebee, I'm sorry, but I just don't feel well enough to go to the park," she had said as she grasped the wall of the building and leaned against it. "I promise you, we will go next time, alright?" Mom had managed a small, tired smile, and Adrienne had wrapped an arm around her, trying to provide the support her mother needed to make it to the car which was parked nearby.

"It's okay, Mom. I had a wonderful time with you today." Adrienne had blinked away tears, sad to see her mother so weak, so fragile. "Crepes with you are better than playing Mario Kart with Rainier any old day."

Colette had chuckled then and threaded her fingers through Adrienne's hair. "My sweet girl. What would I do without you? I promise we will go to the park soon. Cross my heart!"

But there had been no more parks. No more brunches at Muriel's. Mom had gone in for the surgery just two weeks later. A simple thing, they had all said, and Adrienne had kissed Mom on the cheek and ran off to the car where her best friend Sydney and her mother were waiting, turning her back on Mom without realizing it would be the last time she ever saw her.

"These things sometimes happen," her father said, his face drawn, his eyes red and recessed in his face. "The doctors tried everything, but she just fell asleep and never woke up."

No more Mom. And with her had gone any talk of fostering or adopting. No more siblings. And if she were honest, it was the beginning of losing Dad as well. He had already worked long days and spent months out of the year traveling around the world, managing the shipping business, before Mom had died. Now he buried himself in his work, shutting himself away from his children, from their home.

Rainier, four years older than Adrienne, had abruptly changed as well. He stopped going to friends' houses for sleepovers and limited the ones there at the house, even though there was no one to stop him. Instead, every night, weeknight or weekend, he made time to play Mario Kart with Adrienne. It was the only light in their new darkness. After Mario Kart came checkers, chess, cards, and Scrabble. In the months following their mother's death, during which Gerard Cenac was conspicuously absent from the family home most evenings, Rainier filled the role of a parent to Adrienne. He would help her with her homework, order food or make something simple, and then the siblings would play games until it was time for bed. And thus, their lives had gone on, until everything turned on its ear once more, less than a year after Colette Cenac died.

Adrienne opened her eyes with a start. How long had she been sitting here, leaning against the tree? Long enough that her body felt stiff, her joints popping in protest as she shifted in place. She had to get up the embankment, back to the road, and find shelter, find somewhere safe.

She moved her legs, which felt numb, and pushed off from the tree. It exhausted her, through and through, but she had to keep going. Lightning cracked overhead, and she could see she still had a long way to go. One hundred feet, maybe more, to get up to the roadway above. She sighed and climbed. It was painful, slow, and she shuffled along, grasping at tree roots, limbs, and boulders as she fought for every step up the hill.

Her breath soon came in ragged gasps and, once again, consciousness became a flighty creature, ready to escape at any moment. The lightning flashed in a quick burst, jagged strips of light that hurt her eyes and simultaneously lit her way. Twenty more feet. It felt like forever. A sharp branch dug into her leg, drawing a fiery burn as it cut her skin. She kept going. Climbing. Hands grasped for roots, trees, whatever looked stable enough to hold her weight as she fought her way up the hill. It had taken seconds to fly down it, but now? Now, every foot gained was a struggle.

The rain continued. At one point, Adrienne looked up and saw the drops falling from the sky like a shower of jewels rushing towards her. A beautiful moment, just a second of beauty before reality interceded. She was cold, sopping wet through and through. Her body ached from the accident and the myriad of abuses it had seen over the past few days. Her skin burned from the cold. She stopped, her breaths coming in sharp rasps, the mud and rocks and plants digging into her knees, her hands. She couldn't go on much longer. All she wanted to do was curl up in a ball and close her eyes.

Instead, she looked up and saw it. The edge of the road. Just a few feet now, just a couple more. She surged forward, pushing all of her energy into making her body move forward. Fingers abraded, knees sore, shoe missing, dress torn. Gasping breaths of cold, wet air into her lungs until, finally, she felt the rough macadam under her fingertips. One last handful of gnarled tree root and she was up, onto the road itself, where she collapsed on the ground. No matter the cold or the rough ground under her body, her grip on consciousness slipped away yet again and Adrienne knew no more.

The Lady in Blue

J ack strained to see the road. The wind lashed the trees, and the darkness was nearly absolute, the rain pouring in great sheets from the sky. The only sources of light were his headlights and the occasional crack of lightning illuminating the sky in bright flashes. He had slowed the sports car to a tame thirty miles per hour. It still felt too fast in the inky black of the night, and the engine surged irritably, fighting the weight of his foot on the brake pedal. If it were a living thing, it would growl with impatience at the sedate pace he was setting, but at the moment he was far more afraid of running off the edge of the road. On one side was a tall cliff, with the occasional tree fighting for purchase along the dark rock wall. On the other, a thick forest and steep embankment away from the road. Except for branches and leaves, there was nothing but a dark abyss.

The party had been the typical Hollywood scene, plenty of high-end booze and vacant-eyed women who were afraid to eat from the buffet and talked about their modeling careers like it was an art form. It had bored him in minutes, and he had stayed for as short a time as possible and then made his escape. It had been tricky; some women could sniff out money as if it were made from chocolate. One had attached herself to his arm like a lamprey eel and refused to let go. Eventually she had grown bored, however, and wandered off "to the little girl's room," which was code for getting high on the complimentary trays of cocaine in the overly gilded bathrooms.

He had watched her go and made his escape seconds later.

The lightning flashed, slamming into a tree up ahead. The light was intense, blinding, the earsplitting crack and boom of the thunder simultaneous. Jack felt the sound pass through the vehicle and he slowed the car even further. This act saved his life, and the car's, as three deer, a doe and two fawns, came barreling across the road. He slammed on the brakes and fishtailed slightly before coming to an abrupt stop in the dark, rain-soaked road.

He rocked with the car, his body pushing against the tightened seatbelt. "Jesus H.," Jack swore, his heart hammering in his chest. That had been close.

He sat there as the deer disappeared from view, leaping from the roadway into the dark abyss and passing by something crumpled by the side of the road. "What the...?"

He put the car in park and unbuckled his seatbelt, grabbing a small Maglite from the center panel. The rain instantly soaked his hair as the downpour continued. He pressed the button and turned the Maglite on, playing it across the edge of the road. Rocks, tree branches, ferns, and a body. *A body.* "Oh shit."

He ran over to it, this crumpled lump of blue on the ground. Pale white legs, bruises, one shoe on, the other missing. She had scratches on her legs, filthy and bloody. The bruises weren't recent. At least, not from a car crash. His eyes caught on the abrasions and dark bruises at her ankles, her wrists. She wore a blue dress that was torn, bloodied, and the rain had plastered her hair to her skull. Twigs and leaves snarled in her long, honey blond hair. Her eyes were closed, her lips a bluish gray. His phone was back in the car and Jack felt torn. Did he dare touch her and see if she was alive or simply run back to the car and call the police?

"Miss?" he asked. He touched a hand to her shoulder. Her skin was cold, but he could see the rise and fall of her chest now. She was alive. He had to get her off of the hard ground and out of the rain.

Was it safe to pick her up?

Jack looked around. There were tire tracks, furrows, cut deep in the mud at the edge of the road. Far below, he could see the glint of metal, deformed, and bent. If she had come from there, she had climbed a steep embankment to get up and out.

I doubt I'll hurt her by picking her up then.

"Miss, I'm going to need to pick you up and get you out of the rain, okay?"

He gently slid his arms underneath her and stood up easily; he dead-lifted weights heavier than her four days a week. Her head lolled back over his right arm and she moaned slightly. He had to get her out of the deluge. That was the first order of business. He was thankful there was no one else on the road. They were in a blind curve and any oncoming vehicle would have seconds to react. Those gouges in the mud on the side of the road showed how it had gone for her. A car accident for sure. Could there be anyone else still down there? He tried to stare down through the trees and see if he could glimpse the car somewhere below but, despite the bright light show in the sky, he couldn't see anyone else.

He shook his head, spun around, and walked to his car, gently balancing the woman's unconscious body against his as he fumbled with the passenger-side door open and gently settled her inside. Her eyelids fluttered, but she didn't move.

Jack ran around to his side of the car and slid inside, wiping the water from his eyes. The heavy rain soaked him through. The windows fogged up. Her eyelashes fluttered again, and she opened her eyes a crack, shivering from the cold. Jack damned himself for not having put the emergency kit in his car.

She flinched as Jack spoke. "Miss? I need to get us off the road and out of the way of oncoming traffic. Were you in a car? Was there anyone with you? Anyone we need to go back for?"

She shook her head and whispered, "No" before closing her eyes again.

"Okay, my house is just up ahead. Hang in there. I'll turn on the heat until I can get you inside and warm." He reached out and flipped the heat to max, started the engine, and clicked his seatbelt into place before straightening the car out and continuing down the road. The rain had slackened somewhat, for which Jack was very thankful. He could drive faster, and within minutes he was turning onto the long private drive and passing through the gates. The water dripping from both of them had soaked the seats and he could hear a steady drip from her dress onto the floor of the car. Her eyes were closed again, her skin pale, her lips blue from the cold. He probably needed to call the police, but at the moment all he could think to do was to set her in front of the large hearth in the great room and warm her up.

The garage door closed silently behind them and the Ferrari purred to a stop, the heat from the vents ceasing the second the engine stopped. The girl still didn't move. In the bright, harsh light of the garage, it was clear how young she was. Perhaps twenty, possibly younger. Jack slipped open her door and leaned in, murmuring gently to her as he lifted her out of the car. A few quick strides took them from the spacious six-car garage, through the mudroom and into the back hall. It was a few more seconds' walk to the great room, where a fire burned merrily in the hand-cut, imported marble fireplace. The warmth of the fire enveloped them, and Jack set the girl gently in a chair near the fire.

"I'll be right back," he said, covering her with a thick, luxuriously soft blanket.

The half bath yielded a first aid kit nearly obscured at the back of the sink cabinet. Jack grabbed it, along with a handful of towels, and glimpsed his reflection in the mirror. His shirt, a black silk Versace tee, was muddy and soaked. His pants weren't much better. Water still dripped from his hair down the back of his neck. He grabbed a fluffy robe with his free hand.

He turned and walked back into the great room. The young woman was still there, staring at the fire, shivering uncontrollably.

"I've got a first aid kit and some towels. And a robe if you would like to get out of those wet clothes." She shook her head, and he wasn't sure if it was her shivering or telling him "no."

He knelt at her feet and gently slid off the remaining shoe, lightly wiping at the sticks and leaves that covered her pale skin. She flinched, and he looked up at her, realizing with a start that she was stiff with fear.

She's terrified of me.

Her pupils were enormous.

Is she on drugs? Afraid the police will catch her driving under the influence?

"I won't hurt you. You're safe here," Jack said softly, gently. She reminded him of a cheetah, and he half-expected her to spring away from him and streak away into the stormy night. "I should call the police, they could help..."

"No, please, no police." Her voice was soft, almost pleading. "It's not what you think."

"Honestly, I don't know what to think," Jack replied, focusing once again on her legs. The left knee was a snarl of mud, blood, and chewed-up flesh. "If it hadn't been for the deer running across the road, I never would have seen you. You could have died out there."

He felt rather than saw her nod, and her knee jerked back at his touch. She sucked a breath in, wincing as he gently cleaned the wound. Her legs held bruises, the ankles a mess of abrasions. The bruising didn't look as if it had come from a car crash, but as if someone had restrained her.

A shudder went through him. And Allie's face flashed before him. Her eyes were different, and of course Allie had been younger, just sixteen, but still.

This, whatever it is, is more than just a car crash.

"My name is Jack, Jack Benton." He waited for her to recognize it, but she didn't respond, just stared at him. A surge of relief went through him. She didn't know who he was. There had been no look of recognition, no change to a coquettish flirtation, like the girls at the party he had just come from, the look that betrayed their glee at meeting a billionaire, and a single one at that.

This girl, whoever she was, turned away instead, saying nothing, biting her lip. He waited, but she didn't speak.

And then it hit him. "You're scared, aren't you?"

The gentleness of his tone had an effect. When she looked up again, her eyes were full of tears. They spilled down, even as she tried to brush them away, to wrest back control of her emotions. She nodded, still shivering in the blanket.

"I can help you. No strings. No expectations," Jack said, turning away from her tears, focusing instead on the knee. "I guess you could say I've made a career out of it."

She had likely fallen on the hillside on the long climb up. There were pebbles and dirt in the torn flesh. He stole another glance at the abrasions on her ankles, took in the other bruises. They were recent, but different. Someone had hurt this girl, terrified her, abused her, and restrained her. And somehow, she had gotten away, possibly been in a car crash, run through the night and the rain, and collapsed on the side of that lonely road.

"Look, let me get this knee cleaned up, and there is a large guest suite upstairs that you can use. The door locks from the inside. You can take a shower, change out of your wet clothes. I'll fix you some tea or coffee; perhaps you would like something to eat? And then we could talk, or not, about your options. How would that be?" He looked back up at her face, so pale, so frightened, and she nodded, a small jerk of her head.

What or who was she so frightened of?

"Okay. I'll clean this up and bandage it, and don't worry if it loosens up in the shower; I have plenty more and we can just re-apply it. I've got the dirt out and this might sting a little." She winced as he sprayed on the Bactine. "I know, they always said it's not supposed to hurt. Ouch-less spray and all that B.S. Or perhaps I was just overly sensitive as a kid, but this stuff always hurt like hell." Jack caught the small smile that ghosted across her lips and just as quickly vanished.

Their trip upstairs was slow. She moved slowly, gingerly, her feet likely bruised and swollen. At the top of the stairs was a long hallway on the right, which took them past several doors. "I'm that first door on the left, at the top of the stairs, and I'm going to put you over here, in the guest suite," he said, his arm gently supporting her as she hobbled on the thick, plush carpet. "It has a full en suite and there are some clothes in the closet that will probably fit you. You are welcome to use them." They stopped at the doorway and he opened the door, revealing a spacious suite with a high ceiling, modern fixtures, and a small sitting room off the bedroom. "Let me know if you need anything. I'm going to go change and then I'll be downstairs. Okay?"

She nodded and walked inside. As Jack turned and made his way toward his room, he heard the door gently close and the lock engage.

Fair enough. She doesn't know me.

He walked into his room, an extensive suite that included his office, a library, a smaller workout room, and a spacious bedroom and bathroom. Except for food, he could spend most of his days in here and never need to leave. He didn't, but living here in this giant house felt rather lonely, even with Malcolm's silent presence. When Allie had been here, it hadn't felt like it did now. Allie had been full of life, and it had been impossible not to notice how she filled everything she touched with energy and light. Of all the properties he owned, it was here, deep in the Los Angeles hills, where he felt her absence the strongest. She had loved the house, loved the remote feel of the place with the nearest neighbors a good half mile away.

He pulled off his shirt and tossed it into the hamper in the corner of his walk-in closet, reaching for a charcoal silk T-shirt, and looked down at his pants in surprise. Burrs ran down the length of one leg. Off they went as well, and he slipped into a pair of Rag and Bone denim jeans, kicking off his shoes and leaving his feet bare. He took a moment to towel out the last of the rain from his hair.

As he walked downstairs, he could hear the water in the guest suite running.

The kitchen was large and rustic. The heavy wood beams met the sleek matte black of the appliances. Jack reached into the Sub-Zero fridge and pulled out a carton of eggs, a haunch of prosciutto, mushrooms, and cheese. He set the heavy cast-iron pan to heat on the range and set to slicing the mushrooms. Jack had just finished slicing the ham off in paper-thin slices and had a pile of mushrooms and a small diced onion already sautéing to a golden brown when he heard the water shut off. He added a dollop of butter to the pan and it sizzled as it melted. Jack whipped the eggs into a froth and poured them into the buttered pan, adding the cooked mushrooms and onions and the shredded cheese, and flipped the omelet over with a practiced hand as he heard the door open from the guest suite above.

"Do you prefer coffee or tea?" he called, glancing over at her. She was wearing a pair of yoga pants and a T-shirt that disappeared into a zip-up sweatshirt. A pang of sadness hit him. Allie had loved that outfit.

"Coffee," she answered, paused, and then added, "Please."

"Help yourself," Jack said, and nodded at the coffee station. "There's cream and sugar if you want it. And I've made an omelet. I figure it's after midnight, which makes it morning, so it's breakfast time, right?"

A tiny smile. "Thank you."

He slid the omelet out of the pan and cut it in half, slipping one half onto her plate and the other onto his. He ate his slowly, fascinated as he watched the girl tuck into hers with an appetite he had not expected. Moments later, the plate was clean. Half of his food remained. He slid the plate over, smiling, and received an actual smile in return as she demolished it in a handful of bites.

Her hair was quickly drying into a mass of blond and honey-brown ringlets. Some color had returned to her cheeks. She sipped her coffee and his eyes fell on the bruises on her hands, the red chafe marks on her wrists.

She noticed his gaze and pulled the cuff of the sweatshirt down, trying to hide the marks. "Thank you for the food. I can't remember when I ate anything that good." It was by far the most words in a row she had said aloud since he had found her.

"So, shall we start with your name?" he asked, hoping she was ready to talk.

"The less you know about me, the better. Especially my name."

"I see." He sipped his coffee and thought on that. "Well, I have to call you something."

The girl was silent for a moment.

"Call me Kaylee. I've always liked that name."

Jack smiled. "Ah, it brings back memories of *Firefly*. I met Nathan Fillion at a party a few months ago. He's a nice guy."

The girl blinked at him, and Jack thought he saw the ghost of a smile cross her lips and then disappear.

"So, Kaylee, what can you tell me about yourself?"

"Nothing."

"Nothing?"

She reached up and rubbed her temples. She looked exhausted. "Honestly? You seem nice. Really nice, and I don't want anyone else to die because of me."

Search Party

"**I**s it possible she came this way?" Stephan asked.

Rohan shifted his attention from peering through the rapidly fogging windshield and heavy rain, to trying to see where his partner was pointing. He slowed to a crawl.

"I see nothing." He reached his hand out and jabbed at the defrost button.

Is this thing even working?

Stephan batted his hand away. "You just turned the damn thing off."

Rohan growled at his partner, "Then fix it so I can fucking well see. Because right now, it looks like we're in a goddamn fogbank from 'Cisco instead of L.A."

Stephan's mouth twitched, and Rohan could see the kid grit his teeth. He suppressed a smirk of satisfaction. Stephan was born and raised in San Francisco. Rohan knew city natives hated their beloved city being called 'Cisco. The kid was snarky, pretentious, and Rohan took no small joy out of digging at his junior partner's professional façade. This was especially true tonight when it was all Stephan's fault the girl was loose. His head, at least the larger one, had not been in the game. *Think with your dick and you'll end up losing both heads, you stupid little shit.*

He dug his lens cloth out of his pocket and wiped at the windshield; the car slipping to the edge of the road and the built-in edge alert sent a deep thrum through the vehicle. Rohan edged it back into the lane, wishing he could see the middle line better. Not that it mattered, there wasn't a car in sight. Goddamn rain. The view of trees and winding road was picturesque during the day. Who wouldn't love a sun-dappled, tree-lined drive through southern California? At regular intervals were nondescript private drives that led to some of the richest celebrity homes in the area. Right now, however, at just past midnight, it was a nightmare to navigate. The rain was heavy, so much so that there would surely be reports of mudslides somewhere in this mass of twisting, narrow roads by morning. The trees bent down, leaves ripped from them by the force of the rain, a mass of green and wet that reduced the unwieldy town car to a slow crawl. She had gotten Stephan's keys to his piece of shit beater car. If she had stolen the town car, they would have been able to track it through OnStar, but as luck would have it, she had given the kid a set of aching balls and wrestled the keys from him. Pretty slick, considering the trust fund bitch had been restrained when Rohan left for a coffee run. If they didn't find her, though, it would be both of their heads on a platter, no matter that the kid had been the one to try to get some in the space of time Rohan had taken to go get them some coffee and a couple of half-stale donuts that had to be nearly a day old. The same coffee that was sitting back at the facility, likely stone cold by now. They had to find her, and soon. How far could she have gotten, anyway?

Who am I kidding? We might have passed right by her standing on the side of the road and not seen a thing.

"How are your balls?" he snarled at the kid. Stephan mumbled something indistinct, which sounded suspiciously like fuck off. "Yeah? Well, guess what? We don't find her and I gotta call this in, I'm tossing your stupid ass under the bus. I'll be goddamned if I'm going to get sanctioned just because you can't keep your small head in line."

Stephan muttered something else, his head turned away.

"What's that?" Rohan asked as he yanked hard on the steering wheel to avoid a fairly large branch in the road.

"She said she needed to pee."

Rohan barked out a short laugh. "And you fell for that? Damn, how stupid are you?" He laughed again. "And here I thought it was all about you getting your dick wet."

"She was all of a hundred pounds soaking wet," Stephan protested.

"Yeah, so? Those trust fund babies get specially trained on how to get out of dangerous situations. Her family is worth tens of millions. Hell, maybe more. You think they don't teach 'em young how to get out of an unpleasant situation? That they don't know what to say, or hell, how to say it, and then fight dirty the minute they get an opportunity?" Rohan shook his head and let the car drift into the other lane to avoid what appeared to be the top half of a tree covering their side of the road. "Were you born yesterday?"

Stephan said nothing, just stared out of his window into the darkness.

Rohan returned his attention to navigating the road. The rain wasn't relenting, and the windows continued to fog, despite the air pumping away full-blast on defrost. "Shit, we're never going to find her. That girl is likely miles from here, we just need to..."

Stephan interrupted him with a shout. "Stop the car!"

The town car skidded on the tarmac before lurching to a stop. Stephan threw open the door, his feet sliding in the thick mud and leaves as he fought to maintain his balance. A moment later he had nearly disappeared from sight, and Rohan could only see the weak light of the young man's flashlight bouncing along some ten yards behind the car. It slowed, then stopped, as Rohan threw the car in park and got out, swearing under his breath as his shirt absorbed the torrent of rain falling from the sky, blinding him. He had the sense to close his door, unlike his young, impetuous partner. He slipped twice on the leaves coating the tarmac, wishing he had a ball cap to stop the fire hose from the sky from damn near drowning him in water to where he couldn't even see where the tarmac ended and the forest began.

Stephan's flashlight bounced impatiently and then left the side of the road. Rohan couldn't really see more than the outline of him as he tried to negotiate a descent. The incline was steep but littered with smaller trees to hold on to.

"I got tire tracks going down the side. I'm going to go check it out," Stephan called out, his voice already fading as he slipped and slid down through the mud.

Rohan spat out the water dribbling down into his mouth, bent forward, and struggled to stay upright in the slick mud. "Yeah, you do that."

Stephan's light quickly faded from view, popping up occasionally as he moved from tree to tree, slipping and sliding down the steep embankment. Finally, the kid must have entered a far thicker canopy of trees, because the light disappeared entirely, leaving Rohan blanketed in darkness and wondering if he should return to the vehicle. He couldn't see a damn thing, and he was soaked to the bone and cold. It wasn't adding to his positivity, not at all.

The minutes ticked by and his eyes ached from straining to see any light at all in the forest below. Had the kid actually seen anything? Or was he just full of hope that somehow that crazy little trust fund bitch had slid off the road and removed herself from the equation? The boss wouldn't care if the girl ended up dead. In the end, that was her fate, anyway, once they had made sure she hadn't spoken to anyone else past her brother and the journalist. And a few more well-placed questions after the drugs had taken effect would've done the trick. He'd just needed a jolt of energy. A simple cup of coffee, maybe a doughnut, and the coffee shop was just five minutes away, for Christ's sake. Ten, fifteen minutes tops, and it had been long enough for her to sucker Stephan into loosening her bonds to where she could fell the kid with a solid kick to the balls. By the time Rohan had returned, coffee in hand, and saw the car gone, he knew it had been Stephan's car that had passed him on the road. But Rohan had to make sure. So he had run inside, only to find Stephan, still in a haze of pain, moving slower than an octogenarian, a small trail of puke wetting his shirt. She'd nailed him dead center in the 'nads. The kid could barely walk. From what little he had said, she had knocked him out. Then she'd grabbed his keys and hung the lock on the outside of the storage container door, preventing him from following. Not that he'd tried. When Rohan arrived, he was still on the ground, next to a pile of puke. That girl was a hellion.

"Anything?" Rohan called out into the void. There was no response. Or if there was, he couldn't hear past the downpour. He was just about to head back to the car when he saw Stephan's flashlight bobbing in and out of the trees. It took longer for Stephan to make it back up the hill. By the time he did, he was covered in mud, a steady stream of curse words tied together as he slipped, crawled, and wrestled his way up the hill. When he made it to the top, the kid stopped, his sides heaving, then pointed to the car.

They squelched back to it, and Rohan realized as he slipped into the cool interior, that it really didn't matter that he had closed his side. The wind and rain had been fierce enough that everything inside of the vehicle was as soaked as the outside. He reached over and turned the dial to the hottest possible setting, not giving a damn if the inside fogged up.

"Well?"

Stephan sat there, his jaw set, a steady drip issuing from his hair onto the upholstery. "She drove it off the road, ran it into a tree. Airbag deployed. No blood that I could see. But she wasn't anywhere in sight. I couldn't tell for sure, but it looks like she might have come up the embankment onto the road. Fucking rain took out any sign of footprints, so for all I know she's in the forest somewhere. Don't know."

"We've got to call this in," Rohan growled. "She's going to be pissed."

"How pissed?" Stephan asked, not even trying to hide the look of concern on his face.

"Let's just hope we catch her in a good mood."

"Shit." Rohan watched as Stephan clenched and unclenched his hands. The kid hadn't been in this line of work for long, and if their boss was in a foul mood, he wouldn't have time to make another mistake. How many had "reported to the office in person," never to be seen again? Damned if he was keeping count, but if she ever told him she wanted a face-to-face, he would ditch everything—car, phone, hell, even his clothing and identification—burn or cut the damned tattoo off his wrist, and disappear. He'd seen enough to know that you didn't get fired or written up, not in this business, and not working for these people. You disappeared. He was just damned and determined that it would be him doing the disappearing with no help from Management. It was every man for himself, though, and Stephan had brought this on his own head.

Rohan clipped on his seatbelt and put the town car in gear. He was cold, soaked to the bone, and the girl was in the wind. He'd make the call when they got back to a motel and toss the kid under the bus. Hell, he'd probably end up under there with him, but his track record was far better than the kid's. It would likely save his ass from the grinder. If he was lucky, they wouldn't stick him with someone so green again. He needed to work with someone far more competent, who didn't get sucked in by a set of big brown eyes and the promise to be good. The kid had it coming, and Rohan knew better than to feel sorry for him. In this business, you did the job, or else.

They drove in silence. The rain continued to pummel the windshield, and he drove slowly, rounding each curve carefully, the tires occasionally slipping on the thick coating of leaves on the road. She was here, somewhere. Perhaps she had slogged her way towards one of the houses tucked into the cliffs and valleys. Stephan's car was toast, but it also meant she hadn't made it out to the highway. She was still here. And even if it meant waking up the boss, it could also mean that he didn't go down in flames with the kid. He could help figure out where the girl had gone. He had to update her...now.

"What are you doing?" Stephan asked, as Rohan pulled out his phone and pressed a few buttons on the shiny new Samsung Galaxy that Management had issued him last week. He didn't bother responding. It was enough to drive through the maelstrom and hold the phone to his ear. She answered on the third ring.

"It's late," she said, her voice gruff. "I trust this is important."

"Yes, ma'am. We have lost the package you were expecting us to open."

"I see." He could feel a thread of frost emanating through the connection. "And who is responsible for this...loss?"

He didn't answer her immediately, and she sighed. "Was it the newbie?"

"Yes, ma'am." Project Throw Partner Under the Bus was officially in motion. "But the package is definitely in the area. Requesting additional feet on the ground to help locate it."

"You'll have them in one hour." He had his finger hovering on the End Call button when she spoke again. "I'll expect a full explanation when this is complete."

"Yes, ma'am." He pressed the button and slid the phone into his pocket.

"Is she pissed?" Stephan asked. "What happens next?"

Rohan jerked the wheel to the left to avoid a large branch. "What happens next is that we find the girl. Now shut up and watch for her. You never know, she might have headed back towards the road."

The kid heaved a sigh of relief. Rohan kept a pleasant expression on his face. The kid was a fool. Hell, he was a walking, talking dead man. But that was fine. It wasn't his ass that was going to burn. He'd damn well find the girl, torture the information out of her, and bury her with the others. And he'd keep doing the job he was paid so damned well to do, keep himself out of trouble, and run like hell if Management called him in for a face-to-face.

Rohan was in it to survive.

I Can't Sleep

He had gotten nowhere with his questions. Kaylee, or whatever her actual name was, had proved quite reticent. And really, could he blame her? Whatever had happened to her, she was scared.

Instead, he had handed her a small brandy after the meal and changed the subject. Instead of focusing on her, he had told her about the house after seeing her gaze travel over the walls, studying it with an intensity that betrayed her interest in architecture.

"Frank Lloyd Wright." Jack said, anticipating her next question.

"Excuse me?"

"He was a famous architect," Jack explained.

"Yes, I'm familiar with who he is," Kaylee said, a small smile on her lips, "And I certainly can recognize his work. This house has many elements of Falling Water, but the upstairs is different."

Jack nodded, a little chagrined. He hadn't meant to talk down to her, and of course she would know who Frank Lloyd Wright was...who didn't?

"It's reminiscent of John Henry Howe's style," she added. "I studied Wright last summer as part of my application to Cornell. John Henry was his chief drafter and occasionally made changes like the ones on the second floor. It was not without controversy, however, even if Wright usually allowed the alterations."

Jack blinked; this girl knew her architecture. "That's impressive. You obviously have studied it because this building was designed almost exclusively by John Henry Howe. He was a friend of my grandfather's. They went to school together. Most people have never heard of him, so it is easier to just attribute Wright to this house." He cocked his head and stared at her. "Cornell is a long way from California."

She shrugged. "I never got to go. My dad nixed the idea. My brother went off the reservation, took a gap year, and found himself—so I got tapped to carry on the family business." She downed the brandy and stared off into space. "So much for doing what you love." She ran her fingers lightly around the raw skin around her wrists. "In reality, I would have sucked as an architect."

"Why is that?"

"I am obsessed with Victorian architecture," she admitted, pursing her lips. "Nothing else fits." She gave a small shrug. "I mean, I tried to study other architecture, I really did. I focused on Wright as part of my application, and said all the right things, but in my heart of hearts, what I really want is to do nothing but reproduce and live in ridiculously ornate, over-the-top Victorian homes. There is neither the market, nor an affordable way to do so in this day and age." She held out the glass, her other hand showing she wanted a small amount more. "I would have been miserable."

Jack refilled her glass and nodded thoughtfully. She seemed grounded, not moody or flighty, not like the actresses and Hollywood debutantes he encountered every day. It was surprising for someone as young as she obviously was, but he could see why her father had chosen her to carry on the family business.

"I can relate," he said, tipping the decanter and adding a splash more brandy to his own glass. "My parents really pushed for me to get a juris doctorate, which I did, and it has come in handy over the years, but I couldn't do it full-time. I can't stand the immorality of it all, so I have found other ways to thrive. My family already had a variety of holdings, and I've started one or two myself. It doesn't bring in the almighty dollar, but I enjoy it."

Jack looked at his watch and realized it was after four. "You should get some sleep, Kaylee. Tomorrow, well, later today, I'll be happy to take you anywhere you want to go, and you are also more than welcome to stay here."

He took a chance and reached out, taking her hand in his. It was warm now, a stark departure from the icy, damp hand he had first grasped just hours before when searching for a pulse. He could see the angry, raw ligature marks where she had been restrained. "You are safe here, Kaylee. I promise you."

She had stiffened in the first seconds that he took her hand. She took a deep breath, and let it out, visibly trying to relax. "I can't sleep. I just, I just can't."

Jack could see the exhaustion in her eyes. Whether she realized it, she was inches away from collapsing. Sleep was precisely what she needed.

Her hand was still in his and he rubbed his thumb near the edge of her raw flesh, avoiding the bruised and torn skin. "I understand, I do. How long has it been since you've had a decent six hours or more?"

Her eyes welled up again, and she paused for a moment before replying, "I can't even remember. Maybe," her forehead wrinkled as she concentrated, "What day is it?"

Jack glanced at the clock. "Now? It's Sunday."

"Sunday?!" She pulled her hand away and rubbed her eyes. "I think I last slept on Friday. On a plane."

So, she had flown here from somewhere else.

Jack gave a low whistle. "I could give you something to help you sleep."

She snatched her hand back. "No drugs, nothing that will incapacitate me. No. I'll be... I'll be fine."

He raised an eyebrow. "I was going to suggest chamomile tea."

Kaylee blushed, obviously embarrassed. "I'm sorry, I didn't mean..."

Jack recaptured her hand. He knew he probably should give her space, but something just felt right about holding her small, fine-boned hand in his. "It's okay, really. Chamomile and a bedtime story, what do you think?"

Her expression changed from embarrassed to confused. "Um, a bedtime story?"

He grinned. "Well, actually, at the moment I'm making my way through poetry...Keats, to be more specific. I read it aloud, so if you would prefer the couch here, you are welcome to it, and I could fix you a cup of chamomile tea and read from Keats. I'm up to *Ode to a Nightingale*, which is one of his more well-regarded poems."

The girl blinked at him and he watched as a smile slowly lit up her face. "You are a very interesting person, Jack Benton."

"I'll take that as a yes," he said, letting go of her hand reluctantly. The warmth of her hand in his gave him a sense of peace. "Give me just a moment."

Moments later, he had brought her a soft blanket and pillow and a cup of chamomile tea. He had lightly sweetened it with the honey he had purchased last weekend at the farmer's market a few miles away, and a dollop of cream to cool it.

"I hope you like it with honey and cream," he said as he placed it on the glass and steel table next to her, then sat in the seat next to her and opened a weathered book.

Jack watched her as she sipped from the chamomile tea and closed her eyes, a look of contentment spreading across her face. Her honey-brown hair was still damp in spots. Her hazel eyes looked enormous in her pale, expressive face. It struck him hard in that moment, an overwhelming feeling that he was in the presence of someone very special, beautiful, and kind. How he wanted to ask her what had happened, and who had hurt her. He wanted to reach out and take her into his arms and keep her safe from the world. And as these thoughts raced through him, her eyes opened to meet his gaze.

"What?"

He shook his head. "Nothing, it's nothing." He focused on the page in front of him and read the words slowly, deliberately.

"My heart aches, and a drowsy numbness pains
My sense, as though of hemlock I had drunk,
Or emptied some dull opiate to the drains
One minute past, and Lethe-wards had sunk:
'Tis not through envy of thy happy lot,
But being too happy in thine happiness,—
That thou, light-winged Dryad of the trees
In some melodious plot
Of beechen green, and shadows numberless,
Singest of summer in full-throated ease."

Jack looked up. Kaylee had set the empty cup down on the tray and relaxed her body against the chaise lounge. Her eyes had been slipping closed, and she gave a small smile. "Please, continue. I'm enjoying it."

Jack looked back at the page and continued reading.

"O, for a draught of vintage! that hath been
Cool'd a long age in the deep-delved earth,
Tasting of Flora and the country green,
Dance, and Provençal song, and sunburnt mirth!
O for a beaker full of the warm South,
Full of the true, the blushful Hippocrene,
With beaded bubbles winking at the brim,
And purple-stained mouth;
That I might drink, and leave the world unseen,
And with thee fade away into the forest dim:"

He looked up. Kaylee's eyes were closed, her long eyelashes a dark fan against her pale skin. Her breathing was regular, deep. She looked so fragile, so small and delicate, lying there in Allie's clothes, the blanket tucked around her tightly.

Jack felt his heart contract. At first glance, in those clothes, he could only think of Allie. But having spoken to her, having watched her for this handful of hours, he could see how different she was from his sister. Whatever was making his heart do somersaults like this, it felt different, intoxicating.

"Don't stop reading," Kaylee said, breaking him out of his reverie. Jack started in surprise. He had thought she was asleep, but a small smile told him differently. He returned to the poem in front of him. Losing himself in the reading, he plunged into the images wrought by words written over two hundred years ago.

He read it without pausing, the rest of the words falling from his lips until the last line...

Fled is that music:—Do I wake or sleep?

He whispered it, his eyes on the girl curled up in his dead sister's clothes.

Kaylee was truly asleep this time, and Jack debated whether he should risk waking her by picking her up and carrying her to her room. He settled instead for making a nest for himself on the other couch a handful of feet away.

Rebound

Adrienne felt as if she were sinking into a soft, warm cushion of comfort. She could hear Jack's voice reciting the poem, and the words were reassuring, regular, punctuated with inflection. She descended into the depths of unconsciousness, deep into memories of another voice gently reading to her, a voice she knew she would never hear again.

Rainier had just turned the page, pausing as he did so, and Adrienne hunched on the couch, eyes large, shaking with anticipation as she waited for Rainier to resume, when their father walked in. For Rainier, whose mouth turned down in a frown, Gerard's appearance was an unwelcome distraction. He had just gotten to the most intense part of *The Order of the Phoenix*, something he had been looking forward to reading to his sister, and now, here was their father, standing there, expecting them to drop everything. He frowned and set the book down as Adrienne jumped up to hug her father.

Gerard smiled at her indulgently and nodded to the book. "I remember your mother reading you the entire series, Rainier, I'm happy to see you keeping the tradition."

Adrienne watched as Rainier nodded woodenly but said nothing. She missed her mother terribly, and Gerard's absence had felt like abandonment, but she hugged him anyway, frowning at her brother's reaction.

"It's good to have you back, Father. We missed you!" Gerard hugged her in return, lifting her off of her feet.

"I missed you as well, Bumblebee. And I have a bit of a surprise."

"Turkish Delight? Rosewater?" Adrienne asked, her eyes sparkling. Gerard had been on a business trip in the Middle East for two weeks. He usually brought back something unique and glittering for Mom, and a regional confectionary for Adrienne. She bounced a little on her heels, wondering if she might now get a glittering piece of jewelry.

"Well, yes, but... I, uh, I met someone and, well, I know it has been difficult for all of us with your mother gone." Gerard looked at his feet, and he shuffled them awkwardly before continuing. "And Julianna will never replace your mother, but, well..."

Adrienne looked over her shoulder at Rainier, who was scowling now, shooting daggers first at their father and then toward the front door. There stood an elegant woman. In several long strides of her stiletto heels, she was standing at Gerard's side, an overly bright smile plastered on her face.

She glanced quickly at the scowl on Rainier's face before focusing on Adrienne. She reached out and took Adrienne's small hands in her own. "You are every bit as beautiful and sweet as Gerard described you to be. I'm so pleased to meet you."

"I'm, uh," Adrienne turned to look at Rainier, who was shaking now, his eyes filling with unshed tears. "I'm uh, pleased to meet you too." She looked at the beautiful woman, her father, and then back at Rainier. "I don't... I don't understand."

"She's our new stepmother," Rainier ground out, a single tear tracking down his cheek, his face twisting into a snarl. "Father missed Mom so much that he went and got married again." Her brother spit the words out and Adrienne struggled to understand them. Rainier sounded bitter.

"Rainier!" Father began, but Rainier was on his feet and running out of the room. And in his wake, Adrienne followed. She wrenched her hands from Julianna's and ran after Rainier, partly out of fealty, partly out of fear of this strange woman in their home. Who was she? And why had their father married her? Her brother's door slammed seconds before she arrived and Adrienne stopped, unsure whether to go back or to hide out in her own room. She decided on her own room, closing the door behind her quietly. Rainier had never acted like this, and Adrienne felt lost. What should she do? What could she say? She sat down on her bed, trying to understand how her father could have gotten over Mom so quickly.

She heard a creak outside of her door, then a quiet knock, before the door opened a crack. "Adrienne? May I come in?"

Adrienne couldn't trust her voice, so she simply nodded and Julianna slipped in, closing the door behind her. She was tall, taller than Mom had been, and dressed in a cream silk pantsuit. Her lips wore a bright red lipstick and her skin was flawless, her body toned. She was beautiful and Adrienne felt a flash of guilt for even thinking that. How could her father have married so soon? Hadn't he loved Mom?

Julianna smiled at her. "Can I sit next to you?" Adrienne nodded and she sat down, inches away, and her gaze swept the room. "You have a lovely room, Adrienne. Did your mother decorate it for you? I hear she was very talented at interior décor, and painting, and from what I've seen so far of the house, and especially your room, I can see she had impeccable taste."

Adrienne shrugged, unsure of how to respond. She had a few memories of Mom redoing her room when she was younger, perhaps five, and Sydney always told her how she wished she had a swing in hers just like Adrienne did. The egg-shaped wicker swing sat in a corner, filled with cushions and a large stuffed dog. In the days after Mom had died, she had slept in it each night, nestled against the big stuffed animal, the swing gently swaying. She stared at it now and wondered what she was supposed to say to this woman who was here to replace her mother.

"I told your father that we should have given you both some warning, and eased into this," Julianna said, her hands twisting in her lap. "I know how hard this must be for you."

Adrienne said nothing.

"Adrienne, I am so sorry for this surprise. I know you want nothing more than to have your mother back, and I am a poor substitute. But I hope you will let me try." She reached out a hand and gently took Adrienne's hand in her own. Adrienne marveled at Julianna's elegant nails painted the same blood red as her lips. A delicate gold bracelet with a single charm dangling from it encircled Julianna's wrist. "I think you should call me Julianna, not Mother, if that's alright with you." She smiled at Adrienne, and Adrienne did her best to smile back and manage a small nod.

Their father must have been having a similar conversation with Rainier, although from the raised voices, it wasn't going so well. There were plenty of raised voices in the weeks to follow, and Rainier and Julianna's relationship remained strained. Adrienne, perhaps because she was younger, found Julianna to be kind and patient. She acted more like a big sister, and they bonded over a myriad of home-baked delicacies that were mouth-watering and plentiful enough for Adrienne to share with her friends. Just as Adrienne and her mother had gone to Muriel's, or to the park to feed the crows, now Adrienne would spend an afternoon or two each week baking scones or whipping up delectable, melt-in-your-mouth beignets filled with creams and jellies. Rainier stayed in his room or spent more and more time with his friends at their houses, avoiding interacting with Julianna at all costs.

Their father was busier than ever. With their marriage had come an influx of new business and Gerard was busy with it, returning home late at night, long after Adrienne was in bed. One night, raised voices woke Adrienne, and she left her nest in the swing to get some water. The drinking glass from her bathroom was missing. She would have to go downstairs. As Adrienne opened the door, she was suddenly aware of the anger in her father's voice. Rainier was sitting at the top of the stairs listening, and he raised his finger to his lips in warning. Adrienne sat down next to him, curious and unwilling to walk down there when her father sounded so angry.

"Who is this Oladni Corporation, Jules?" Their father sounded upset, angry.

The siblings could barely make out Julianna's quieter reply. "Gerard, my brother's done business with them for years."

"Really? Because I can't find anything older than two years back on them and, frankly, Tom's concerned about what's in the containers we are shipping."

"Darling, stop being so paranoid! They changed names a few years back. I told you that."

"Cenac Shipping has always maintained a high reputation, Jules, and of all of those who have risen and fallen, we have proven ourselves reliable for transporting legal merchandise at all times."

"Of course you have, Gerard! And that will always be the case. The Oladni Corporation also values privacy, because of the cargo it ships around the world for its clientele. There's nothing to be concerned about, Darling. I promise!"

Her words were soothing, but their father's voice remained raised.

"I don't care whose toes I step on, Jules, the next shipment will go through Customs and be thoroughly vetted, just like any other shipments on board Cenac's cargo ships. Is that understood?" Adrienne gave a small shudder at the steel she heard in his voice.

"Of course. Now please, let's have a drink and stop worrying about things that aren't an issue. I'll give my brother a call and ask him to clarify things with Oladni so that this doesn't happen again."

Their voices faded as they moved into the den, and a heavy door closed behind them.

"What was that all about?" Adrienne asked, yawning.

"Something that was shipped didn't go through Customs," Rainier answered, frowning.

"Is that bad?"

"Well, usually if they somehow make it so that the cargo doesn't go through Customs, it could be because there is something illegal inside that they don't want anyone to see." Her brother looked troubled. "Father would never let that happen, though. He says Cenac Shipping is the best because we turn away dirty business and focus on the good."

Adrienne yawned again and turned back toward her room. She would just drink from the tap. She didn't want to go downstairs after all of that.

"She's bad news, Adrienne, and she isn't someone you should trust," Rainier said under his breath.

She turned around to say something back and somehow defend Julianna. But her brother had already disappeared into his room and shut the door. Adrienne returned to her room. Sleep eluded her. She tossed and turned, Rainier's words echoing in her head. Julianna was nice to her. She'd spent time with Adrienne, taught her how to make delectable desserts, painted her nails, and wasn't trying to take Mom's place, or force Adrienne to call her Mother. But something undefinable niggled at her, keeping her from sleep until finally, exhausted, Adrienne finally succumbed to sleep.

She would have overslept the next morning if it hadn't been for Julianna waking her up. As it was, she could barely keep her eyes open in History, one of her favorite subjects. Later, in P.E., she lagged behind the others, her body slow, her brain sluggish. It took the teacher calling her name twice before she looked up, blinking in surprise to see Julianna standing at the door of the gym, her eyes red and swollen. Mrs. Walker, the vice-principal, flanked her.

Mr. Jenkins laid a hand on her shoulder. "Adrienne, your moth-...er, um, your stepmother is here to pick you up. There's been an accident."

Adrienne's brain spun as she gaped first at her gym teacher and then over at Julianna, now advancing across the gym floor. She reached Adrienne, took her hand, and leaned down to hug her. It wasn't as if Julianna hadn't hugged her before. She did it often, really. And Adrienne had liked it, felt soothed by it, even.

This hug was different. Julianna was shaking. "Darling, we have to go to the hospital. Your father, and Rainier, well, there was an accident."

"An... accident?" Adrienne could barely make words move past her lips. The last time she had been to the hospital, Mom had died. She didn't resist as Julianna released her from the hug and pulled her along after her. She could feel her classmates' eyes on her, silent as she was swept from the echoing gymnasium, out to the car, and on to the hospital.

Julianna filled the journey with a nervous monologue. They had scheduled Rainier for an exam, a follow-up visit after pulling a ligament a month ago during soccer practice. "And, well, I would have taken him, but you know how your brother is, and so Gerard took him and the police said the car just went straight off the road down an embankment. And I'm sure they'll be fine, Adrienne, I'm sure they will, but they said something about Gerard needing surgery and I..." Her perfectly manicured nails clasped the steering wheel and turned it hard to the right, going slightly up on the curb as she screeched to a stop in the parking lot and heaved a big sigh. "I just thought you should be here with me."

"Thank you." Adrienne forced the words out of her mouth. Her stomach roiled. Her exhaustion evaporated, replaced with a painful ache of fear creeping up the back of her neck.

Her throat had closed up as they jogged through the hospital doors and into the large front entrance. The smell wasn't unpleasant, only a hint of antiseptic, but enough that it reminded her of returning to the waiting room with Rainier. She could still see her father's tall frame bowing in despair at the news that his wife's routine surgery had turned into tragedy.

Hours later, the sun had set outside, pinks and reds and golds giving way to the blackness of night, interrupted only by the glow of the city and the parking lot lights. Adrienne sat on the hard plastic seat in the waiting room, her stomach growling for food, but the muffin Julianna had bought in the gift shop remained untouched by her side. She stared out into the darkness. Beside her, Julianna had wedged herself into a reclining position and her breaths came regular, deep, spaced.

"Mrs. Cenac?" A doctor in blue scrubs stood near the entrance to the room, his eyes tracking around it. The others in the waiting room had stirred when he made his appearance, but dropped their heads at the unfamiliar name. It wasn't their loved one he was here about. Julianna responded to Adrienne's hand, shaking her, and the doctor advanced.

"Mrs. Cenac, I'm Doctor Watanabe. I just wrapped up the surgery on Mr. Cenac and young Rainier."

Julianne stood, smoothing her clothes free of wrinkles. "How are they, doctor?"

Dr. Watanabe nodded and smiled. It was a brief thing. It appeared and then disappeared again. "Your son Rainier will make a full recovery. His leg had multiple fractures which require immobilization. It will be a few months of healing, followed by physical therapy. Your husband, however, received extensive injuries to his spine, Mrs. Cenac. Myself and Dr. Batanides, who specializes in spinal cord injuries, did everything we could, but the damage is extensive and, unfortunately, looks as if it is permanent."

"Spinal injuries?" Julianna responded, her fingers covering her mouth.

"Yes, I am very sorry to report that Mr. Cenac has suffered a permanent paralysis. It looks as if he severed his spinal cord at the same time as he crushed the T4 vertebrae in the accident. If Mr. Cenac had been wearing a seatbelt, like young Rainier was, he likely would have been fine." The doctor winced at his own choice of words. "That is, he wouldn't have sustained such permanent injuries."

Julianna wiped away tears, asked to see both Rainier and Gerard, and then turned to get her coat and purse.

The doctor walked away, then stopped in the doorway and turned back to them. "Mrs. Cenac, I know this is difficult, but your husband and your stepson are alive. And after a one hundred and fifty foot fall off of the embankment, that's quite a miracle."

"Indeed, it is, Doctor Watanabe. Indeed, it is. I am so happy they both have their lives." As she swung her purse over her shoulder, Adrienne glimpsed an expression on her stepmother's face that looked anything but happy. It was there and gone in mere seconds, replaced with a look of grateful hope that had Adrienne instantly doubting what she had just seen. Julianna was kind to her, after all. She was even kind to Rainier, who was rude and standoffish. They were all lucky to have her.

She's just worried about Father and Rainier.

Julianna strode from the waiting room, and Adrienne scuttled after her.

Rough Night

Jack lay there on the couch and listened to Kaylee's slow, rhythmic breathing. He would be a fool not to admit that he liked her; more than that, he felt drawn to her, an attraction that had nothing to do with protecting her slowly building.

She wasn't like the women he dated. Where they were hard, she was vulnerable. Where they were devious, Kaylee struck him as intelligent and troubled, but determined. He had quickly eliminated any concerns of her being involved in drugs or really anything illegal. Despite looking as if she were under the influence when she first came to in his car, he was just as sure that she was the injured, and innocent, party.

Her lips were parted slightly, and he could see her eyes moving in the quick back-and-forth movements of REM sleep. Her eyelashes, thick and dark, fanned out over the dark shadows under her eyes. He wondered what she was dreaming about as her face twitched and she huddled deeper underneath the blanket.

The skin on her left cheek was abraded. Had she fallen? Had they abused her? Anger rose in him at the thought of whoever it was who had hurt her.

Every part of him wanted to hunt them down and make sure they never had the chance to hurt her again. And his last thought as he fell into sleep, and into the dream, was how it would feel to run his lips along her jaw and capture her lips with his own.

The dream, more like a memory, really, was the same. It never varied. Despite knowing exactly how it would end, Jack could not wake from it, or escape it. He had to let it play out, just as he had for the past ten years, each misstep a reminder that his choices and mistakes had led to the life he had now.

It started, as it always did, with the day before it all came apart...

Jack kissed his mother on the cheek. "I'm heading out now."

"Darling, please be safe. And try not to stay out too late," she said, hugging him. "Your father wants to get an early start."

Jack rolled his eyes. "I know, I know. Although really, Mom, I'm not much for skiing."

"But you love it! We haven't missed our annual trip to Tahoe since you came down with strep at age six. It's a family tradition."

Jack laughed. "I loved snowboarding until I ran into the tree and broke my clavicle. Now I far prefer drinking at the chalet, finding some cute snow bunnies, and shooting pool. But don't worry, I'll be home by two, maybe three at the latest. I can sleep on the plane."

Renae Benton smiled up at her son. "Don't forget you promised your sister you would spend some time snowboarding with her. It will ease my mind to know you are with her on the slopes."

"Crap. Yeah, okay. A promise is a promise. Gotta go!"

He slipped out the front door and was nearly to the car when William Benton's voice floated out over the courtyard. "Where are you off to?" Jack turned to see his father close the door to the office and head his way.

"Just going out for a few games of pool with some friends, Dad. I'll be home soon."

The elder Benton scowled. "You aren't planning on drinking all night, are you? And it's your friends, not Jerry, right?"

Jerry Banks, who he had known since high school, was two years older and served as their pilot. William had hired him soon after they opened a branch of the investment firm on the East Coast and another in Canada. Most weeks, the elder Benton was traveling from one destination to another and not here to judge Jack's party-going enthusiasm. Today, however, was different.

"Nah, just meeting up with a couple of friends, nothing crazy."

His reassurance did nothing to change the grim look on William's face. "Mahoney called me this afternoon. You're failing one of your classes."

Jack kept his face calm with difficulty. If it wasn't bad enough having Dad insist that he pursue a law degree, William Benton had also made sure it was a college he chose, not Jack's first choice of UC Santa Cruz. He had scoffed at Jack's suggestion, called it a place where you went to get a doctorate in partying. He wasn't wrong, but it had stung. Instead, Jack's dad had pushed Jack towards Stanford, where his friend was Dean. Considering Jack's lackadaisical approach to his schooling in high school, he was lucky to get in there. He certainly hadn't earned it, but money and connections made all the difference in the world. They couldn't, however, magically convert him into a straight-A student.

"I've brought home my books; I'll get it up to snuff in no time."

The look on his father's face betrayed his lack of confidence in Jack's smooth answer.

"I'll be back soon, couple of hours, and I'll be sure and take Allie out on the slopes, and keep an eye on her."

Mom was protective, but Dad? He wrote the book on overprotectiveness when it came to his only daughter.

"See that you do." William turned away from him and, with it, dismissed Jack without another word.

Hours later, creeping home in the car at the lowest rate of speed possible so that his alcohol-soaked brain kept the bright red sports car on the road, Jack could feel the hangover headache snaking its tendrils into him. How many shots had he done? How many had Banks had? He'd lost count between the shots, dancing with twin redheads. They were identical and with piercing green eyes, by God. A fight in the bar between two short, dark-haired men had broken the dancing up and he had lost track of the girls and Jerry Banks and realized it was three in the morning. He'd spent an hour, possibly longer, weaving among neighborhoods, avoiding sobriety checkpoints and getting lost. Now, as he slipped off his shoes and made his way into the house, the dark black of night was turning to gray.

Christ, my head is killing me!

The house would soon be waking. The parents were both early risers, as was his sister. Jack was the black sheep. Given the chance, he would sleep all day and rise as the sun set. It had made his morning classes especially difficult, hence the failing grade.

"Dad's pissed." Allison's voice from the darkness nearly had him shooting out of his skin. "I just heard him talking to Mom."

"Christ, you scared the crap out of me!" Jack could just make out her form, stretched out on the couch. "Wait. He's up already?"

"Uh, yeah," Allison said, in a derisive tone she had cultivated over the past year as she moved into her mid-teens. "It's after five."

"No, the clock in the car said it was four." Then he smacked his head. "Time change. Crap, I keep meaning to fix that."

Allison laughed. "It's two weeks until we fall back. Might as well keep it where it is."

"Yeah, yeah." Jack moved towards the panel door that led to his basement bedroom. There would be no time for sleeping now. Plus, he hadn't packed. Who would have thought that the first snow of the season would come so early? Normally it wasn't until Christmas break, or later, that they flew up for their annual trip to Tahoe. This year, however, snow had come early. The Halloween decorations were still up, but they would be gone by the time they returned. A bunch of servants would pack them up and put them away in storage, then lay out the autumn colors for a month before moving on to Christmas.

A half-dozen staff ran the Benton estate with precision and a quiet efficiency.

An hour later, Jack slid into the back seat next to Allie and wished he had taken a second aspirin. His head was in agony, his heartbeat like pulsing fire in his forehead. He was tired, hung over, and had already gotten a reaming from the elder Benton. Mom said nothing, but that was typical. She let her husband handle the uncomfortable discussions, and that left her to the gentler pursuits and kind reminders. He had never seen her lose her cool, except maybe over Malcolm. His lips thinned at the thought of his baby brother stuck in some damned institution. Just because he was different, just because he didn't live up to their father's expectations of what was acceptable or not.

They had stopped without him even noticing, and Jack's father was already out of the car and snarling at anyone who came near him. Jack's mother leaned over and placed several pills in his hand, saying, "Sweetheart, take another of these; you'll feel better. Vitamin C, multivitamin, and another aspirin. You'll be right as rain in no time."

A gray drizzle was falling, and the temperature was plummeting. Jerry reached for Jack's bag and winced, then grinned. "Where the hell did you go? The twins took the party back to their place. We looked for you, you know; Izzie really had the hots for you, but Lizzie was more my type." He stopped, frowning. "Or was it Izzie who was hot for me? Well, hell, I've got their number for next time you want to hit the town."

Jack slapped his friend on the back. "You're going to have to give me the details later, man. Damn! I'm sorry to have missed that!"

Later, far later, he would remember their conversation. And for years after, he would try in vain to remember just how many shots he had bought for Jerry, and which one of them had been the one that pushed it too far. Maybe all of it. Maybe none, if Jerry had continued to drink with the twins, Izzie and Lizzie, in the hours after. No matter, the guilt remained heavy, constant. It was borne in the screams of his mother and his sister, as the plane, coated with ice and piloted by a man who was sleep-deprived and hungover, dove toward the deep lake. The same guilt sunk as deeply in his psyche as Jerry, his parents, and the plane did when it sunk into the icy waters. It was laden deep in the questions from the investigators afterward.

The guilt festered as he sat by Allison's side in the ICU as he waited for his little sister to wake up. She looked so small, so vulnerable there in the bed. Allison didn't look fifteen in those moments. She looked as she had at ten. The makeup had long washed from her face, which was battered and bruised from the impact with the water. She had been closest to him, with his window already shattered on impact. It had been all he could do to get her seatbelt and his off, to drag her out of the window and kick, kick, kick his way through the icy water to the life-giving oxygen above.

The guilt had exploded inside him weeks later as he watched her face crumple at the news that she had lost her beloved mother and father.

The counselor was mandatory, and Children's Division was steadfast. "If you wish to take your sister home and have custody of her, we need to know you are fit to care for her."

For once, his family's money held no sway. Not in the face of a nosy, bureaucratic machine.

He had submitted to their demands. He sat in an exceedingly plain office across from a man who spent an entire year earning what Jack's family investments made in a day. The hospital psychologist was middle-aged, balding, and his cheap tweed jacket frayed.

"I see here that you have refused pain meds for your fractured humerus." The psychologist looked up from his notes. "My father-in-law had a fractured humerus. It was exceedingly painful."

Jack said nothing, just shrugged his uninjured arm. The pain from his arm throbbed through the thick haze of his grief. He had difficulty thinking through the pain, yet somehow it was easier to feel the pain than to be numb. He didn't deserve the numbing gift of the painkillers. This was on him, his fault, his guilt, his mistake.

Jack and the psychologist sat in silence for a moment, then another, each staring at the other. "This will go better, quicker, if you could tell me what you are thinking about. How you feel right now, sitting here in my office."

Jack had sighed, the air rushing out of him, a great exodus of despair. "How do I feel? I let them down. My parents, Allie. Hell, even Malcolm."

"This is your..." the psychologist consulted his notes, "...younger brother, is that correct?"

"He's a non-verbal autistic. My dad had him put in an institution two years ago, when he was ten. I haven't seen him since."

"Would you like to?" the man asked, his pen held at the ready. "How did it make you feel to see him taken away?"

The questions had gone on, seemingly endless. All Jack wanted to do was return to Allison's side, where he had stayed, day in, day out, as she slowly recovered. Besides a serious head injury, she had suffered two broken ribs and a bruised spleen. The doctors had also diagnosed her with a heart arrhythmia, the first either of them had heard of this, and Jack hated to leave her side, even for an hour at a time.

After two meetings filled with invasive questions, the man had finally relented and written a letter of recommendation to Children's Division to release Allison into Jack's care.

The next month had passed quickly. Dean Mahoney had reached out to Jack and offered him access to a sped-up online course instead of in-person learning. Jack, suddenly juggling caring for Allison, and now Malcolm, marveled at his newfound focus and completed the course early, despite the heavier study schedule.

"You aren't off partying all the time," Allie said, her face nearly healed, and the last of the bruises hidden under a careful application of makeup. "If you count up the hours spent doing that, and especially the time recovering from it, you can see how much of a difference it is." She hadn't been wrong. As it was, he was on track to take the bar exam in

six more months at this rate. It wasn't his dream job, but he could see that it was something that would move him forward with building his own legacy in the Benton clan's fortune.

The social worker still came by monthly, but Jack could see a change in attitude from the woman. Any day she would sign off on Jack, and Children's Division would step away and leave the Benton family alone. Allie had recovered some of her exuberant self once her ribs had healed, and having Mal back had been a huge, yet welcome change. Nadine Roberts had asked Jack to consider giving her daughter Azule a position in the office now that she had graduated, and he hired her immediately. He had known Az since they were both small, and she was practically family. When she had seen Malcolm struggling in those first few days, it had been her suggestion to give the boy some magnetic words and see what happened. The results had been instantaneous. Jack couldn't help wondering how long his brother had been waiting to talk, to communicate. He certainly had it now. The simple box of magnetic words had quickly expanded to a folder. And their lives, these three siblings together in the house their grandfather had built, with the billions in wealth from three generations of savvy business dealings, slowly found a pattern and pace. It had been a good time, despite the terrible loss; if only they had stayed together.

Jack shifted, the dream ending, consciousness slowly returning. He was on the couch, and Kaylee's form, her back to him now, was visible in the dim morning light. The memories of his behavior, of the plane crash, and of the cruel turns that life still had yet to deal out, haunted him. He wondered if they always would, if he even had the right to want more, or better, from his life.

I Should Go

Kaylee shifted, one foot slipping out of the warmth of the blanket. Her eyes flew open, her body reacting in a moment of panic, disorientation. "Rain!"

Whatever dream she had been having seemed to scatter in fragments. She sat up, gingerly, and winced, no doubt from the myriad of scratches and bruises that covered her body.

Jack, stretched out on the couch just feet away from her, sat up as well. "Good morning. How are you feeling?"

She gaped at him.

"I, uh." She paused, took in a deep breath. "I'm fine. Um, better. Bad dream." Her eyes drifted to his bare chest, stuck there for a moment, and then looked away.

Jack moved slowly, first stretching, then slipping on the discarded T-shirt he had left on the couch. Kaylee reminded him of a frightened bird, one he was hoping would not fly off. She looked nervous, like she knew or at least suspected that he had been watching her sleep. Jack hoped he hadn't creeped her out too much. She'd looked so peaceful lying there, her lips parted, her breaths slow and regular.

It was daylight outside, and from the angle of the sun, it was quickly on its way to mid-morning. It surprised Jack that he had stayed on the couch as long as he had, watching her sleep, but it had been mesmerizing. He had so many questions, and perhaps today she would talk, and perhaps share her story. He wanted to know why she was so frightened, who had hurt her, and why she was unwilling to speak to the authorities.

Kaylee tried to stand up and hissed in pain. Her left ankle, which had been puffy and bruised a few hours earlier, was mottled dark with bruises and it had swollen significantly. It didn't look broken, but a sprain was possible.

"Here," Jack said, slipping an arm around her, "Let me help you."

"I'm fine, really I..." She hissed again as she tried to put her weight on her left foot.

"Let me help you, Kaylee."

She smiled then and nodded gratefully as he helped her navigate her way to a chair at the breakfast bar. There was a small click from the far wall and Kaylee gasped as she looked over Jack's shoulder, her body tensing.

Jack's brother Malcolm stood there, his lanky, long hair covering his eyes.

Jack smiled. "I'm sorry, I didn't mention my brother Malcolm."

Malcolm stood there, saying nothing. He had a thick binder tucked under one arm.

"Morning, Mal, you hungry?"

Malcolm nodded slightly, then shifted the binder so the front of it showed. It had a word on it. The young man tapped it, but said nothing.

AVOCADO

"Avocado and cheese omelet it is."

Kaylee stared at him and tilted her head in confusion.

Jack shrugged. "Mal communicates using magnetic letters and words." He said it in a matter-of-fact way, as if he was used to explaining it to others. "The therapist suggested it as a communication tool early on. Avocados are one of his favorite foods. I usually make him a cheese and avocado omelet for breakfast. Would you like one?"

She nodded, her eyes fixed on Malcolm and full of questions.

"Where did he come from? It was like he appeared out of nowhere!"

Jack chuckled quietly and pointed to a long expanse of wood-paneled wall. "Press gently on the third panel from the left."

He turned away and opened the refrigerator while she slowly limped over to the wall.

The wood panels were a rich blend of gold and brown wood, and one could see the craftsmanship in each of the inlaid pieces. The wall was a work of art. It was only when she was a foot away that she leaned forward, spying the hairline crack on the right side of the third panel. Jack watched as she pressed it. The wall swung open silently. Inside there was a small landing, an enormous expanse of wall covered in beautiful paintings, and a set of circular stairs leading down to the basement below.

"My parents loved secret doorways and passages. Every house we own has them, either from them commissioning their installation or me keeping up the tradition. Mal lives down in the basement in one bedroom."

"Wow," Kaylee said, gently closing the door. The wall resumed its proper shape with only a ghost of a click. "That's amazing."

Malcolm had slid into one of the tall seats at the breakfast bar, his binder open. Kaylee limped back, and then slid into her own seat, leaving a chair in between for Jack. She could see what appeared to be hundreds of words, all black on white background, arranged neatly on magnetic sheets.

Malcolm flipped the sheets, returning AVOCADO to its open spot. He arranged it precisely on its black box, neatly edging it until it was straight, then returned to the back of the binder for another word. Kaylee watched in fascination. Before long, the boy pushed the binder toward Jack. There were two words on the front...

WHO SHE

Jack read it and said, "She's a friend, Mal, someone who needs our help."

Malcolm tilted his head and gave a quick nod. His hands moved words around and he slid the board back to Mal.

NOT BITCH

Kaylee stared up at Jack, eyebrows furrowing in concern.

Jack grimaced. "No Mal, she's not." He turned to Kaylee. "I'm sorry. I had a... well, there was this woman and she..." He paused, gathered his thoughts, and said, "I was with someone and it didn't work out. She wasn't comfortable with Mal, and he wasn't comfortable with her."

Mal said nothing, just tapped the words with his finger twice and tilted his head so that he could give each of them a sideways glance. Jack watched his brother's eyes slide over her quickly. He was curious about her, and that was a good sign. Mal rarely liked visitors enough to ask about them.

"Do you have other siblings?" Kaylee asked, staring at Malcolm.

Jack's smile disappeared. "I did, but now it is just Mal and me." He turned away and focused on the omelets.

He could hear Mal shuffle through his binder of magnetic words, flipping pages upon pages. With a tiny sideways glance at Kaylee, Mal cupped his hand, blocking her view as he slid it forward.

Jack turned back, a perfect omelet on the plate with a row of neatly sliced avocado to one side, and placed the plate next to Mal's cupped hand. His eyes took in the words, flashed an apologetic look in Kaylee's direction, and then pushed the board aside.

"Enough questions, Mal. And you know it is impolite to not show the words. Eat up."

Mal's impassive face held a flicker of a frown, and he nodded slightly. His baby brother dug into the omelet and seconds later, Jack pushed another perfectly cooked omelet in front of Kaylee.

"Salsa? Sour cream? Hot sauce?" he asked as she took a bite and closed her eyes in contentment.

"Hot sauce, if you have it. This is fantastic, by the way." She managed a smile. Jack pushed down the sudden flush of attraction he felt seeing it. She was beautiful. He had sat there watching her sleep and trying to steer his thoughts away from dwelling on what it would be like to kiss her.

He slipped into the seat in between Kaylee and Mal with his own omelet a moment later and dug in. He looked up and caught Kaylee watching him in the wavy reflection created by the kitchen's backsplash of expensive, shiny tiles.

Who is this girl? Why is she so afraid of the police or hospital?

Mal finished first. No words, magnetic or otherwise, before he slipped out of the tall seat and walked his plate and fork over to the sink and hand-washed it. He disappeared just as quickly, heading back to his lair, most likely to read. Jack had brought him a stack of science fiction novels by Greg Bear and Mal appeared to be tearing through them, judging by the small stack of finished books he had left near the front door.

As soon as his brother disappeared through the secret door in the wall, Kaylee turned to Jack. "Your brother, he's autistic?"

"Yes. It's classified as non-verbal autism. However, as you saw, he has plenty to say." He shrugged. "How he learned to read is beyond me, but he just knows."

"My best friend growing up, Sydney, she had a cousin who was autistic. He spoke, but he really struggled." Kaylee sighed. "He would come for a week every summer to Sydney's house. He was excellent at checkers and chess, beat us soundly. Then his mother died, and they put him in a group home."

"My parents did that to Mal. He was eight. I brought him home after they passed away four years later. He belongs here; this is his home as much as it is mine."

Kaylee smiled and opened her mouth to say something more, when a soft chime sounded.

"There is a vehicle at the gate," intoned the security system.

Jack grabbed his phone and opened up the app. The wait icon blinked for a second before showing the vehicle, a town car with two men inside.

There was a small gasp from Kaylee as she saw the men and jerked away from the image on the phone. "Is this two-way?"

"No."

"Can they hear us?"

"No," Jack repeated.

Kaylee's skin had paled, her lips set in a thin line, her shoulders curved in, and she backed away from him and stared out of the windows. She looked like a wild animal desperate to escape.

The chime sounded again. "There is a vehicle at the gate."

"Kaylee, tell me what's wrong."

She shook her head, tears forming. "I should go. Please, don't tell them I was here."

She limped to the base of the stairs, casting about for the nearest escape as Jack said, "I won't let them in or tell them anything. Just...stay here. Don't run. I promise, you are safe here."

He pressed a button on the phone, holding a finger to his lips before he did. "Yes?"

The driver held a card up to the camera. "I'm Detective Daniels of the Los Angeles Police Department."

"Okay," Jack responded and waited.

"We're investigating a crash and missing woman. We found her car off the side of the road, about a mile from here, and we were just wondering if you have seen anything."

"Sorry, but no," Jack answered.

The driver showed a photograph next, one that was certainly Kaylee. "She's wanted in connection with a string of robberies, so if you see her..."

"I'll make sure and contact the LAPD right away, Detective," Jack answered.

A few more pleasantries later and the car backed up, maneuvered into the turnout, flipped around, and headed back towards the main road.

Jack watched the town car disappear from view and then shut the app down. He looked up at Kaylee. She was shaking her head.

"They're lying. I've never even shoplifted mascara!"

Jack blinked. He wasn't sure shoplifting mascara was a thing, but she looked absolutely scandalized at the idea that she was a burglar. "Look, I believe you."

He raised his hands. She still looked ready to flee. "Kaylee, sit down before you fall down. Please."

She nodded and rubbed her arm before sinking down onto the bottom step. "Was that live or recorded video?"

"Recorded. You want to see it again?" She nodded, and Jack said, "Okay. Hang on. I can put it up on the big screen."

It took a moment for him to pull it up and Kaylee limped slowly over to the couch, sitting down on the edge of one cushion. Jack watched her look repeatedly out the large windows of the house.

"We lock the gate, Kaylee. It's a six-foot-high fence all around." He pressed a button. "Here we go."

Kaylee's eyes locked on the enormous television screen and she grew pale as she stared at the images. Jack zoomed in, selecting and cropping the pictures.

"What are you doing?" she asked, glancing back at him.

"I'm going to find out who these men are," Jack said, as he pulled up his email and sent a message to Teeny.

"Who is Teeny?" Kaylee asked.

"He would say that he drinks and knows things," Jack answered as he shut down the email client and went back to the full image of the two men.

Kaylee pulled her feet up onto the couch and rested her chin on her knees. Jack glanced over and saw the corners of her mouth twitch.

"So, *Game of Thrones*?" she asked, color returning to her cheeks.

"Indeed. He's a midget, so the name isn't a play on words; he truly is tiny." He sat down in the chair to her right and stared at the screen. "Were these the same men who did that to you?" He pointed at her bruised wrists and she pulled them closer, out of sight, before returning her gaze to the screen and giving him nothing but silence.

"Well, just for the record, Kaylee, I'm not in the habit of handing women over to their abusers, in case you were wondering."

He waited for her gaze to return to his. After a moment of silence between them, she tore her gaze away from the screen and met his eyes. "Thank you for not telling them anything," she said.

"That's it?" Jack asked, raising an eyebrow.

Kaylee's face looked conflicted, and he could see she was struggling with what to say. Finally, she spoke, "They would have killed us all. They still might, if they think I'm here. I should go."

Jack nodded, keeping his voice calm. "Where would you go, Kaylee? Where would be safe?"

Her face dipped down behind the safety of her knees and her hair, which slipped down over her eyes. She sat there silently for a moment, and when she looked up, her eyes were brimming with tears. "I don't know, I don't think anywhere is safe. And I, I just don't want anyone else hurt."

Jack nodded again. "And they hurt others?"

"The others are dead, Jack." It burst out of her, a desperate whimper of fear, followed by more tears.

A crying woman had never been a turn-on for Jack. But in that moment, all he wanted to do was scoop her up in his arms, silence her tears, and then wrap his body around hers. He was falling for a girl he had met less than twelve hours ago, in the worst of situations, and all Jack knew was that he couldn't let her go.

He knelt in front of her and gently tugged on her hands until she unwrapped herself from her hunched position. "I promise you, Kaylee, I'm here to help. And I'm far better prepared to defend myself, Malcolm, and you than you might realize. I need you to trust me. I've sent the images off to Teeny. Let him do his magic, and while he does, you and I will watch a movie. How do you feel about Thai for lunch later? I'll have it delivered at the gate."

Kaylee's hands trembled in his own. She nodded wordlessly, and he released her hands and reached for the remote.

As the movie began, Julie Andrews' voice rang out from the meadow and Kaylee gave him a sideways glance. "You like this movie?"

"It's one of my favorites," he said, and grinned at her.

Take the Day Off

Sunday had slipped by with several movies, takeout from Ayara delivered to the gate as promised, and Kaylee falling asleep in the middle of the third movie, the remains of her Pad See Ew still clutched in her hand. Monday morning had been pleasant, but Kaylee had barely touched her breakfast. Now she was staring out of the window towards the front drive, her eyes round.

Jack followed her gaze out of the window, confused by Kaylee's panicked expression.

"Don't worry, that's Azule. She works for me."

His employee's car was making its way down the long, twisting drive. He glanced at the clock in the kitchen. Right on time. Every weekday morning at five minutes before nine, Azule's car would appear, regardless of traffic jams or road closures. He wasn't sure how she did it, but her ability to arrive at exactly five minutes before the hour was a talent he had seen day in and day out for over ten years. Traffic jams, tremors, not even the wildfires knocked her off her schedule. He couldn't believe he had forgotten she was coming. The weekend with Kaylee and Malcolm had blasted past far too quickly.

His words, meant to reassure her, only panicked her more.

"No, no one can know I'm here."

She stood up, wincing as her injured feet hit the ground, but just as determined to escape before anyone else knew of her presence in the house.

"Okay, okay, hold on. I'll just go out and ask her to work from home today." He held out a hand. "Just stay here, okay?"

Kaylee nodded silently; her expression tight, fearful.

He could feel Kaylee's eyes on him as he walked outside, barefoot. The cement was cool under his feet and Azule braked as he held a hand up.

Her window rolled down.

"Morning, Boss." Her round, brown-skinned face frowned for a moment. "What's wrong?"

Jack struggled to think of an excuse. "Hey, Az, listen, I uh, I've had a tough weekend with Mal. I uh, I hate to ask you this, but do you think you can work from home today?"

"Work from *home*?" Azule's face held a mixture of suspicion and shock. "You feeling okay, Jack?"

"Yeah, Az, I'm great, it's just..." he stumbled over his words. "I need a day. Alone. Here with Mal." He hated having to lie to Azule, but he had promised Kaylee he wouldn't say anything. He'd given her his word.

Azule's eyes narrowed. They strayed to the house as if she were trying to see into the windows, determined to discover what he was hiding. "What about the shareholder information you wanted me to work on? I need to have file access, which is here."

"I need you to postpone that meeting until next week."

"But, Boss..."

"Please? Azule, I promise I'll explain everything later. Just, right now, I need you to work from home today. Can you do that?"

Azule frowned further and then nodded slowly, her eyes troubled. "This isn't some dolphin in the jacuzzi bit, is this?"

Jack stifled a laugh. Azule's mind was like a steel trap. She forgot nothing. Years ago, when she had first started working for him, he had told her there were certain key phrases he needed her to memorize, for her protection and for his. You didn't get to be a multi-billionaire without having safety measures in place. He picked different catch phrases for different things, but the phrase, "The dolphin is in the jacuzzi" was code for "Call the police."

"No, Az. No dolphins in jacuzzis around here. Promise. It's all good. Take a day on my dime, Az. Relax. I'll explain everything when I can."

Azule chewed on his words for a moment. "All right, Boss. I'll go home. But you need me, you call."

"Will do, Az." He backed away from the car and Azule rolled the window up, still frowning. He had twenty-four hours, tops, to figure out what had happened to Kaylee, and how to help her, before Azule would be back.

He watched her pull away, waving at her as he did. Azule wouldn't rest until she had her answers. It was something that he depended on most of the time, but right now, it was a real pain in his side.

As she drove away, Azule Roberts could not think of a single day she had missed work. Nor could she think of a single instance, except for a 4.2 quake two years past, when Jack had told her to stay home. There had been a good reason for that edict. The road outside of her house in Compton had dropped five feet, crumbling into an impassable sinkhole. Every weekday for three months after, Jack had sent a car to pick her up just past the blocked street. He'd even arranged for grocery delivery.

She saw him wave and then turn away and walk back into the house. Then she turned onto the curvy road and quickly lost sight of the house in the trees. It was a long trip back into the city, and Azule felt a minor annoyance flash through her. Why hadn't he called and told her not to come? He had looked distracted, not upset. And wouldn't he be upset if Malcolm was having a hard time?

I can't say I've ever seen the boy have a tough time, what with Jack caring for him like he does.

Azule knew that, before Jack had taken over the family business, and before his parents had died in a plane crash, Jack's parents had seen fit to have Malcolm institutionalized. It had seemed an extreme reaction to the boy being diagnosed with non-verbal autism, something her uncle's youngest son had. Isaac was difficult, far more so than Azule's near-daily interactions with Mal, and he had been violent. But Mal was mild in comparison. She tried to imagine the boy striking out or being destructive and simply couldn't.

She had often wondered why Jack's parents had felt it necessary to send their youngest child away, even if it was a far better place than most folks in the same position would ever see. Money bought things, and that was for sure.

Azule had started working for Jack shortly after the plane crash. She'd been there when he first brought his brother back and watched him interact with Mal. The boy had been a mess. On the edge of turning thirteen, he was uncommunicative and withdrawn.

Jack had pulled him out of that. So had she, for that matter. She had come up with the idea of the binder and magnetic letters, and Jack had acted on it immediately.

Watching Malcolm come out of the dark place he had been in had been as good for the boy as it had been for Jack.

And that is why none of this made sense. It raised her hackles. Even if Jack had laughed off the dolphin phrase. Could he still be in trouble?

The trees thinned and the narrow, two-lane road appeared. She slowed and waited for a town car with two men to drive slowly by. They stared at her, brazen, curious, and Azule felt another twinge of concern. Their car looked out of place and so did they.

Might be casing the area, looking to burglarize some homes.

Azule watched as they eased by and made a mental note of their license plate. She would ask Teeny to run it later, just as a precaution.

She frowned as she maneuvered her car onto the busy, congested highway and headed for home.

"Auntie, I'm home!" Azule called, dropping her keys in the drawer near the front door before locking it behind her. It had been unlocked, which was odd, since she distinctly remembered locking it when she left. "You left the..." She stopped in mid-sentence as her cousin Marley came into view.

"Hey, Az." He grinned at her; his two front teeth yellowed but edged with gold.

"What are you doing here, Marley?" Azule ground out. Her cousin was trouble, no denying it, and from the look on his face, he sure hadn't expected her to come walking in right then.

"I just come to see Mama, that's all." He gave her a shit-eating grin she didn't return.

"Yeah? How much you borrowing from her this time?"

Marley rolled his eyes. "Now, Az, I don't see as how you need to worry yourself over..."

Lorna appeared behind him, a vacant smile on her face. "Hi, Azule, honey. Is it already time for dinner?"

"No, Auntie, it's still morning. I had a short day today." She didn't want to get into it, not with Marley standing right there.

"Still working for that rich white dude?" Marley asked. "You know I got this investment opportunity that..."

"Save it, Marley. He ain't interested and neither am I," Azule gritted out. "Auntie, I need to have a word with Marley in private." She gestured towards the door. He grinned at her and stood his ground.

"Now."

He made a show of playing the dutiful son with Azule's aunt as he hugged the older woman. "Mama, I'll come again real soon and see you. Play canasta with you, okay?"

"Alright, son, you do that. And you bring me those clothes you need fixin', I ain't too old to take care a'you, y'know," she called out as Azule unlocked the front door and hustled Marley out of the house.

Azule shut the door firmly behind her and spun around, hands on hips. "So how much you hustle from her this time?"

Marley raised his hands in front of him. "Honestly, cousin, I don't know why you think..."

"Save it, Marley. Don't you dare bullshit me. I asked you how much."

"Just three hundred." He looked off in the distance, avoiding her eyes.

"And how much do you owe?"

"C'mon, Az, I tole you, I'm looking for..."

"How much?" she barked at him.

Marley stole a glance at her, then stared at the ground, silent. He scuffed the broken concrete with his foot. "A hell of a lot more than three hunnert."

"She can't help you, Marley." Azule folded her arms over her chest. "And I'm not going to either."

"Az!"

"Don't you 'Az' me, Marley Remus Black." He backed away from her as she lashed out his full name. "We've had this discussion. You know we have. Last year I went and pulled out the last of Auntie's money, and paid off that damn bookie after you went and fucked up. I take care of Auntie, and I send Jamal enough in prison to keep him from bein' the bottom of the damn pile in there. And that's it, Marley. You gotta help yourself and figure out a way out of this. I'm done fixing your mistakes."

Marley's mouth moved the way it had when they were kids and he was trying to come up with something to say, some way to change her mind or convince her to give him the last of her pocket change. They'd grown up together. He'd been a baby when Azule's grandparents had died and Azule's mother had moved in with Aunt Lorna. Decades later, when Lorna needed help, Azule's mother Nadine had insisted she come and live with them. Marley had been a few years older than her. Back then, he had been a lot more effective at getting what he wanted. She'd learned a lot in the decades since. If she didn't stand up to Marley, no one would, and he'd run amok on her savings enough as it was.

"Don't bother arguing with me, Marley. I'm done. And I'm done with you takin' what little your mama has."

"And how you gonna stop that?" he snapped at her. "I'll just come back tomorrow, or the next day. You ain't gonna be here to stop me."

Azule smiled then. "She won't have any more cash on hand, Marley. Unlike you, I keep my money in bank accounts, CDs, and an investment portfolio. When Aunt Lorna asked for that three hundred, it was me who went to the bank and got it out."

The smug smile slipped from Marley's face.

"Because it was my money, not hers. You drained her dry two years ago, and I have been taking care of her ever since. And that's fine. I'll keep taking care of her. I promised Mama I would. But I'm telling you now, cousin, that this here well has run dry."

And with that, she walked back into the house and then turned and slammed the door in her cousin's face.

"Azule, honey, is everything okay?" Aunt Lorna was sitting in her rocking chair, a pile of knitting in her lap. Her face was smooth, only a few wrinkles, but her mind had begun to slip nearly a decade back. It was one reason Aunt Lorna could no longer care for herself. Marley, and Jamal before him, had rummaged through their mother's meager savings until there was nothing left.

"Everything's fine, Auntie," Azule answered, her insides roiling. That no-good Marley. He was just as bad as Jamal, worse. He was the youngest of three, and Lorna doted on Marley. At least he hadn't ended up a gangbanger like his two older brothers. Terrell, Lorna's oldest, had died in a shootout when Marley was barely ten years old. Jamal had been in prison for the past ten years, caught selling drugs and unwilling to rat anyone out for a reduced sentence. Azule figured he'd be there for another fifteen at this rate.

"Is Marley coming back?" her aunt asked, a small frown on her face. "He said he needed a little more for that stock he's a'gonna buy. I told him that was all I had, but..."

"Don't worry about it, Auntie. He said he had someplace he had to be." Azule knew she would need to talk to her aunt soon about not giving Marley any more money, but that was something she didn't look forward to. Lorna's mind came and went like the tide. No matter what she remembered about her finances, which wasn't much, she always had an excuse for her youngest child. Just as she had had for her husband, who would have gambled away every penny of their life savings if he hadn't died in the middle of a card game shortly before Marley was born. He hadn't even known his dad, so how had Marley followed in his father's footsteps so well?

Azule shook her head. That was irrelevant, really.

If Marley can't get his shit in order, that's his problem.

She hadn't even brought up Demetrius, Marley's four-year-old son. At least the boy had a wonderful mom. Nia struggled, but she managed three square meals a day, kept the boy clean, and put a roof over his head. Nia had kicked Marley to the curb when Demetrius was just three, and it had been a sound move, if not long overdue. Azule sent them two hundred dollars every other week to help them out. Nia thought it came from Lorna, and Azule preferred it that way.

"It wasn't enough, was it?" Lorna asked, her fingers working away, needles clacking. "The way he asked if he could get more, that boy has gone and gotten himself in deep, hasn't he?"

"Marley is a grown man, Auntie. One who has got no place coming to his mama begging for money," Azule answered.

The older woman nodded and said nothing, the needles clicking rhythmically. It was a soothing sound.

"I could take on some work."

"Auntie, he'll be fine," Azule said, although she wasn't entirely sure of that.

"Why are you back so early?" Lorna switched colors, and the needles resumed their steady clickety-clack.

"Jack said for me to take the day off or work from home."

"Huh."

"I'll be back tomorrow. Meanwhile, why don't I call and see if ShayTwin Hair has an opening for one of us to get our hair done and then I take you out for lunch? It's been a minute since we had a meal we didn't cook," Azule suggested. "Would you like some Chinese at Sunny's?"

Lorna smiled, setting her knitting down and standing slowly. "I been hearing of this soul food place called Not Your Mama's. Janine's baby daddy works there as a line cook. She says the mac and cheese there is better than mine."

Azule whistled. "Well, that's gotta be wrong. But sure, we'll go give 'em a try. Now that you mention it, I heard something about peach cobbler, and you know how I feel about cobbler."

The day passed swiftly, and it wore Lorna out by the time they returned, the sun already low in the sky. The older woman had sat and knitted while Azule had her hair done in braids and swept up onto her head. They had eaten at Not Your Mama's and, while good, the mac and cheese fell short of Lorna's. The cobbler, however, had been exceptional.

As she locked the heavy security door behind them, Azule's thoughts fell once more on Jack Benton.

What was going on up there? Tomorrow morning, come hell or high water, she was going to find out.

Fever Bright

Jack walked back inside and waited by the window, watching as Azule drove away.

I've got twenty-four hours to get some answers before Azule comes in and wrests them out of this girl.

He turned and gave Kaylee a smile. "She's gone. I imagine she'll be back tomorrow with a thousand questions for me. Az is one of the best, and you will see what I mean if, well, *when*, you meet her."

Kaylee had settled back into her seat at the table and she poked at her breakfast half-heartedly.

"Tired of my cooking already?" he asked.

"Sorry, I'm not hungry right now." She pushed the plate away from her. "And you are an amazing cook. Could I have some more water?"

He took the glass from her, his fingers brushing hers. Her hand was warm to the touch, and he was suddenly aware of how flushed her cheeks looked.

"Are you running a fever?" He reached over, ignoring her flinch, and touched her forehead. It was burning up. "You are! No wonder you don't feel like eating. We need to get you back to bed."

"Jack, I can't stay here. I..." She swayed slightly in place, her skin paling. "I need to..."

"You need to rest, Kaylee." He strode over to her side and slipped a protective arm around her.

Malcolm, whose plate was empty of food, held up the binder. It read...

JUICE

WATER

SLEEP

"See? Even Mal agrees. C'mon. I'm going to make sure you make it all the way up those stairs."

The heat rolling off of her was fever bright, and Jack wondered if he should call a doctor. All of those hours out in the chilly rain had done it, he was sure of it.

She leaned on him, despite her objections that she was fine, and stumbled slightly, clearly unsteady on her feet. By the time they made it up the stairs, he was practically carrying her. How had he not seen how sick she was this morning? How had he missed the red cheeks and clammy, sweating skin?

She felt so small in his arms at the top of the landing when he lifted her up, off of her feet. Kaylee didn't even protest, her eyes fluttering and then shutting as he carried her the last few feet to her room and gently placed her on the bed. She showed some signs of life when he tried to cover her with a blanket, shoving it off as she turned on her side with one feverish kick.

He turned away from her and nearly slammed into Malcolm. His brother stood there silently, eyes on the floor, two pills outstretched in one hand and a glass of juice in the other.

"Thanks, Mal." He took the pills and juice from him and flashed back to Azule. From the look on her face when he had talked to her and given her such a flimsy excuse, she had seen through it. Azule knew Malcolm nearly as well as Jack did. It had taken time, but Malcolm was far better now than that shell of a boy Jack had found locked away in the institution. Why Dad had found it necessary, he would never understand, just as he couldn't stomach why Mom hadn't objected to it. Mal would never live what others would consider a normal life—there were no kids or a career in his future—but he didn't deserve to be locked away like some animal.

Mal was all Jack had, just as Jack was all Mal had. That's just the way it was. Azule got that. So really, it wasn't any surprise that she didn't buy his flimsy excuse to send her home. He was half-shocked that she had actually left when he asked her to, instead of digging her heels in and insisting on the real reason for him sending her away.

He grabbed a pillow and seated it under Kaylee's head, gently raising her shoulders and then extending his palm with the Tylenol towards her.

"I need you to take these. They'll lower your fever. Mal brought you the last of the fresh-squeezed juice."

Kaylee's eyes flickered open. She shakily took the pills from Jack's hand and put them in her mouth before reaching for the juice. Her entire body was shaking now.

"Mal, do you remember where the thermometer is?" Jack asked, as he steadied the glass in her hand. Seconds later, Mal pressed the thermometer into Jack's hand.

Jack activated it and held it against Kaylee's forehead. Her fever seemed to have grown in just the few minutes. The thermometer flashed twice and then gave a discordant beep. The number 102.9 glowed, back-lit in red.

"Christ."

Kaylee's eyes fluttered closed as she sank back on the bed. "I should, I should go."

"Kaylee, you are running a high fever. You need to rest." He touched her shoulder, felt the heat of the fever on her skin, and damned himself for not having realized she was sick earlier. "You are safe here. Now get some rest."

Jack left the room, closing the door gently behind him. Malcolm waited outside, binder in hand.

Jack read the list of words his brother was holding out.

FOOD

QUIET

I WATCH

He nodded, surprised at the last line. Mal kept to himself. Anytime there were others in the house, he slipped away, down into the basement, hunkered down in his room, and avoided the others.

"I'll place a grocery order for delivery later this afternoon," Jack said in response. "Are you sure you are okay with keeping an eye on her?"

Mal nodded. It was nearly imperceptible, but Jack was used to Mal. His brother communicated volumes, if you only knew how to see the signs.

"Okay, well, I need to check in with the team and a few other tasks. I'm going to go over to the office. You let me know if I'm needed here, okay?"

Another small jerk of Mal's head and Jack left him there. When he reached the bottom of the stairs, he looked up and saw Mal seat himself in a comfortable chair on the landing a few feet from the door, his binder in his lap, his hands busy flipping the pages.

I've never seen Mal react like this to anyone except Az and me. Well, possibly Luke, as well. But never protective or concerned.

It was a first.

Jack walked briskly towards the far end of the house, then outside, to the building at the far end of the garden. Here the architecture remained the same, but they'd designed the building with business in mind. It blended in perfectly with the clean lines of the house, but inside there was a distinct business-like feel.

There were four offices, a galley kitchenette with coffee station, two bathrooms, and a spacious conference room. It wasn't often that they needed the conference room, only a handful of times in the year, but it came in handy when meeting clients. Jack had added onto the back part of the building nearly a decade ago, eradicating his father's putting green and instead installing an atrium with several small fruit trees that reached up to the tall, glassed-in ceiling. The center of the atrium held a pond that burbled and gushed. It held a cluster of fish and there were seats, several bistro tables, and chair sets scattered about. Jack often ate lunch here with Az on the weekdays.

Az will be back tomorrow with a barrage of questions for me, guaranteed.

He needed to check in with Jesse and Shane, who were both on separate jobs. Shane was busy with a minor mob boss turned informant out of Atlanta, along with the guy's hyena of a wife. Jack suppressed a grin at Shane's description of the woman. Apparently, his charges had been fighting like cats and dogs since they arrived at the safe house and showed no signs of calling a truce. The client was due in court to testify in another month, and Shane was as unhappy as they were.

Protecting the seedier characters like this minor mob boss paid for the other work, and the clients who didn't have money. And since Allie, well, Jack knew he was filling a need. Battered wives, abused teens, and dozens of innocents with no money or options, they got the help they desperately needed. If his guys had to babysit some shittier players in order to provide the seed money for making a difference in the lives of innocents, then that is what they would do.

Jack varied the clientele among his guys. Right now, he had Jesse protecting a battered wife and her two small children in Mississippi while they waited for the divorce and custody hearings. The court had released the husband from jail with no monitoring two days after he had put his estranged wife in the hospital and broke his six-year-old son's arm when the boy tried to protect his mother. The bastard was still walking free while the prosecutor's office took its time trying to decide whether they had enough to charge him.

Jack shook his head, his lips a thin line of disgust as he read his emails. Jesse had moved the woman and her two kids to a secure location, and things were quiet for now. There was a message from Shane informing him that the ex-mob boss and his wife had actually gotten into a fistfight. The other two men on assignment had checked in as well, with nothing to report, and a third was on vacation. He'd sent a photo of a giant catfish he'd caught on Lake Powell in Arizona where Jack had a houseboat.

He believed in paying his men well, contributing to their retirement funds, and letting them make use of the properties he had scattered all over the United States and the rest of the world.

Hell, why not? The houses were just sitting there, after all.

Jack pulled up the Bristol Farms website and began preparing an order. It was something that Az typically handled, a task which always looked effortless when she did it, but took him nearly an hour. He ordered the basics, along with some specialty cheeses and meats, and sent the order in. Seconds later, his email chimed, informing him they would deliver it after two. He set an alarm on his phone. Mal refused to answer the gate notifications, and the delivery guy always needed a signature.

With the general housekeeping duties and email checked, Jack could now dig into Kaylee, if he could find anything at all.

False name, for sure, and likely there won't be anything on the police scanner, but I should check.

He dug in. Jack wasn't half as efficient as Azule would have been, but he managed. He responded to three new inquiries for Benton Security Services. One was for rich kid bodyguard detail for three months. He could put Aidan on it since the detail he was on was ending soon. He refused the second one out of principle. A protection detail for a well-known pedophile? No way in hell. The third was a general inquiry, and after a fair amount of searching through the files, he found the standard fee list and attached it to a form reply and sent it.

In between emails, Jack called Teeny and asked him to keep an ear out for any missing woman cases, car accidents in the area, and recent murders.

"Where's Az?" Teeny asked, sounding surprised when he heard Jack's voice.

"Out today."

"She's okay, though, not sick or nothing?" Teeny persisted.

Jack's eyebrows raised. "Uh, no. She's fine, Teeny." He listed out his requests and Teeny promised to message Jack's phone with the lists in an hour.

Jack grinned to himself. Teeny sounded a bit lovestruck over Azule.

Just as he set the phone down, an instant message popped up.

COME BACK

"Shit." If Malcolm was asking for him to come back this soon, something had happened. He jumped up and headed for the house, taking the long, low steps two at a time.

"Mal? What's wrong?" Jack called as he loped into the house, the door shutting behind him with a slam. He saw instantly what the problem was. Kaylee was standing in the doorway of her room, clutching at the door frame for support, a jacket in one hand. Mal stood next to her, his eyebrows furrowed, silent, clutching the cell phone in one hand while steadying Kaylee with the other.

Jack ran up the stairs, reaching out for the girl just as she collapsed.

"I'm sorry," she said weakly. "I thought, I thought I was feeling better."

He pressed his hand against her forehead. Her fever was down, but she was still warm to the touch.

"I need to go," she whispered.

"Kaylee, I promise you, I will take you anywhere you want to go." Jack leaned down and scooped one arm under her trembling knees. The heat rolling off of her was concerning, and he was beginning to second-guess keeping her here. Perhaps she needed a doctor. He wasn't looking forward to explaining to hospital staff the marks on her ankles and wrists. They were livid bruises now, a deep purple and black in some areas, fading to a sickly yellow in others. "But please let me help you right now. I promise you; you are safe with me."

She weighed nothing. At least, nothing compared to what he dead-lifted three times a week with his trainer. Jack carried Kaylee easily back to her bed and set her gently down on the soft mattress. As he did, his nose grazed the side of her neck and he breathed in the faint scent of lavender and sandalwood.

"It's not safe for me to stay here," she whispered. "You aren't safe. He's not safe." Her eyes darted to Malcolm before returning to his. "I can't let them hurt anyone else." Tears pooled in her eyes.

Jack brushed a stray tear away with his thumb.

She's worried about me. About Malcolm. Not herself. What happened to this girl? Who has she lost?

"Kaylee, listen to me, please. You are safe here. I am safe, and so is Malcolm. I promise you that. But if you don't take care of yourself, if we can't get this fever down, then I will have to take you to the hospital."

"No hospitals."

"No hospital, no police, Kaylee..." He stopped, took a deep breath. Close behind he heard Malcolm shuffle through his binder and then it appeared next to him.

TELL HER

Kaylee read the words as well. A look of fear crossed her face. "What does Mal mean? Tell me what?"

Kaylee certainly fell under that category. Whoever she was, wherever she had come from, and whatever she had been through—it was all still unknown. But nothing about this girl struck him as being anything other than a victim here.

"Tell me what?" she repeated.

"I run a security service, one that protects those who need it most."

"A security guard business?" The look on her face made it clear she was unimpressed.

He fought down a laugh. "No, the people I protect are usually running for their lives, Kaylee. Like you. Women who are looking to escape abusive husbands. Witnesses of crimes who the police can't or won't protect." He reached for her hand, turned it gently, and traced the bruises on her wrist. "Someone hurt you, Kaylee. I can also see from your wrists that this same person restrained you for hours, possibly days. You don't trust the police, and you don't trust anyone, really. Considering what you have been through, that's completely understandable. But you need to trust me. I can help you, Kaylee, so please, rest. Please trust me to keep you safe. And when you are feeling better, I'd like to know what happened."

Kaylee nodded slowly. "Okay."

Jack smiled, relieved that she wasn't jumping out of the bed and running for the door. She needed to rest. Mal rattled the bottle of pills in his hand and bumped it against Jack's arm. "And that's Mal reminding me you are due for more Tylenol. That and a large glass of water," he added as Mal shoved two pills and a glass into his hand. "Apparently he is worried you are dehydrated."

Kaylee smiled at Jack's brother, her eyes warm. "Thank you, Mal." She didn't act concerned when Mal turned around and walked out of the room. Mal's silence, a hallmark of his autism, typically unnerved people, but Kaylee wasn't like the others. And somehow, that made Jack even more curious. What was her background? Who was she?

The questions kept piling up. Eventually, she was going to have to trust him enough to answer some of them.

No Recovery

S he took the Tylenol, drank the water. Despite everything that had happened to her in the last week, Kaylee felt relatively safe here. More than anything, she was afraid of bringing down danger on more innocent people. Hadn't there been enough of that already? Learning that Jack dealt with dangerous situations, and could protect others, had eased many of her concerns. He had steered those two men away yesterday, and they hadn't returned. And then his employee this morning, which showed he could be circumspect, but battered wives were a far cry from international trade deals and multi-million-dollar illegal activities.

Whoever the Oladni Corporation really was, and what part Julianna might have had in it, was still unknowable. It made her question everything she thought she had known about her stepmother. Not to mention what role Cenac Shipping had in it all. The company was hers, her family's, and she was supposed to be running it just as her father did before her.

The heat from her body faded, the Tylenol taking effect, and as she slipped into sleep, there were two very different thoughts in her mind. One, what part did Julianna have in all of this. Two, what kind of man was Jack Benton and why, oh why, did she find him so attractive?

Memories of the days after the accident interceded, and Kaylee fell into a memory-filled dream...

Adrienne was relieved when they finally allowed her into Rainier's room. Father was in the ICU and the doctor had glanced at her before shaking his head at Julianna, explaining that his condition was still critical and that they allowed no minors on that floor. Her brother was on the floor below, recovering, and still woozy from the surgery that had been necessary to reset the bones in his legs. The nurse on duty seemed to take pity on Adrienne who, according to hospital policy, should have stayed in the waiting room.

"Just a few minutes, mind you." She leaned close and whispered, "If you see a doctor walk by, duck. You can't be in here without a parent."

Adrienne whispered an equally quiet thank you back, but the nurse had already disappeared down the hall. The room was quiet and empty except for Rainier's bed. She sat down in a chair on the far side, out of sight. She was small for her age, and with the hospital bed in the raised position that it was, the top of her head wasn't even visible. Rainier looked so pale, lying there in the bed, and Adrienne held her breath until she saw the steady rise and fall of his chest. They had immobilized both of his legs in bright, lime-green casts that ran from his ankles to his hips. There was a line of neat stitches along the side of his face, and she wondered how he had gotten it. The doctor had said Rainier had stayed in the car, thanks to his seatbelt, but that Father was thrown from the vehicle.

The embankment had been steep, some hundred feet or more of a descent before trees had stopped them. Adrienne had heard paramedics talking about it as they had walked by. They had needed the Jaws of Life to cut Rainier out.

No wonder his legs had been broken.

His eyelashes fluttered and Adrienne felt her tears spill over onto her cheeks, a relieved gush of them, as he opened his eyes and stared at her there next to him.

"Hey," he croaked and tried to shift in the bed. His lips thinned, and he winced.

"Hey," she said back and cried harder.

"Is Dad..." Rainier stopped, winced, his face twisting with pain. "Is he...is he okay?"

"He's in the I..." Adrienne hiccupped and sniffled, reaching for a tissue box, "...the ICU. He's hurt bad. They won't let me see, but they told Julianna that he was going to make it." She wiped her tears away, but they kept on coming, falling faster. "I was so scared, Rainier, and the doctor says Father might never walk again. And you," she said as she pointed at his casts, "Are you going to walk again?"

"Yeah. I'll be okay. It just really hurts right now." Adrienne could see that Rainier was crying too. Just a single tear tracing its way down his cheek, but definitely a tear. She had seen Rainier cry only one other time before. Last year, when Mom had died.

"What happened?" she asked, struggling to understand how they had ended up in such an awful accident.

Rainier shrugged and shook his head. "I don't know. One minute Dad was driving me to the orthopedist in Ponchatoula because she had screwed up and scheduled me for there instead of New Orleans like I normally do. Dad said he had a meeting out that way and so he would take me. The next thing I knew, the brakes stopped working. We were on Route 22, near that spot where it gets all twisty, and Dad just kept pushing down on the pedal and swearing. We couldn't slow down. And then the road took a real sharp twist, and we just weren't on the road anymore."

Another pair of tears leaked from his eyes and he brushed at them furiously, as if their existence on his cheeks was simply unacceptable.

Rainier stared at the empty room in silence before adding, "I bet she did something to the brakes. I bet she wanted us dead."

"Rainier! That's not fair. Julianna is nice," Adrienne protested, feeling defensive of her stepmother. "If you weren't so mean to her, you would see for yourself."

Her brother bit his lip. "You're just a kid. You just don't get it."

It hadn't been long before the kind nurse had returned. And with Adrienne now standing, hands on hips and looking ready to do battle, she was ushered back to the waiting room where Julianna, pinch-faced and looking angry, had appeared moments later. With a swoosh of her arm, she had grasped Adrienne's hand and pulled her towards the parking lot, Adrienne struggling to keep up with her stepmother's long stride.

"Julianna?"

"Put your seatbelt on, Adrienne."

Adrienne did as Julianna directed, the seatbelt barely in place before Julianna reversed out of the parking slot, tires screeching a complaint.

"Julianna?" she asked again. "Is Father going to be okay?"

Her stepmother yanked on the wheel and zoomed out of the parking lot, the car bucking over the speed bumps, waving a free hand dismissively at a security guard signaling at her to slow down. She didn't respond for a long time. By then they were on the freeway, heading home, and Julianna had cut off several other motorists, causing a cacophony of car horns in the process before she slipped past, moving over into the fast lane, and pushed the speedometer past 75 and kept speeding up, weaving among cars as she did so.

"Your father will need to be cared for, Adrienne. He'll need nursing care, now, and likely for the rest of his life." She passed another car, missing clipping its bumper by inches, and Adrienne flinched as the driver rolled down his window and screamed at the pretty red sports car that had nearly run him off the road. "The doctor is sure he will never walk again. There will be pain as well. Likely severe, and for the rest of his life. Thanks to the severe nerve damage." She sighed. "It looks as if I'll need to step up and take care of most of his business dealings. Thank goodness my family business runs itself."

As if she suddenly realized she was speaking to a nine-year-old traumatized by the events of the day, she looked over at Adrienne. "Oh, my dear, I am so sorry. I didn't even check on Rainier." She slowed the car. "Should we go back?"

"I saw him," Adrienne said, releasing the death grip she had on the side of her seat. "He's in two leg casts."

"Well, it's past dinnertime and I doubt you have eaten anything, have you?" Julianna nodded at the exit. "We'll stop and eat. Go back to the house and see if you can't get something to keep Rainier occupied for a while. He's going to be laid up in bed for weeks. And I'll need to contact a contractor to handle the renovations."

"Renovations?" Adrienne asked, faintly.

"Yes, the large room on the east side of the main floor. I'll convert it into a suite for your father. He won't be able to make it up the stairs, after all." She continued to talk, but for Adrienne it was all static. The room that Julianna was talking about had been her mother's art studio. It still was. The sun had filled the room with a natural light in the mornings, and Mom had spent hours painting and sketching. When they had come back from the hospital without her, it had been the one room Adrienne would spend hours in, just sitting, sketching buildings and columns, recording the details of the ornate wood carvings above the mantel, like she had when Mom was alive. Nothing had changed in that room since Mom had died.

The antebellum mansion had been in the family for nearly half a century, and extended family for a century before that. Adrienne felt a little ill at the thought of what Julianna could mean by the term "renovations." What would happen to her mother's artwork and her supplies?

"A suite?" she asked, trying to visualize what Julianna could mean to do with the enormous room. The wood inside of the room was all original, the floor planks Cyprus and oak. Her mother had taken such care, laying down thick oilcloth to protect the floors, her paints, brushes, and more neatly placed in cabinets.

"Yes. It will need a bathroom installed that is fully wheelchair compliant. I hope we don't need to take out any of the wall on the north side to handle the pipes and wiring." Julianna turned abruptly into a parking lot in front of a greasy spoon diner. "They'll likely need to remove that monstrous fireplace and mantel as well." The tires spit gravel before coming to a stop. She pawed through her purse, then looked up to see Adrienne's look of horror.

"But you, you can't, Julianna."

A shadow crossed Julianna's face. She stared at Adrienne, tilting her head to one side, and the look on her perfect face chilled Adrienne. "I beg your pardon?"

"The, the, the room." She tried to stutter out an explanation. "Mom told me that the fireplace is original and the wood has never been painted, not in over 150 years. It's, it's, it's our heritage," she finished in a whisper. Bad enough that they would clear the room. In Mom's absence, just as it had been when she was alive, the room was a refuge, a place of peace. A place she could step inside and walk quietly through, touching the things that Mom had touched, breathe in the smell of paint and mineral spirits, note the paint that had flown down to the oilcloth below and tacked it in a spray of aubergine, of salmon pink, and a serene cottage blue.

Where would she remember Mom? Where would she go when the world outside became too complicated and loud and she felt as if she would lose her place in it? And to paint it. That would be a cardinal sin. Even Father would never agree if he knew.

From the moment that she had first met her stepmother, Julianna had been kind. Adrienne had never seen her grow angry, or frustrated, not even in the face of Rainier's obvious dislike of her intrusion into their family unit. The look on her face earlier in the day, when the doctor had told her how lucky it was that neither Rainier nor Father had died, Adrienne had already convinced herself that she hadn't really seen it. It disappeared just as quickly, and it could have meant anything, *really. Father wouldn't have married just anyone. Not so soon after losing Mom. Julianna had her own business, her own wealth, she didn't need Cenac Shipping; she had her own business too.*

But now, in the car's quiet, Adrienne saw someone different. This was not the woman who had laughed and rolled the dough out on the long marble countertop in the kitchen. She wasn't the one who had shared her lipstick one night after giving Adrienne a manicure, despite her ragged, bitten stubs of nails.

And then, just as before, the look vanished, replaced with concern. Adrienne could hear a burst of noise erupt from the greasy spoon diner as the door swung open, and a family breezed down the steps, laughing and talking, a bag of leftovers held in one of the teenager's hands.

Julianna reached out and took Adrienne's hand in her own. "Forgive me, Adrienne, I didn't think. Your mother's art, her supplies, and..." she said as she closed her eyes, rubbing her forehead with her free hand, "...today has been overwhelming. Of course, you are right, we will figure something out, so that your father will have a place that can accommodate him and we won't be changing the property. I'm just panicking a bit." She opened her eyes and smiled warmly at Adrienne, giving her fingers a warm squeeze. "I'm hungry and trying to problem solve. It's never a good mix. We will eat and I'll pack a bag for Rainier, all the pieces for him to futz about with his video games while he's laid up in the hospital, and we will talk to someone about getting a chair lift installed. How does that sound?"

Adrienne managed a smile in return. This was a side of Julianna she had never seen. Then again, her father and brother had nearly died today.

Julianna is just upset, like me. Except she doesn't get to cry or panic, because everyone is depending on her.

Still, the look on Julianna's face continued to haunt her long after they finished eating crawdads, etouffee, and gumbo at Big Sal's and headed home. A few weeks later, and both Rainier and Father were home. It felt weird. Rainier lay in his room, housebound, with only visits by the physical therapist for company for twelve long weeks as the bones slowly knitted themselves together.

Father was a changed man. The active, always on the go businessman replaced with a broken shell of a man. He rarely used the chair lift, preferring to stay upstairs in the suite of rooms he shared with Julianna. Adrienne would pass by his door on the way to her own room at the end of the hall. Usually, she would find him staring out of the window, his face slack and expressionless.

Rainier transitioned from the bed to a wheelchair and eventually to crutches. Spring gave way to summer, and summer moved into fall. It was nearly time to return to school, and Julianna had promised Adrienne she would take her shopping for a fall wardrobe in Baton Rouge. She skipped upstairs to grab her purse and slowed to a stop outside of Father's bedroom. Rainier was there in the doorway, watching, his eyes troubled.

"He takes too many pills," he mumbled. Father sat, unmoving, slack-jawed and staring.

"Julianna says they will help him feel better," Adrienne protested.

"Sure, if you want to be a zombie." He scowled. "She gives him too many pills."

Adrienne stayed silent. Part of her thought Rainier was wrong, but the person her father had become frightened her. It was as if that sharp business executive was gone, replaced by a ghost of a man who only looked like her father.

In the end, Julianna's voice had floated up the stairs and Adrienne had run away, relieved to leave the ghosts behind.

Move Aside

Jack checked on Kaylee every few hours throughout the afternoon and into the night. Her fever shot back up, barely responding to the over-the-counter medications.

Malcolm, who was dependable down to the hour and minute, maintained a vigil in the chair outside of Kaylee's door, waking Jack whenever the girl's temperature climbed past 102. Jack had seen nothing like it. Ever since Jack had brought his brother home ten years ago from the institution his parents had put their youngest child in, Mal had been a silent fixture in the rambling house. Jack had questioned whether Mal would be better in a group home, around others like him. He had even asked Malcolm if he wanted something different, and his baby brother had produced the same answer each time.

NO
HAPPY HERE

What was happiness for Mal? Jack couldn't detect a single iota of it on his brother's face. The only communication, the only sign, came from the binder of magnetic words. Over the years, the smallest of changes in Mal's pattern showed the most.

When Alexandra, his latest short-term dalliance, had invited herself over, and done her best to move in, Malcolm had made his displeasure known by slipping the following words to the front.

SHE GO HOME NOW

He hadn't even bothered to cover them. Every morning, without fail, Malcolm had shown the words to Jack until, six long weeks later,

Alexandra had set her sights on an easier, and far older, target. It had been a relief for all involved.

Mal liked Kaylee and showed concern for her welfare. Well now, that was something more than unusual. It was a good sign, really. And Jack nodded to his brother as the last of the night gave way to the bright morning sun. Kaylee's temperature was still over 102 degrees, and she was slow to respond to his efforts to have her drink more water, turning away before finishing the glass.

Azule's car turning into the drive at a quarter past eight was a surprise. Normally she arrived at a few minutes before nine, and Jack was sure it had to do with his assistant's curiosity. She cared little for being kept in the dark about anything.

Jack walked down the stairs and met her at the front door.

"Move aside, Jack." He suppressed a smile. Azule had a forceful personality. If he had ever wondered who the real boss was, he recognized the truth then: she was.

"Morning, Az."

"Well," Azule said as she turned to face him, hands on hips, "Who is it and where are you keeping them?"

"Her name is Kaylee, and she's upstairs in Allie's old room."

Azule nodded and headed for the stairs. Jack followed. In some ways, it relieved him Azule was here. She would know how to get the girl's fever down or likely die trying.

As Azule stared down at Kaylee, who slept on, unaware of the attention she was receiving, the older woman noted the thermometer and half-full glass of orange juice. Malcolm walked in, board in hand, and nudged Azule with it.

FEVER HIGH ALL NIGHT
ON THE RUN
NO HOSPITAL

Jack blinked. It was the most he had seen his brother communicate in a long while. And it showed he'd been keeping up as well.

Azule read the words and met Jack's eyes. "On the..." She shook her head. "And a high fever all night? Are you two trying to kill her?" She dug into her purse and pulled out her cell phone.

"Who are you calling?" Jack asked, and she gave him a frosty look, raised her palm towards him, and walked away to the far end of the room.

"Marley? I need Diamond at Jack's house. Tell him to rattle his dags too." She stabbed the End Call button with a fingernail and her eyes swept the room. "He'll be here in an hour."

"Who?" Jack asked, mystified.

"The doctor, of course." Azule walked away. "I told him to hurry, but there's traffic."

The short black man clad in ragged jeans and a T-shirt with Snoop Dogg emblazoned on the front with the words "Paid the Cos' to be the Boss" did not look like a doctor. Despite this, he set up an IV, complete with a collapsible IV stand, with a few quick, efficient movements.

"Um..." Jack stepped forward as the smaller man wrapped rubber tubing around Kaylee's arm.

"Don't worry, she'll be fine. I'm starting with a cocktail of antibiotic fluids on her," Doctor Diamond said, his voice cultured and reassuring. "Once she is awake, have her take these twice daily for five days and call me if you don't see improvement by tonight. She's receiving the first round via the IV." He set the bottle of pills down on the nightstand. Jack could see from the label that it was a common antibiotic. The doctor closed up his satchel. "That'll be one gee for the house call and antibiotics. I left my card there in case you need me again. Just return the stand when you get a chance, Az, I've got spares."

Azule slid past Jack and handed him a small stack of hundred-dollar bills. "Thanks for getting here, D, give my regards to your mama."

The man nodded and said, "Will do, Az. Hey, her birthday is on Saturday if you can make it. I know it would really make her day if you came by. I'm pretty sure she likes you better than any of us, anyway." He turned his gaze to Jack and offered a hand. "Pleasure doing business with you, Mr. Benton."

Jack shook the man's hand. "Thank you, Doctor." He watched as the man left the house, got into a van that had seen better days, and drove away.

"Who the hell was that, Az?"

"I grew up with him," Azule answered. "I've known him my entire life. His mama's house is just down the block." She shook her head. "Diamond there, he got out, was on track to be a bigshot neurosurgeon until his cousin went and borrowed his car. A week later, Diamond gets pulled over. The police want to search his car."

"Why did they want to search his car?" Jack asked, interrupting.

Azule gave him a look. "Because he was black, Jack. Why else? He was black, driving a nice Mercedes in a nicer part of town. So of course, they wanted to search the car. And he didn't think he had anything to hide, so..."

"So, he let them search it, and..."

Azule snorted. "It wasn't really a choice for him; he said yes so they wouldn't break a taillight or something worse." She stared at him with a look that spoke volumes and then shook her head. "Anyway, his cousin had neglected to remove all the cocaine, or had tried to skim it off of the top of the shipment. We never learned the entire story because the fool died of an overdose the week after they arrested Diamond."

Jack blinked. "So he has a drug conviction?"

Azule nodded. "Served five years, lost his license, and now he handles medical care for folks who can't go to a hospital without raising suspicion or causing the authorities to get involved."

"I'm guessing he does business with gangs?"

Azule gave him another withering stare. "And playboy billionaires who hide pretty girls away in their luxury homes. Diamond doesn't ask questions; he just takes care of his patients. He does what they trained him to do: be a doctor."

Jack nodded. "Fair enough, Az." She gave a harrumph and slung her purse over her shoulder.

"I took it out of petty cash, just so you know. I'm going to see what else you messed up in the office while I was out. You know where to find me." She headed out of the house without a backward glance, and he watched her make a beeline for the office.

He glanced over at Mal. His brother's fingers were busy with his board and folder full of words.

K BETTER SOON

TIRED

BED

Jack nodded. He slept poorly as well, but Mal had stayed in that chair all night. "You want any breakfast first?"

There was no answer, not so much as a head shake. Instead, Malcolm walked downstairs, pressed the panel, and disappeared inside with a quiet click.

Jack looked back at Kaylee, asleep in the bed, the IV dripping into her arm, the antibiotics on the nightstand.

You aren't doing her any good standing here staring at her like some damned pervert. Get to work, Benton. Find out who those guys were the other day, track down the lead, keep Kaylee safe, and stop thinking about her. She's a client.

That's what he kept telling himself, even if she hadn't agreed to it. She needed help, and that's what he did. Kaylee wasn't one of those models or wannabe actresses who could smell money a mile away. She was hurt, traumatized, and now ill. Once she recovered, he'd get her to tell him why she was running and who she was truly running from. And he could help her then.

He shut the door to the guest suite gently. She had slept through Doctor Diamond's visit, hadn't even twitched at the needle piercing her skin, and he could only hope that this would be what she needed.

He walked downstairs, stopping at the kitchen long enough to grab an apple to take the edge off of his hunger, and headed for the office.

Azule was waiting for him to arrive. She looked pissed. Her hands were on her hips and one foot was tapping in time as she barked out her questions. They were the same questions he had been asking for the past two days.

Who was she?

How did she get those marks on her wrists?

Where did she come from?

Why no police or no hospital?

Jack held up a hand, his lack of sleep catching up with him.

"Az, please, I don't have any answers yet."

The black woman's foot tapped faster until she was practically stomping. "Well, what do you know?"

Jack sighed and sat down in an armchair, relinquishing the power of the room to Azule, whose fiery eyes showed she was questioning everything, including what part he had played in the whole debacle.

"I found her on the side of the road, about a mile from the house. She had those bruises, scratches, and injuries from a car wreck."

"A car wreck!" Azule barked. "She could have internal injuries!"

"Az, please, hear me out. I checked for injuries. She's fine."

"She sure as hell doesn't look fine, Jack." She parsed her words, pausing between each for emphasis. Jack couldn't remember the last time she'd looked this angry.

"The rain soaked her to the bone. It stormed Saturday, do you remember?" Azule arched an eyebrow at him and said nothing. "Look, she likely caught a cold from the exposure. I don't know how long she was out there, but she had climbed out of the wreckage, up the embankment, and was there by the side of the road when I came along at what, one or two in the morning?"

Azule gestured for him to continue and Jack did, explaining the first few hours, her panic at the thought of involving the police, and the two men who had come by the house looking for her.

"Why didn't you tell me all of this yesterday?"

"She was so panicked every time, I just needed to gain her trust more than anything." Jack shrugged. "It seemed the best course of action."

"Well, it wasn't," Azule said, her eyes still angry, a flash of hurt seeping through.

And suddenly, Jack understood. She was worried about him, not just Kaylee.

I upset Az when I excluded her and sent her away. Shit.

"Az, I'm sorry. I should have told you. I should have trusted you and told Kaylee that as well."

Azule raised her chin, nodded, and said, "Apology accepted."

She sat down in his office chair with a sigh, "I worried about this all damn day and night, wondering what was going on that you wouldn't let me in. Well, what's done is done. Now we have to get those answers, find out who that girl is, where she's from, and what the hell happened to her, before someone else comes sniffing around looking for her." She tapped her long nails, painted a deep, metallic green, on the rich wood of the desk. "You think she's on the up and up?"

Jack nodded, relieved that Az was focusing on Kaylee and not him. "I do. She's young, maybe twenty, or twenty-two?"

Azule snorted. "That girl isn't a day over nineteen."

Jack sat back. "What else did you notice?"

"Manicured nails, eyebrows been shaped, and her hair might have been colored. She's got dark eyebrows, but brown hair with blond streaks. I'd have to hear her talk, but I'd guess she comes from money, like you."

Jack gaped at her. "Damn, Az, that's a lot of noticing for just a few minutes with her."

"What was she wearing when you found her?" Azule asked, a flicker of a smile on her lips.

"A dress. Blue. It was pretty torn up; I tossed it in the trash."

Azule stood up and walked out of the office without a word. Moments later, she was back. "Gucci."

Jack shrugged; he never looked at labels, or price tags. "And that means?"

Azule gave him another one of her looks. "The girl is a trust fund baby, just like you, Jack Benton."

"So, a kidnap victim?" he mused.

Azule shook her head. "Not if she was afraid of the police."

Jack rubbed his forehead. A headache was forming, and it exhausted him. "I don't know what it could be then. She's too young to be a battered wife. A kidnap victim wouldn't be afraid of the police. And she's too scared to be playing games and be the one up to no good here."

"And she won't tell you anything?" Azule asked, frowning.

"No, nothing. Other than she doesn't want me to get hurt." He paused. "Her words were, 'I don't want anyone else to die because of me.'"

Azule folded her arms over her ample chest and stared off into the distance. "We need answers."

Jack nodded. "We certainly do."

Wrong Place, Right Time

The room was quiet, the voices who had filled it, gone. Kaylee opened her eyes. The door was closed, the curtains drawn. She wasn't sure if it was day or night. They'd secured the tubing that ran from the IV bag to her arm, and the bag was nearly empty. She contemplated taking it out. Her fingers moved to the spot, ready to peel away the adhesive, but then she stopped. If there was something inside meant to keep her unconscious, well then, she wouldn't be awake. Perhaps it was to help, not hurt.

Her eyes focused on the bottle next to the bed and squinted at the label. Something ending in "cillin"—which meant an antibiotic. She must have been sicker than she realized.

She remembered Mal's steadfast presence in the armchair outside of her door. How long had he stayed there? It had felt like forever. Jack had been in and out as well, talking to her, reassuring her. Kaylee squirmed with discomfort at that memory. She smelled, she was sure she did, and that was not attractive at all. She wanted to get up, take a shower, feel clean again.

He was hot. Several of her dreams had included him, and man, had they been X-rated.

Am I truly safe here?

The men had come, and he had headed them off. But they might come back. She shivered at the thought. It was an impossible situation, one that she couldn't seem to figure out a way out of. If only she had known to hide, or stay silent. She wished she hadn't overheard what she did, or gotten Rainier involved. If only she had understood the depths of danger that one overheard conversation would put her, and the only family in the world she had left, in. If only she had understood how much was at stake.

She closed her eyes as the memory of that moment came flooding back. It began, of course, nearly two months before, with Father's funeral.

Julianna's hand was warm compared to Adrienne's. The rain hadn't been unusual, but the temperatures, normally warm by early May, had been unusually cold. It seemed appropriate for where they were, and Adrienne shivered under the black tent, shifting on the hardness of the wood chair. Rainier was on her left, and Julianna on her right, the rest of the mourners scattered behind them, the chairs half-empty. The rain fell steadily on the tent, and Adrienne could see that the back of the minister's coat was becoming soaked as he stood, his back to the rain, and extolled the virtues of a man who had once headed a shipping empire. Julianna squeezed Adrienne's hand as the man, a stranger who knew nothing of the past decade's slow and inevitable descent into addiction and despair, continued to speak of "dedication to his family" and "forward-thinking" and all the rest.

"Garbage, all of it. Who is this guy?" Rainier grumbled next to her. He said it low, but it was loud enough for Julianna to hear, apparently. Her grip on Adrienne tightened.

Moments later, the minister led them in a prayer and Adrienne wiped her eyes and did her best to smile graciously as the mourners filed past, offering their condolences. What did it matter, really? Father had been as good as dead the moment his car went off the cliff nearly ten years ago. As they lowered the casket into the ground, she could feel the tears wash down her cheeks. For the death of their family unit, the happiness that had once filled their home, and the loss now of both of her parents. She was an orphan.

Julianna handed her a tissue and rubbed her shoulder. Rainier cast a dark look at the woman and Adrienne felt ill. Even here, even now, his antagonism towards their stepmother was so obvious. To her credit, Julianna never responded or grew angry, and that somehow made it all the worse in Adrienne's eyes. She loved her brother, but would it kill him to be kind? To be polite?

She shot Rainier a look, and he looked away. The mourners had dispersed and now the gravediggers waited, likely hoping that the rain would abate long enough for them to do their job.

"Come, they are waiting for us to leave. There's a reception back at the house and the others will be waiting." Julianna tugged at Adrienne's lapel, pulling the black coat closed around her. "This weather, it will make us all ill if we stay out here much longer."

Adrienne stood and walked with Julianna, only to realize that Rainier was not next to her. She turned back, and he shook his head. "I'm not going. None of those people care. They barely knew Father."

It was her look of anguish that seemed to change his mind. "Okay, but I've a flight out this evening."

"Rainier, there are financial matters to discuss. Your father's will, and his wishes," Julianna interjected.

"Father's wishes were that I run the business after he passed. But you seem to handle that well on your own, Julianna." He waved his hand when she protested. "Please, we all know who has been in charge of Cenac Industries since the accident, and likely even before that. I want no part of it. Besides, I have finals next week."

Adrienne suppressed her tears. She had missed him, dreadfully, in the past two years. The day he turned eighteen, just two days after graduation, had been the day he moved out. He had enrolled in a college on the west coast, chose a major of marine biology, and had avoided visiting home for the holidays two years in a row.

She told herself it was for the best. He had been miserable since Father married Julianna, even more so after the accident. And while she hadn't believed their stepmother had had anything to do with the accident, Rainier had held onto it, even tried to have it investigated, which had of course come to nothing.

He had been closest to Father. And as their sole remaining parent had slowly faded away in front of their eyes, lost in a sea of pain and addiction to the pain medication and his now severely limited life, Rainier too had pulled away. He would escape each weekend to his friends' houses and no longer wanted to have them come to his. It was hard for both of them, but far harder for Rainier.

"Rainier, please stay the night," Adrienne asked, her voice hitching with emotion. "For me?"

Her brother looked at the ground. "I'll see if they can reschedule the flight to tomorrow morning. But I am not staying for the reading of the will." He shot a glare at Julianna. They were now at the parking lot, and he stood still for a moment before looking up at Adrienne. "I'll drive you home, Sis." He had rented a car and it sat a short distance from Julianna's sleek forest-green Jaguar.

Julianna said nothing. She squeezed Adrienne's shoulder and nodded, turning away. Moments later, they followed her car in silence, the rain still falling, and the windshield wipers steadily clicking away.

"How is school?" Adrienne finally asked.

Rainier sighed. "It's great, actually. I love it there. You should come and visit this summer."

"I'd like that. A lot."

"Where are you planning to go in the fall?" Rainier asked, his fingers tapping out a rhythm on the steering wheel in time to the windshield wipers. "Did you settle on Cornell?"

Adrienne gulped past the tears that were threatening again. "No. Father said I should study business instead. I'll intern at Cenac this summer and enter Harvard in the fall."

Rainier frowned. "And Father suggested this? Or was it Julianna?"

"Well, of course it was Father, Rainier. I mean, Julianna told me, but she was just repeating what he had said."

"And when was that, Adrienne?" her brother pressed, his fingers tightening down on the wheel until his knuckles turned white.

"I don't know. Months ago, I guess. I mean, come on, Rainier, you know all I want to create is the Victorian era in buildings. I would have been hopeless as an architect." She shrugged. "Father is just looking out for me."

"And Julianna gets just what she wanted," Rainier hissed. "She's getting you out of the way, just as she did Father. You'll spend the next six years in college and come back to a business you don't even recognize."

"At least I'm coming back to it, Rainier! Father wanted you, not me. As if I had a choice. As if you even cared!" The last words flew out of her mouth and she dissolved into tears again. The last thing she wanted was to fight with him. Rainier was the only family she had left. As kind as Julianna was, she wasn't Mom.

They pulled into the driveway in silence, and Adrienne dried her tears. As she slid out of the seat, Rainier said quietly, "Don't trust her, Adrienne. She does not have your best interests at heart. She doesn't care about either of us."

One month later, she had walked into Cenac, her stepmother by her side, for the first time in years. Adrienne had dressed in a slim pantsuit, one of a new wardrobe full. Julianna had taken her shopping days after Rainier had left without another word early in the morning.

"Now, we are starting you out on the ground floor, Adrienne. A simple girl Friday kind of position. This is only for a short time, but you need to understand how this company works, from the ground up," Julianna said, beaming. "That pantsuit looks absolutely lovely on you! I'm so glad we went to White House Black Market; their line fits you well."

Adrienne smiled in return. It felt awkward, strange. There had been little to smile about. Graduation from high school was supposed to be the beginning of it all, but it had felt so anti-climactic instead. Her friends were going to far-off places, but none to Harvard, and certainly no one was working this summer as she was.

An hour later, she filed thick folders, all alphanumerically, then assisted the mail clerk in delivering the interoffice envelopes. She had even taken notes at a meeting. In some ways, it was just what she needed. She remembered with great fondness when she would visit Cenac with her mother for lunch with Father. Some faces were familiar, but much had changed in the years. The support staff, the guards, the mail clerks, and the receptionist in the front all smiled and told her how much she had grown, but the secretaries and many of the managers and other higher-ups were unfamiliar, different.

"How was your first day, Adrienne?" Julianna smiled at her from across the table. It was a small bistro, one that she had never visited before. Julianna had ordered a watercress salad and roast duck. Adrienne had settled on a seared salmon over wild rice.

"It was strange to be back there. I used to go often with Mom and we would make a day of it after taking lunch with Father," Adrienne answered, picking at her salmon. "It was familiar, and yet not, at the same time. So many unfamiliar faces."

"The nature of business, dear. People come, they move up, they move on," Julianna said and slipped a bite of her salad in her mouth.

"Father used to say that he didn't believe there should ever be turnover. It showed the company was unwilling to grow with their employees, or vice versa."

Julianna blinked, and for a moment Adrienne saw a flicker of something move across her face. It disappeared the next second as her stepmother smiled and said, "My goodness, I did not know he had talked about the business with you. I'm happy that you remembered such a conversation. It bodes well for the future of Cenac in your hands, Adrienne. Once you have finished your studies, of course."

Adrienne smiled back at her stepmother, Rainier's words from the day of the funeral bouncing about in her thoughts. She focused on her food and tried not to think any more about it. After all, Rainier had never given Julianna a chance, never warmed to her, and certainly spent no more time in her presence than he had to. He had to be wrong. He just had to be.

The next week, however, changed everything.

Adrienne had moved from one department to another, receiving brief overviews of how each interacted with the other. The thrill of it coursed through her. This would be her company one day. Her employees. Overall, everyone was friendly and took the time to answer her questions, of which she had many. The unfamiliar faces were predominantly in power positions, and when she would ask about their predecessors, there were few answers. It was as if they had simply disappeared. She brought it up again with Julianna, only to receive a dismissive wave of the hand and an offhand comment about how many had reached retirement age. It made little sense. Most of them had been Father's age, and certainly not ready for retirement. And their replacements were in their late forties to early sixties, so it just didn't add up. And if that had been the only thing different, Adrienne wouldn't have given it another thought. But the atmosphere in the company had changed, drastically. She questioned her memories over and over, comparing them to the daily reality as she walked the halls. The managers were polite, willing to answer her questions, but she could feel a reticence, an almost invisible wall, one that stood between her and the others. It was unnerving, and she wondered why Father had truly wanted her to take her place here.

It was a Thursday, in mid-June, when everything came crashing down. She was working in a small office outside of a conference room, filing documents, when she heard the voices. She recognized them instantly—they were both high in the ranks—and Julianna had introduced them as her "right-hand men because in a world like this, you need two!"

"Hastings bungled it big time, and if we don't get on top of this, we are toast," Tom Denkins said, his voice cracking.

"Well, Julianna already knows we didn't fuck it up, so there's hope." The second voice was gravelly and belonged to Jerry Einsdale, the VP her stepmother had said she hired personally shortly after Father's accident.

Tom swore. "She rushed it. She ordered it dumped, and soon, and Hastings did as she asked, and now we've got three hundred dead or dying villagers to deal with. They'll track it back."

"Not to us. To Cenac," Jerry replied with a short, barking laugh. "That was the plan all along. Lay it all at the feet of Gerard, then Julianna and the rest of us walk away scot-free as long as we get rid of the evidence."

"Yeah? And how the hell are we going to do that?" Tom asked, his voice rising. "The village is steeped in toxic waste and the deaths are increasing."

"We burn it to the ground," Jerry responded calmly, and Adrienne felt the hairs on the back of her neck rise. "Tactical strike. Say they were hiding insurgents, and that backwater country's military will take care of the rest. Why do you think she donated millions to Cruzar's campaign?"

Adrienne could not believe what she was hearing. Part of her quivered in fear as well. If they were willing to kill hundreds of people to cover up something, what would they do if they found her?

"So, burn it to the ground and kill the trail back to us, and Cenac, and it buys us time?" Tom's voice had leveled out. "Damn, that's brilliant."

Jerry laughed. "Don't mess with the best. I'll propose the strike, in case she hasn't already thought of it, and the rest will just go away. No one's going to build a new village on the bones of the dead. No one will discover the toxic waste's source, and it will dissipate in the Pacific quick enough. Then it's back to status quo for another six years, or longer if that girl is slow at her studies."

Adrienne sucked in a breath. She felt cold seeping into her bones. They were talking about her. She had to get out of here. Now. She looked around the room wildly. There was only one way in or out of it, through the conference room that was currently occupied by the two men. There was also nowhere to hide. She reached for her purse, for the phone inside. Perhaps she could call the police, or Rainier, or... The change she had received for the soda sitting on the filing cabinet jangled. Not a loud sound, and nothing that should have been noticeable above the two voices...if they had still been talking. Instead, the noise had come at a lull in the conversation.

"What was that?" Tom asked, suddenly alert to her presence. The door to the room was open a crack. And Adrienne did the only thing she could think of at the moment.

She slipped her earbuds into her ear, turned away from the door, and faced the filing cabinet and hummed as if in tune to the music. In the seconds before the door was flung open, Adrienne quickly hit Play on her music and shoved the phone into her pocket, gyrating her hips. She slid the folder into its alphanumerical slot and, pulse pounding, turned to pick up the next. Tom Denkins stood there staring at her and she jumped slightly, then pulled the blaring earbud out of her ear.

"Oh, hi!"

He stared at her, and Jerry appeared behind him, a pleasant grin plastered to his face. It didn't reach his eyes.

Tom had paled slightly, and now he reddened. "What are you doing here?"

Adrienne forced a vapid, half-bored look on her face. "More of this boring filing stuff. It's, like...endless." She paused and did her best to morph into a confused, somewhat put-out look. "Was, like, the room scheduled or something? Do I need to come back later?"

Jerry smiled wider, showing his teeth. "No, no, not at all. Carry on."

"Okay. Whatever." Adrienne shrugged, her heart hammering in her chest, and turned away, slipping the earbud into her ear and surreptitiously turning down the volume to zero. A moment later, she heard them leave. She stood there for seconds, maybe minutes, trying to calm her heart rate, to stop the shaking that had overcome her.

The façade of working for her family's company, the dream of becoming their future CEO evaporated, and suddenly all Adrienne wanted was to run away. She slid her phone out of her pocket and dialed the number. It rang three times before the voicemail engaged. She waited for the beep and said, voice shaking, "Rain. You were right. Call me back right away." She paused for a moment, then added, "I'm scared, Rain, I need you."

I Dreamed of You

His lips grazed hers, and she wrapped her arms around his neck. She had to stand on her tiptoes to do it, but the heat of him and his musky scent were intoxicating. The kiss deepened, and he groaned, his tongue entwining with hers, his hands roaming down her sides to grab hold of her ass and pull her up, suspended from the ground, pushed against the cool, hard wall, her body touching his. She could feel him throbbing against her lower belly.

"Adrienne," he breathed, pulling back to meet her eyes, "I want you."

His hands moved back to her hips, the left one sliding its way along the edge of her panties, the fingers working their way to her clit even as his mouth broke away from kissing her, headed towards that sensitive spot behind the ear. Bursts of sensation blew through her every time his fingers moved and she moaned, digging her fingernails into his back as he continued to stroke her, teasing each new spark of sensation until she couldn't think of anything past this moment, this man.

The feel of his strong, muscled back under her fingers, not an ounce of fat, just pure muscle was intoxicating. It put the boys she had dallied with in high school to shame. They didn't hold a candle to Jack. Adrienne gasped as his fingers continued on their quest, pushing her closer and closer to ecstasy.

The bird fluttering its wings and squawking loudly nearby shattered the dream into pieces.

Kaylee blinked, stretched, and felt a tug on her arm. The room was dimly lit; it was sunrise or sunset by her glance out of the part in the curtain, and the gloom spread long shadows in the room. The door was closed, and she noticed with some alarm that there was an IV bag, empty now, hanging from a pole next to her bed and a tube trailed from it to a neatly wrapped bandage on her arm.

Did he drug me? Wait, this was here when I woke before, wasn't it?

Her panic subsided as she read the side of the bag and surveyed the bottle of pills. Antibiotics, a saline drip, not drugs. Well, at least, not any bad ones, from the looks of it. She wanted the IV out of her arm. Her fingers gently pulled the IV out, then tossed it aside. It hurt more to pull the bandages off as they caught at the fine hairs on her arm.

She felt...better. Less groggy, less hot. The fever seemed to have passed. Had they called a doctor? They must have.

I need to get out of here. A doctor will talk.

She swung her legs off of the bed and stood up. A wave of dizziness hit her and she sat down again.

Okay, so not completely better yet.

The dizziness eased and instead was replaced by two things: body odor and a growling stomach, neither of which she could fix by sitting on the side of the bed. She stood up, swaying a little, but feeling less dizzy. She needed a shower. Thankfully, there was one just fifteen feet away.

Kaylee looked down at her clothes. She was still wearing the borrowed pants and shirt. She hoped it was okay to borrow something else. Moments later, clothing discarded in a hamper, she leaned against the cool tile of the shower and let the water cascade over her. The heat of the water was invigorating, and she felt better than ever. Stronger. It was as close to ecstasy as she was going to get. Outside of the dream that still lingered in her mind, that is. She could still feel Jack's mouth on hers. His fingers, his... Kaylee shivered with desire. The man was undeniably hot. In another place or time, would she act on her desires? Most definitely.

Kaylee chewed on her lower lip, closed her eyes, and her fingers traveled down to that sensitive nub, her own finger tracing it gently, imagining it was Jack here in the shower with her. She rubbed harder, faster, and the water continued to cascade down her neck, tenting over her hand, swirling around the drain. She watched the fireworks explode behind her eyes as she came and opened them, only to find Jack standing there, mouth open, his eyes traveling up and down her body for a brief second before he wheeled around and put his back to her.

Kaylee gasped, reaching for the tiny washcloth on the handle, as if that was enough to hide her body from him.

"I apologize," he said, his hand raised in defense. "I just woke up, heard the water running, and wasn't thinking. I'll, um, just go downstairs now."

Kaylee's face felt flushed and hot. He had walked in on her in the shower. That was bad enough. But to catch her masturbating? And oh my God, masturbating to her dream of him!

She shut the water off, exited the shower, and grabbed a towel before peeking through the open door. The bedroom was empty, the door to the hall firmly closed. She toweled herself off and picked an outfit out of the closet. Whoever had occupied this room before her, they had been the same size, even down to shoe size. Her mind briefly flashed on a sudden paranoid thought.

Did he have all of this ready for me? Is this all an elaborate ruse of Julianna's to discover what I know or what evidence I might possess?

And just as quickly, she realized she was truly being paranoid.

Complete with an autistic brother and a house that was obviously owned by someone with considerable wealth? Right.

It was far more likely that Jack was just who he said he was. That he was wealthy was obvious. He talked and walked and acted like everyone else she had ever grown up with. As she pulled on the yoga pants, crop top, and a light sweater, she wondered if this is what he meant when he said he "used to" have other siblings besides Malcolm but didn't any longer. Was she wearing a dead girl's clothes? She had a quiver of discomfort with the thought, but then instead her thoughts flashed back to him coming into the bathroom, seeing her naked, her fingers between her...

He was staring at me. I should be creeped out by that, but I'm not.

Instead, it left her embarrassed and weirdly turned on. Her fingers slowed and paused as she bent to tie the shoelaces of the shoes she had found neatly arranged on the bottom shelves of the closet. She felt horribly self-conscious. Could she actually go down there and look him in the eyes? Perhaps she could just make a run for the door.

Right. Run out of the man's house. After all, this is probably the only safe place in the world for you right now. After all, they can track you with the first swipe of a credit card. The police seem to be in on this, and every person you love is dead.

She finished tying the shoes and then stood up. The truth of the matter was she didn't know how far Julianna's reach extended. And she wasn't willing to risk her new friends' lives finding out.

Face it, girl. You can't even tell him your actual name. That's how scared you are.

She stood up and straightened her clothes, ran her fingers through her damp hair, and let out a long sigh.

The person you were. She's dead. Adrienne Cenac is dead, or as good as.

All that mattered now was survival. Somehow, she had to disappear. Completely. How did one do that without access to her family's money?

Kaylee realized she had been standing there, immobile for several minutes. Her stomach growled, and she shrugged.

Time to feed the beast and figure a way out of this.

She walked to the door, flung it open, and walked down the hallway before she lost her nerve. Jack was in the kitchen, vegetables sizzling in one pan, bacon in another. She felt the flush creep back up her neck and face. She paused on the stairs, then squared her shoulders, walked down them, and slipped into a seat at the breakfast bar. Jack turned towards her. "Kaylee, I am so..."

She held up her hand to stop him, her eyes avoiding his. "Please, it's fine, really." She could feel her own blush start up again. "Let's just forget it ever happened, okay?"

"Right, okay." He turned away, back towards the stove. "I'm fixing omelets again. Honestly, it's the only meal I'm good at."

Kaylee smiled at his back. "You make an excellent omelet."

The smile he flashed her before turning back to his work made her weak in the knees. It was devilish and sweet, all rolled into one. Was it any wonder she'd had such an X-rated dream of him?

"I'm uh, glad to see you are feeling better," he said, glancing back at her. Her cheeks burned. He was playing it straight, except for a twist of the lips, and she giggled first, her face in her hand. When she looked up, he was smiling in a way that turned her insides to jelly.

Before she could stop herself, the words fell out of her mouth. "I had a dream and you were in it."

He turned off the burners and slowly turned towards her. His hands held his weight as he leaned across the countertop, drawing closer to her than he had been since that first night when he carried her inside of his house. This close she could see the shadow of hairs on his cheek, neck, and chin. His lips looked as kissable as they had in her dream, with a rakish tilt at one corner of his mouth. His smile had vanished, replaced by an intense gaze that turned her insides to jelly.

"Was I?"

It suddenly felt like there wasn't enough air in the room. Her body thrummed as she watched his gaze slide from her face down to her crop top, before stopping at her belly-button piercing. The one she and Sydney had gotten on the same day last summer right before their senior year began.

She didn't trust herself to speak. Couldn't speak, actually. His eyes, dark brown with flecks of gold, sparked a sexy smile sliding across his lips.

Kaylee wondered if he was going to ask her if that was what she had been thinking of when he caught her there in the shower, but he didn't. Instead, he let the moment between them stretch, elongate, and heighten. Suddenly, Kaylee didn't give a damn who was chasing her, or what the days before they had met had been like. Their eyes locked.

He'd seen her naked. And not just naked but... touching herself. He moved closer, inches away now, and his lips parted slightly, betraying a set of perfect, white teeth.

"What if I told you I had a dream about you as well?"

Kaylee's body reacted, the thrum inside of her increasing, searching her mind for something witty or sexy to say. She felt, no, she *knew* she was out of her league. He had at least ten, maybe even fifteen years on her, and she knew countless women had likely warmed his bed. In comparison? She had gotten hot and heavy with all of two boys. And they had been boys, not men.

If the moment had not been interrupted by two very anti-climactic reasons, Kaylee knew that other far more deliciously sinful, pursuits would have been engaged in. But just as their lips hovered millimeters apart, her stomach ruined the moment by growling loudly. Malcolm's sudden appearance sealed the deal when he chose that moment to slip out of his basement lair with a tiny creak and click of the door.

If Jack's brother noticed how quickly Jack and Kaylee jerked away from each other, or how red Kaylee's cheeks became, his face did not show it. His binder under one arm, Malcolm slid into his customary seat, set the binder on the breakfast bar, and began plucking words out to add to the magnetic front. He slid it towards her and flashed her a sideways glance.

K BETTER
YES?

Kaylee smiled, trying to cool her burning cheeks down with her fingers. "Yes, Mal. I am feeling better. Thank you for asking."

Jack, who had returned to cooking, turned to give her an appreciative smile, nodding slightly, as if in approval.

Malcolm's hands were busy plucking words out once he put the first ones away.

K LIKE WORD GAME?

"Word game?" Kaylee turned to Jack, questioning, eyebrows raised.

"Mal wants to know if you like playing Scrabble. He's mad for it. It's okay if you don't; he takes rejection well," Jack explained as he cracked eggs and whisked them together.

Kaylee grinned and clapped her hands, turning to Malcolm. "I happen to *adore* Scrabble, Mal. I used to play it with my mom and my brother. I would love to play a game with you later."

She was picking up on Mal's tells. It wasn't easy. For most people, it might appear as if he had no expression on his face, but the tiniest flash of emotion showed, if only one paid attention. A tiny flicker of a smile appeared and then disappeared just as quickly, along with an almost imperceptible nod of the head.

Kaylee knew she should think about leaving here. She needed a plan. She needed to find a place to hide, to start over, if possible. Somewhere no one would think of her, no one would know who she was. But the thought of it, it was so overwhelming, frightening, really. She had played Scrabble with Mom, and later, with Rainier. It was a series of happy memories, one that meant far more to her than she could put into words. She should think about leaving here, before she brought danger crashing down on all of their heads, but in a few minutes, all Kaylee could think of alternated between kissing Jack and playing a game of Scrabble with Mal.

Jack slid a plate with a perfect omelet on it in front of her. He met her eyes when he did it, and her stomach flipped at the intensity of his stare. She had almost kissed him. And right now, if Mal hadn't been there, she would have grabbed ahold of his black silk tee and gone for it. Kaylee shelved that desire with an effort and looked away from Jack, down at the food. Her stomach rumbled again.

"This looks divine. Thank you, Jack." She dug in her fork and tried not to react when he walked around and slid into the seat next to her, his fingers brushing her shoulder as he did. She trembled slightly in response; her nerves alight, sensitive to the slightest touch.

"Azule will be here soon," he said, and cut a piece off with his fork. "We have an early meeting. A conference call with one of our offices on the East Coast."

Kaylee grew rigid, anxiety filling her again. She set her fork down.

Jack put a hand over hers reassuringly. "You may not remember, but Az arranged for the doctor. She will say nothing, and neither will the doctor. I promise you."

"She already knows about me?" Kaylee asked, the past forty-eight hours mostly a blur from the fever.

Jack smiled, his hand still over hers, warm, strong. "Yes, she saw you, actually. It rather annoyed her that I sent her home on Monday instead of 'fessing up." He grimaced. "There isn't much of my life that she doesn't know about. Her family has worked for mine for the past four decades, possibly longer, and I trust her implicitly."

Sitting there, her hand enveloped in his, Kaylee felt torn between wanting him to hold her and keep her safe, or kiss her and do far more than that. Her stomach growled again, and her cheeks flared red.

"Oh my God, seriously." She glared at her belly and Jack laughed and released her hand.

"It's a good sign," he said, eyes twinkling, "that you have your appetite back. Eat up."

Kaylee picked her fork up and closed her eyes as the first bite of omelet slipped into her mouth. She couldn't help wondering what else he could do besides serve up luscious, mouth-watering, perfect omelets.

Those hands, for example. Such long, dexterous fingers.

The Walls Have Ears

Rainier didn't call her back that day.

Adrienne pled a migraine the next morning, complete with a cool cloth over her eyes. When Julianna knocked on her door, her keys jingling in her hand, Adrienne felt every bit of the part she was playing. She hadn't slept, not at all. Her head was pounding and her stomach roiled as the door creaked open.

"Oh honey, you look miserable," Julianna said, her voice oily with concern. Adrienne wondered if her stepmother had always sounded that fake and that she just hadn't noticed, hadn't wanted to believe it.

That Rainier was right all along. That she's a liar, that she doesn't care about me or Rainier, or even Father.

Her mind had taken her all kinds of dark places last night.

"Perhaps I should stay. Maybe take you to the doctor?"

That was the last thing Adrienne wanted. "No, I'll, I'll be fine. I just need to rest." She could feel nausea rising in her as Julianna drew closer. "I was reading some early syllabi for my classes in the fall and I guess I shouldn't have read in the dark. It's just a nasty headache. I took two aspirin a few minutes ago. I, I'll be fine in a few hours."

She couldn't see Julianna's face, what with hers being covered with the damp cloth, but her stepmother seemed convinced. She retreated to the door.

"I'll bring you a cup of tea. It always helps me with my headaches. I'll be right back." Adrienne could hear Julianna's steps, purposeful, quick, as she strode away before Adrienne could object. A few minutes later, she could hear her stepmother climb the steps, pause for a moment, and then stroll the rest of the way down the hallway.

"Come on now, Darling, sit up and drink this. I guarantee it will help."

Adrienne hated the thought of Julianna in her room, but it was quite clear her stepmother was going to insist, so she sat up and squinted, the headache intensifying in the dim light. Julianna had dressed in red from head to toe. Adrienne remembered she had an important set of meetings today. She had mentioned it over dinner, going on and on about global positioning and new contracts. She stood there, a smile on her lips, the lipstick blood red to match her suit, stiletto heels to finish it all off.

No wonder Father fell for her. On his arm, they made the quintessential power couple.

Julianna handed her the cup of tea. "I added a touch of milk. It's a special blend and I promise you, drink this and in a couple of hours you will feel as right as rain." She smiled widely, her perfect, white teeth dazzling.

Was she really involved? Directing this? Did she really want all of those villagers dead? It seemed impossible.

Adrienne took the cup from her and sipped. The floral notes tasted odd with the milk, and there was a bitter aftertaste. She wrinkled up her nose and Julianna laughed.

"It isn't that bad, Adrienne. All Chinese herbs and flowers. Very good for you. Drink up."

She sat down on the side of the bed and Adrienne forced another gulp down. It tasted less nasty than the first sip. She wanted Julianna to leave, so she could try to call Rainier again. And it was obvious her stepmother would not leave until she finished the whole thing. Three more large gulps and she finished, a fine sediment of white coating the bottom. Adrienne poked at it with the spoon and shook her head.

Julianna laughed again and patted her shoulder. "Good enough. You will feel fine. I'll come back home at noon and check on you."

The warmth of the tea was settling her belly and spreading out through the rest of her body in a soft glow. Adrienne lay back on the pillows, her head feeling muddy, slow. Her eyes drifted shut, and she opened them to see Julianna watching her, the corners of her mouth curled up, satisfied.

"Get some rest," she said and gently lay the damp cloth over Adrienne's eyes. Adrienne yawned and heard her stepmother's steps as she closed the bedroom door behind her gently and then began walking down the hall.

Her eyes felt heavy. All of her felt slow, muddled, and as Adrienne's eyes slipped closed, she could hear Julianna speaking. It wasn't to her and there was no one else in the house. She tried to focus on the words, tried in vain to open her eyes, to sit up, but she couldn't. Long before the sound of Julianna's Jaguar roared to life and drove away, Adrienne had already sunk into unconsciousness.

She was ripped from sleep by Rainier's voice and his hands on her shoulders shaking her. "Adrienne! Adrienne, wake up!" Sunlight poured into her windows, and Adrienne blinked groggily, confused.

"Rainier? What are you doing here?" She tried to sit up and listed to one side, her limbs loose, uncooperative. Her brother steadied her.

"You called me. Yesterday."

"Yeah." She nodded slowly. Why had she called him? Why did she feel so tired? "I, um, I overhead this conversation, and..." Why did she feel so groggy? And confused? "What time is it?"

"Nearly noon. I've been calling and calling ever since the plane touched down."

"Oh. I didn't know you were coming to visit," Adrienne said, feeling thick and stupid. She could hardly think and it was impossible to concentrate. "Julianna will be home for lunch." She was waking up more now, and her words sounded slurred, slow.

Rainier leaned away from her, picked up the empty mug of tea, and stared into it. "What did she give you?"

"Tea."

"Yeah. Tea and something else. Damn it. We gotta go. Now." He stood up and walked over to her closet and opened the doors.

Adrienne pushed herself up. She had listed over the moment he let her go, dizzy and tired. Everything felt awkward. "What are you doing?"

"Trying to find something for you to wear. You need to get dressed. Now, Adrienne. We need to leave."

She wished he would slow down. He was so impatient, and he was moving way too fast. He yanked a handful of clothes off the hangers and tossed them towards her. Adrienne tried to catch them, but they fell flat, inches from her fingers.

"Would you just wait a minute? I can't, I can't think."

"No surprise there," Rainier said, and shoved her covers off her and pulled her to her feet, reaching down and tucking her clothing in a wad underneath his arm. "She's got you drugged to the gills. Just like she did Father." He took her hand and pulled her after him. "Come on, you can get dressed in the car."

"What? Wait. At least let me get some clean underwear." Adrienne could hear her voice now, her brain waking up faster than her body or her mouth. She was definitely slurring her words, and she was so tired, it was hard to keep her eyes open. She pulled away from him and lurched towards the dresser to retrieve a bra and panties. When she turned around, Rainier was standing, her clothes under one arm, her purse clutched in his left hand.

"Geez, okay, I'll change in the car." She rolled her eyes. It all felt rather dramatic. Even if what Rainier said was true, whatever was coursing through her bloodstream felt nice. She allowed her brother to hustle her along the long hallway, down the stairs, and out to his waiting rental car. The sun was high overhead, and the air was hot and muggy. Her headache had vanished. At least Julianna had been right about that. She didn't resist when Rainier bundled her into the passenger seat and shut the door. His haste to get away from the house was obvious as the car lurched forward and the wheels spun momentarily on the blacktop. They careened out of the drive, Adrienne snugly belted in, feeling rather exposed with only her crop top and pajama shorts covering her.

"I won't look." Rainier pointed to the pile of her clothes between them. "Just get dressed. I'll get you to a Starbucks, get some coffee in your system, flush the meds out."

"At least slow down first!" she protested, and immediately the car slowed as her brother released his lead foot from the accelerator. "Where are we going, anyway? And why did we have to leave the house?"

"Because the walls have ears, Sis. And you aren't safe there, not anymore. Hell, maybe we never really were." He kept the wheel steady as she shimmied out of her pajamas and into the clothing he had grabbed from her closet. As soon as her seatbelt was back on, he sped up. "I don't want to pass her on the road."

"Where are you taking me, Rainier?" Adrienne demanded, feeling more wakeful by the moment. Her body felt strange, numb, and kind of...floaty. What the hell had Julianna given her? She wondered if it had been some of Father's pain meds. There was an enormous bottle of them still sitting there in Gerard and Julianna's bedroom suite. She remembered how Julianna's steps had paused for a moment and then restarted down the hallway, moving slower than normal. Or had she imagined it?

"To the airport," he answered.

"What?"

"What did you find out? Was it about Dad?" he asked, pulling off the highway onto a side road that led to the nearest Starbucks. Adrienne looked down and realized she didn't have shoes.

"About Dad? No." She looked down at her feet. "We need to go back to the house. I don't have any shoes."

Rainier glanced down at her bare feet and swore as he wrenched the wheel hard into the parking lot. The car tires came up on the curb and the car lurched. "I'll buy you shoes on the way to the airport." They pulled into the drive-thru and he glanced at her. "Your usual?"

"Make it a venti instead of a grande."

He grinned and placed orders for both of them and then drove forward to the window.

"So, this isn't about Dad?" he pressed, looking confused.

"No. Why would it be about Dad?" Adrienne frowned as she waited for Rainier to pay for the coffees and hand over her cup. She sipped at it gently as he pulled away from the window, his own cup set precariously between his legs.

"Because I know Julianna killed him. I just can't prove it," he said, piloting the car out of the parking lot and waiting for an opportunity to merge onto the main road.

"Rainier, that's insane!" She took a sip. It was hot, but the coffee washed away the fuzziness she still felt. Her limbs and the rest of her body were coming out of it, but she still felt loosy goosy, high even. Like the time she had smoked weed with Sydney at the back of the bleachers after school. She had hated the feeling of it, her body suddenly uncoordinated, her mind fuzzy and slow.

Rainier shot her a glance that screamed "stupid little girl" and pulled out into an open spot neatly. "Okay, so what did you uncover?"

Adrienne told him about the overheard conversation and how she had played it off with the earbuds and pretended to listen to loud music.

"Huh." Rainier appeared to mull it over in his mind. "This makes sense, really. I thought she married Father for his money, but now I'm wondering if it wasn't something else."

Adrienne took another sip of the hot coffee and willed the fogginess to clear. "Control of the company?"

"Yeah. And the ability to make Cenac a legitimate cover for some far darker dealings." Rainier nodded, thoughtfully. "We need to get to California and talk to Lincoln."

"Lincoln? Who is Lincoln?" Adrienne felt out of touch. There had been a time when she knew every single one of Rainier's friends. Often, his friend's younger sisters or brothers had been her friends as well. She had never heard of a Lincoln.

"He's a friend. A couple of years ahead of me. He just graduated with a degree in Journalism," Rainier explained, as the car edged onto the on-ramp that would lead to the airport. "He's been helping me look into Father's death."

"But Father died from complications from the car accident, Rain." Adrienne was feeling as if she had ventured into the Twilight Zone. Sure, Julianna was up to no good at Cenac, she could see that, but kill someone? That was extreme.

Rainier gritted his teeth. "Sis, I love you, I really do. But you really are annoyingly optimistic. Before I got your call, Lincoln had just scored records showing that Julianna had two separate doctors prescribing medications to Father that could be deadly when mixed. We have the prescription bottles, I just needed those records, and Lincoln found them. But this, what you overheard yesterday, this takes it to a whole new level."

Adrienne rubbed her eyes. "But, Rain, murder?"

Rainier reached over and grabbed her hand. "Come with me to California. I'll show you everything Lincoln and I have cobbled together. See it with your own eyes."

He pulled into a parking lot next to a low-slung building with a large, red Avis sign on the front of it.

"I need shoes, Rain."

"The airport terminal will have some, don't worry." He squeezed her hand and parked the car.

Julianna was sitting in her office when her cell phone rang. She stared at it for a moment, then answered on the third ring. "Yes?"

"The house is empty. There's no one here." The man's voice was professional, no pleasantries given or expected.

"She should be dead to the world in her bed," Julianna barked. "I gave her enough to knock out a man twice her size."

The voice on the other end was unmoved. "All I can tell you is that she isn't here. I checked everywhere."

Julianna felt a surge of fury rush through her as she pressed the End Call button. Where the hell had Adrienne gone? And how? She had watched the girl drink every drop of the tea. She had laced it with two of Gerard's pills. There was no way that girl should be conscious, much less gone. And where could she have gone? She scrolled through her contacts, looking for Adrienne's friends' names. She would have to call each one. Her fingers were shaky. She would call them all before calling her back with an update.

And if you can't find her, you know who you will have to talk to next. You'll have to call her; you know you will.

Julianna felt a thick wedge of anxiety form in her chest. Of all the people she didn't want to call with failure, she was the one. Her stomach flipped, and she crossed her fingers for a moment before locating Adrienne's friend Sydney in her phone and pressing the Call button. She would find Adrienne, get her back to the house, take care of this. She wouldn't have to call her with an admission of failure. Anything but that.

Scrabble Me This

Jack tapped his foot, irritable, eager for the phone conference to end.

Azule had shown up a few minutes before seven and given Kaylee the once-over before chivvying Jack off to the office. As they walked, she kept smiling, but said nothing, just kept eyeing him with sidelong glances and that infuriating smile.

"What?" he finally broke, "It's obvious you have something to say, so, say it."

"I don't know what you are talking about, Mr. Benton," Azule responded with a smirk.

She never called him that.

"Damn it, Az!" he growled, and she laughed, a deep belly laugh that bent her over at the waist.

"She's a beautiful girl," she noted, once she had stopped laughing.

"I hadn't noticed," Jack responded, deadpan.

"No, of course you didn't." Azule took her customary seat in the conference room and leaned back. "Well? What have you learned about her so far?"

Jack sprawled in the chair at the end of the table. "That she likes my omelets and seems willing to play Scrabble with Mal."

"Wait." Az tilted her head. "Mal likes her?"

"Yeah, I think he really does." Jack threw his hands up. "Mal doesn't like anyone but you. He barely tolerates me."

"You know it's true," he insisted, as Az rolled her eyes. "It's the damnedest thing, really. He actually asked her to play Scrabble with

141

him. And she didn't bat an eye. Truth is, she looked excited about it. I can't think of any woman under forty who likes Scrabble."

Azule fixed him with a hostile glare, her head bobbing on her neck. "Oh, you did not say that to me!"

Jack suddenly remembered that it had been Azule who had first introduced Mal to Scrabble. It was what had led to the magnetic letters, which had been a breakthrough that had rocked their world.

"Except for you, Az, of course." He tried to recover from the faux pas while Azule's head bobbed like an angry chicken, her neck gyrating back and forth. "When does that conference begin?"

She glared at him and wrenched the intercom/phone combination over and stabbed at the buttons with a sharp, long, perfectly manicured nail.

"It starts in one minute," she snapped.

Jack winced and hoped it wouldn't take her long to forgive him.

He leaned back in his seat, his thoughts focusing on his brother. Mal was like a puzzle box. It took the right person, with the right combination of inspiration and intuition, to understand the labyrinthine twists and turns of his brother's mind. Mal remained locked inside of his own head, thanks to the autism. In some ways, that had given him a bit of an advantage. Because he didn't talk, or even react, in a way that others would consider normal, often people's reactions were to ignore Malcolm, as if he were a piece of furniture or something incapable of feelings. Just by existing, Mal was a great barometer for measuring the worth of a person as well. Every single woman he had dated, even considered living with, or brought home, had failed that test. Until now.

Jack sat back in his chair as the call connected and wished he could go back to the house. He would even be fine with a game of Scrabble, especially if he got to go toe-to-toe with a beautiful girl.

He flashed back to this morning, both embarrassed and turned on by what he had seen. What in the hell had possessed him to walk into that bathroom? Sure, he hadn't had his morning coffee, but what did he expect to find? Had there been any thought in his head at all?

At least, not a single thought in the *larger* head.

And the sight of it, Kaylee standing there, the water pouring over her, eyes closed, her fingers between her legs, pleasuring herself. He hadn't stood there one or two seconds; he had stood there for at least two minutes, frozen in place, his dick harder than Chinese algebra, eyes locked on her.

What kind of pervert am I, anyway?

He tried to shift his attention to the phone conference. It was impossible. He simply could not concentrate. For each number or percentage rattled off, his monkey brain injected "naked thigh" or "suds rolling off her breasts" pictures, overwhelming any of the more mundane, practical affairs of running a billion-dollar business.

Luckily, he had Azule, along with a host of smart, thoughtful managers on the other end. Az had picked them personally, winnowing out the old-school, predominantly stodgy white men for young, forward-thinking, hard-working men and women. They crossed ethnicities and cut the median age by nearly half. Some of them didn't look old enough to drink, but they sure as hell knew how to double, triple, and even quadruple the business since coming on board. As it was, he didn't really need to be here. The meeting practically ran itself.

Jack sat up straighter and Azule looked confused for a moment, then outraged as Jack stopped the head finance gal in the middle of her report.

"My apologies, all, but I, uh, I have an important meeting I forgot all about."

He ignored Azule's hissed, "What are you doing?" and stood up.

"I'll leave you to it then. Az will give me the highlights." He practically ran out of the door, holding in a laugh until he was out the front door of the office and halfway to the house.

The scene that greeted him looked normal and odd at the same time. If anyone else had happened upon the two of them, it would have looked like Kaylee and Malcolm were engaging in a perfectly normal game of Scrabble.

If anyone who willingly *plays Scrabble could be considered normal.*

For Jack, however, the scene was at the very least odd, if not downright surreal. He stood there watching them, and neither had noticed his return. Kaylee was sitting on the couch, leaning forward to stare at the board and then back at her letters, and Mal also studied the board quietly, without a hint of emotion.

She lay down a short word, just four letters, and Mal made his move seconds later, expanding on her own word and hitting a triple word score.

"Participate? Ugh, Mal, were you lying in wait with that one? Can you see my letters? I swear, I think you can read minds as well!" She said it all with a grin on her face and it was clear she was enjoying herself. As for Malcolm, it was obvious to Jack that his baby brother was happier than he had been in a long time. Happier than he had been since they lost Allie.

Jack's heart panged with loss. It had been over eight years now and it made no difference. The memory of her loss was as painful today as it had been then.

Kaylee looked up with a start and spied him watching them. She blushed again, and Jack suppressed the urge to walk over, swing her up over his shoulder, and march her off to his bedroom.

Suds. Steam. Hands between her...

"I didn't hear you come in, Jack." She smiled and pointed to the board. "Mal is handing me my ass in this game. I think he is up to 230 points to my 98."

Jack smiled back and sat down on the couch next to her. He could tell from the way she shivered that he was affecting her just as much as she was affecting him.

I sure would like to know about that dream she had with me in it. I don't think I would mind reenacting it.

"He got me last week with perambulate. I'm convinced he is psychic or a cheat, likely both."

Mal opened his binder and laid out words in the middle of the magnetic front.

NO JUST BETTER

Jack and Kaylee laughed as Kaylee pointed to the board. "He's right. I'd say he could win at competitions." She turned to Mal and asked, "What about it, Mal? Would you ever like to play in a Scrabble championship?"

She watched as he assembled the words.

TOO MANY PEOPLE

SHAKE HANDS NO

Kaylee tilted her head in confusion for a moment. "Oh, they ask you to shake hands at the beginning and end of a game? I understand. That would be difficult." She said nothing for a moment, thinking, and then said thoughtfully, "It is something you could learn to do, Mal. Just like anything, it takes practice. You could practice with Jack, or me while I'm here, or possibly Azule." Her lips curved up into a kind smile. "I think that if you wanted it bad enough, you could whomp a Grandmaster, show them who is the real boss at Scrabble. If I can help, you just let me know, okay?"

Jack saw Mal's head nod. A quick jerk, really, but far more than he usually did to acknowledge another in conversation. And as impossible as it might have been, it also looked as if a ghost of a smile had just run across his baby brother's face.

"Ooh, it's my turn, isn't it?" Kaylee busied herself with plucking out tiles from the velvet bag before handing it forthrightly to Malcolm. Jack's jaw dropped to see Mal reach for it, brushing his knuckles against Kaylee's. Malcolm normally could not stand another person's touch at all. He had been that way since he was a toddler. Jack hadn't forgotten the earsplitting shrieks from a far younger Malcolm that had sent his parents scrambling to a developmental psychologist. The diagnosis had been swift, brutal, and had set Jack's parents on the path that led them to institutionalize Mal when he was eight.

Jack's hands clenched at the memory. Allison had cried herself to sleep for days. She had been closest to him. It seemed incomprehensible that Malcolm's absence could fracture the family to such a degree, but it had. Jack had never forgiven his father for it. Instead, he had escaped into parties and fast cars and more. Anything but return to a home devoid of his silent youngest sibling.

"Jack? Is everything okay?" Kaylee's voice interrupted his dark memories.

"Hm? Sorry. My mind was miles away." He realized the board was now empty and Kaylee was handing a tile rack to him.

"I was asking if you would play as well. A third player can make the game even more fun. I used to play with my mom and brother all the time when I was a kid." Her smile clouded momentarily as she mentioned her mother and brother, and Jack wondered if she would ever be willing to share her story with him. He could feel her moving closer to that point, though, and moments of normalcy, like this one, could only help.

"Absolutely," he said, taking the tile rack from her. He winked. "If we cheat, I think we could beat him together."

Kaylee laughed and shook her head. "No way, I'm going to beat the two of you fair and square!"

What followed was a marathon of Scrabble games, broken up by a quick lunch, before they all dove back in for another, and another, and finally Jack stood up, stretched, and felt his back crack.

"I'm done for. If I lose another game to you or Mal, I'll be plagued with insecurity for the rest of my life." He shifted his gaze to Kaylee. All morning, through their early lunch and now mid-afternoon, he had felt their connection building, growing, tightening. His hand had grazed hers multiple times and she hadn't flinched when he hugged her the one and only time he hit a Triple Word score.

It was time to act on it. Time to take a moment away from all of this and be alone with her. Maybe he could get the answers he was hoping for. Maybe not. But he knew one thing for sure, if he didn't find a way to be alone with this woman, he might lose the opportunity altogether.

Practice Makes Perfect

"Shift your body to the left, lean back on the ball of your foot, and maintain your center of gravity," Nyra barked at her sister. The girl glared, but obeyed.

"And again," Nyra ordered, and attacked, swinging her staff at Zella, and Zella met it with solid resistance. Nyra feinted right and cracked the girl on the knuckles. Zella yelped in pain and attacked her staff, blurring as she swung it toward Nyra's skull, murder in her eyes.

Nyra stepped to the left and felt the breeze as it missed her head and grazed her shoulder. She grinned sadistically. "Better." Then she grasped her own with one hand and jabbed hard into Zella's gut, knocking the wind out of her. The girl fell on her butt with a small "oof" of pain, followed by a hiss of anger, and her staff whistled along the ground, slamming into Nyra's shin.

Nyra found herself on the ground, looking up as Zella, now on her feet. Zella copied the move Nyra had done earlier, jabbing downwards toward Nyra's guts, her eyes black with rage.

Nyra whacked the girl in the side of the head, knocking her off-balance, and as the stunning blow superseded Zella's bloodlust, the younger girl slumped to the ground. Nyra wrenched her sister's staff out of her hand, climbed to her feet, and stood over her.

"You'll never win if you let your anger take over, Zella Dean." She smirked at the girl lying on the ground holding her skull. "And you sure as hell will never win over me."

Zella mumbled something and spit bright red blood into the dirt. She got up slower than normal, but Nyra could see the girl wasn't done yet. Nyra grinned at her and tossed the two staffs off into the brush and crooked a finger at her sister. Zella charged at her, a wordless scream on her lips. It ended, as it typically did, with Zella on the ground. She was unconscious this time, however, and Nyra laughed and walked away. The girl would learn, just as Nyra had, and a few minutes on the ground in the scorching sun would serve her right.

She left Zella on the ground, and jogged the half mile back to the cabin. She had eaten a sandwich and was reading when Zella finally made it back. Zella's right eye was swelling and her lower lip split, the blood dried and black. She was also sporting a mild sunburn, which would quickly fade and turn her skin an even deeper olive tone.

Zella said nothing, walking past Nyra as she lay in the hammock. Nyra heard her curse again, and walk out of the cabin, practically stomping as she drew to within two feet of the hammock. Nyra didn't look up. Instead, she kept her focus firmly on the words on the page.

"You made lunch and didn't bother to make me any?" Zella growled.

"Losers fix their own meals," Nyra said, and continued to read.

Zella stomped away, back inside, and the pots and pans clattered loudly as the girl made her own meal. Once silence ensued, Nyra sat up and walked back into the cabin. Zella stared up at her moodily from her space at the table, then returned her gaze to her meal. Nyra settled into the chair on the opposite side of the table. She didn't enjoy sitting with her back to the door, no matter how isolated they were from others. She rubbed the tattoo on her wrist, remembering the day she had received it. It had been a day much like this one, only she had been the one lying in the dirt after.

Zella eyed the tattoo and took another bite of goulash, her split lip bleeding. She winced in discomfort but said nothing. "When will I get the tattoo?"

"When I think you are ready."

Nyra's sister grunted in anger. "Well, that'll be never then."

"You need to be more patient. You can't just act like a berserker; there are situations that will require finesse."

Zella rolled her eyes. "Next you'll have me reading that stupid book."

"You would do well to study *The Art of War*, little sister."

"This hand-to-hand combat is bullshit, anyway," Zella grumbled. "Give me a Glock any day of the week."

Nyra shook her head. "There are plenty of times when you will need a quieter alternative. A Glock is loud and draws attention when we need quiet. We kill and we vanish, that's our job."

"I still prefer my Glock. And a silencer works wonders." She scraped the bowl clean, stood up. and took it to the sink.

Nyra watched her move. She wasn't the jumpy, traumatized child she had been a year ago. But the trauma had transformed into a black, roiling anger, and a fury towards men the likes of which would cause waves if their employer caught wind of it. The anger worked for now. It had turned Zella into a thing of deadly beauty as her body, once bruised, underfed, and violated - had toned, strengthened, and grown over two inches since they had come to this desolate place. There had only been one incident, and Nyra had dealt with that. It's easy to make a body disappear in the desert. No one had even come round looking for him. Not that they would have known where to look.

Cut in under an outcrop of rock, the cabin was a perfect hideaway. It was here that Nyra had insisted on coming when she learned of the fire. She had taken a leave of three months to ensure her sister recovered from the abuse she had endured in their parents' home.

When Nyra had left home at fifteen, Zella had been nine, and their father hadn't looked at her twice, not with his sights set on Nyra. That had apparently changed when Nyra left.

Zella had been a shadow of the sister she had left behind. If it hadn't been for the anger she had seen in the girl's eyes, she might well have left her there, standing by the smoking remains of their childhood home. But Zella had set the fire, of that Nyra was certain. And could she even blame Zella? Their father had been a monster, their mother too weak to stop the atrocities from occurring, and Nyra had been too young, too desperate to escape herself to take her sister with her when she ran away.

Her years with the Indalo had shaped her into a killing machine, one that had a pretty face, perfect body, and was just as perfectly lethal. And soon, the Indalo would have two perfectly trained killers. Another year, possibly two, and Zella would be ready, if Nyra could teach her sister to transform her fury into precision and stealth.

"Delta wants you cross-trained," Nyra said, wishing she had a way to take the patience she had learned and shove it into Zella. Her sister's endless capacity for anger and violence was exhausting.

Perhaps if I had gotten her out of there sooner.

But she hadn't. It had taken Delta's voice on the phone to send her scrambling to get back to the backwater hole of a town in the middle of Oklahoma. "Your sister set fire to your family home, Nyra." Delta had sounded calm, unruffled. "Assess the situation and if she is trainable, bring her back." How Delta had known this, when the local law enforcement seemed oblivious, Nyra was unsure.

A town that small didn't have any children's division or social workers—those were all in the next town over. The next-door neighbor, saddled with Zella until they had found suitable placement, didn't argue when Nyra had shown up at their door—especially when Nyra handed the thin-faced, twitchy husband a roll of crisp hundred-dollar bills with the advice to report Zella as a runaway. They looked positively relieved to have the girl out of their house, especially the mother, who held her young daughter close to her the entire time Nyra stood in their living room.

It occurred to Nyra that if Delta had seen Zella first, she would have likely left her there. She would have seen the maelstrom of dark fury the girl held inside of her far more clearly than Nyra had. Instead of assessing, Nyra had reacted on a gut level, powered by fear and guilt. She had gotten Zella out of there and realized later just how damaged she was.

Just as Nyra was about to speak to Zella, the phone, plugged into a solar charger that hung on the outside wall, its cord snaking inside through a rough hole in the wall, rang. The sound of it nearly made her jump in surprise. It had been silent for so long, months upon months.

She had asked for three months, which had turned into six, then nine, and now a year. In all of that time, the phone that only Delta ever called Nyra on had remained silent. It wasn't silent now, however, and both Nyra and Zella turned to stare at it. Zella picked it up and was about to hit the Accept Call button when Nyra warned her off. "Don't. This isn't for you. Not yet."

She took the phone from her sister and answered it. "Yes?"

Delta didn't waste words. She didn't ask how Nyra was, or even Zella. "I have an assignment for you. Details are at the drop site." There was a click, and the phone went dead.

Nyra nodded and set the phone back in its spot, connecting the charging cable once again. She looked at Zella. "Right. We have two weeks of food left, more if I'm not back soon."

"Where are you going?" Zella asked, her eyebrows furrowed. "And when will you be back?"

"I don't know. I'll know more once I get to the drop site."

"I'll come with you," Zella insisted, and Nyra could see the curiosity oozing out of her.

"No." Nyra shook her head. "Until you are one of us, you aren't, and you aren't involved. Delta was clear on this." She spun on her heel, walking out of the cabin with nothing other than the water bottle in her hand.

The drop site was two miles to the north, on the far side of the low hills they sheltered within. Another two miles beyond that was a private airfield. The Indalo kept the utmost secrecy, using dead drops that detailed the target, along with a need to know basis among a select few at the airfield. And assassins like her were nameless and unknown, just as Delta and the other high-ranking Indalo preferred. Nyra picked up the package. It included plane tickets, an ID identifying her as Nancy Smith, and a stack of cash tucked into the pockets of her nondescript outfit. As the tiny plane taxied down the runway, with Nyra as its sole passenger, she read over the dossier for Adrienne Cenac.

They had already dealt with one of the two Indalo who had failed to secure the target. Nyra had met him briefly while on an assignment outside of Los Angeles. The dossier detailed the girl's escape from two Indalo agents whose cover with the LAPD kept them in the know. And thanks to patchy surveillance of the surrounding area, all that the dossier could tell her was that Adrienne Cenac, age eighteen, was likely still in the area where her car, or the car of one of the Indalo agents she had escaped from, had been found.

Nyra leaned back and closed her eyes, aware that the pilot was watching her with open curiosity. She had at least two hours until they arrived in Las Vegas. There she would walk onto a flight to Los Angeles, dressed conservatively and armed with a boring name and an unremarkable identity.

I'll dress as a survey worker and get into each of the properties of at least one mile in each direction of where they found the crashed car. A survey for women only. Yes, that will do nicely. Something to do with makeup.

She typed a text message on the new burner phone and requested a MAC makeup samples case sent to the hotel room reserved for her in Los Angeles. Time for a nap. It would give her a chance to think over her approach if the survey taker angle didn't pan out.

A Walk in the Woods

"Take a walk with me," Jack said, and Kaylee sensed an undercurrent of intensity in his words. The spark between them was growing, feeding on the connection between them. Part of her wanted to stay where it was safe, here in the house. Perhaps challenge Mal to another game that she knew she would lose.

That would have been the safe way out.

Instead, she rose from the couch and slipped on the shoes she had found earlier in the day in a closet near the front door. A glance back at Mal before the door closed behind them and she could see him putting the pieces of the Scrabble game back in the same precise manner he had unpacked them with.

Jack was close, his lips brushing her ear as he spoke, "I want to take you to my favorite place in the entire world."

Kaylee shivered. Since the moment they had nearly kissed, heck, before that, Jack's presence was causing a low hum of anticipation to flow through her body. Despite the complications it created, on top of all the other complications and tragedies of the past two weeks, all she could think about was the way her body had reacted to him earlier.

The attraction between them was undeniable. And of all the men to fall for, someone with his background, his abilities, well, she knew she wouldn't get him killed. She had enough death on her conscience as it was. Rainier, Lincoln, their deaths kept running through her dreams, and they haunted her in the day as well.

"Where are you?" Jack's voice interrupted her thoughts. "You suddenly went a million miles away."

She hadn't paid attention to where she was walking, only to the fact that Jack's hand was in hers. The house was behind them now, most of it obscured in the thick line of trees and shrubs. He paused, squeezed her hand gently, and Kaylee's thoughts of others, anyone but Jack, fled. She stared up at him, mesmerized. He was older than anyone she had ever dated or flirted with. His dark hair was threaded with silvery gray, but his body was fit, lean, and he towered over her by at least six inches, likely more. His dark brown eyes were gazing steadily into hers. The look in his eyes turned up the hum in her body another notch and part of her wanted him to kiss her, now.

"Sorry."

"Don't be. You just looked like you had the weight of the world on your shoulders." He reached up with his free hand, traced the line of her jaw gently, then pulled away. "I promised to show you my favorite place, but it is a bit of a hike. Are you up to it?"

The body aches were still there, but not as bad as they had been in the first few days. Kaylee knew she would be fine, and being outside in the fresh air, away from the others, just her and Jack, well, that was well worth a little discomfort.

"Absolutely."

He grinned, his teeth white and perfect, and he tugged at her hand gently. "It's this way."

The path was well-worn, not just by human feet, but by deer and what appeared to be an enormous dog. Jack pointed at one particular track, deeply embedded in the thick mud that had now dried, hard as concrete.

"Mountain lion," Jack said, and placed his hand next to it for comparison. The track was slightly smaller than his hand, and Kaylee gasped. The pad of the track had three distinct lobes and she could see the hint of claw marks above each of the four toes. "Likely running," Jack said, "normally you can't see the claws otherwise."

He grinned up at her and winked. "Don't worry, she's likely long gone by now."

Kaylee still jumped a moment later at an unexpected screech. "What was that?" She closed the short distance between them, and Jack's arm slipped protectively around her.

Jack laughed. "Likely a parrot; they infest Pasadena, but I keep seeing them here as well."

Kaylee felt embarrassed. "Oh." His arm slid slowly off of her and she stared at the ground, trying to ignore the hum of attraction she felt towards him that had ratcheted up yet again with such near proximity.

"It isn't much further," he said, his stride lengthening, and Kaylee quickened her pace to match.

She looked back over her shoulder, but the house had long disappeared. The forest wasn't quiet, but she couldn't hear a single sound from the city, which she knew was quite near. It felt as if she had stepped into the middle of an untamed wilderness, one that contained just her and Jack, with the sounds of the parrots screeching, the gentle breeze making the trees creak gently, and the leaves fluttering. Kaylee could just barely make out the sounds of their feet scuffing the now-hardened mud.

It smelled different here. The Louisiana bayou had a swampy, almost pungent odor, but these woods smelled of dirt and pine. Kaylee was so caught up in the smells and looking off into the distance that she was unaware of the enormous tree until they stopped at the base.

She gasped with surprise. They had stepped into an opening in the forest, one enforced by the gigantic tree with roots that curled up out of the ground at least twenty feet in each direction, supporting a trunk that split into several smaller trunks, which in turn each climbed towards the sky. Interwoven through the tree was a structure of sorts, more than one, all connected by swaying bridges. The posts that supported it all were at regular intervals along the ground, gently woven among the tree roots in a way that would not harm the tree or disfigure it.

"It's a fig tree, native to Australia, and they planted it in the mid-1880s, according to family lore." Jack's mouth hovered at her ear, sending a shiver down Kaylee's spine. "It's approximately ten feet taller than Big Tree, in Glendora, and stands at over one hundred feet tall. My great-great-great-grandfather planted it. They had sentenced him to the penal colony in Australia. He worked off his sentence and ended up owning a fleet of sailing ships back in the day. He ended up marrying a woman from the Serrano tribe who saved his life. Beginning with my grandfather, a series of treehouses were built with each new generation. We have taken care not to damage the tree, and the tree is still growing. My design is near the top. Are you up for a climb?"

The dirty part of Kaylee's mind visualized their two bodies entwined far above in the branches of the tree.

The way he said it was intentionally seductive, thrilling, and the thrum increased, suffusing her body with desire. Kaylee shivered again, and nodded, not trusting her voice to stay even. They had been teasing, sparring, and dancing around this since she first opened her eyes in his car that first night. She could see that now.

There was a short run of steps up to the first platform, but after that Kaylee could see that it would take some work to get to their goal, the tallest part of the structure obscured by the tree and the network of rope and wood bridges and other small platforms and treehouses that wrapped around the tree.

Jack stepped forward, his long legs carrying him up the steps and onto a small platform. He turned and held out his hand, a devilish grin on his lips. His button-down shirt and linen trousers weren't intended for climbing trees, yet somehow, they looked perfect on him. He was handsome and sexy as hell, and Kaylee felt a flush of desire course through her. What would he be like as a lover?

Climb the tree and find out, girl.

She ignored his outstretched hand and reached for the first handhold, a rope looped gently around a thick branch, and climbed.

Jack followed, and when she looked back, his eyes were on her butt, right where she wanted them. She wasn't a fainting lily, she could take care of herself, and now that her bruises were fading and her body had recovered from the fever, he needed to know that she wasn't just some damsel in distress. She wanted to meet him on a level playing field, not have him think she was weak and in need of protecting. That kind of thing was only interesting for so long, usually until the next damsel in distress came along.

She stretched and pushed herself, despite the healing bruises and sore joints. She slipped then, one foot loose from the rope net, her arm jerking as she felt the other foot slip.

"Careful." His arm was around her waist, his lips hovering near her neck. A wave of desire crashed through her. If it hadn't been that they were at least thirty feet in the air and not in a safe position, she might have acted on that desire. As it was, she placed her feet in the net and continued to climb. Two nets, a well-constructed rope and wood bridge, a quick peek inside of one treehouse, and several moments for them to both catch their breaths, and they finally made it to Jack's treehouse.

Whatever Kaylee had expected, it wasn't this. It was small, perhaps five feet by eight, but not childish, not at all. The roof was clear, and she was thankful the sun wasn't overhead any longer, otherwise it would have been stifling inside. The walls were wood, sitting on what appeared to be a steel beam. A window on either side, once opened, provided a gentle breeze. In the center of the floor was a thick carpet and a dozen or more soft, thick pillows. A telescope sat nestled in one corner; in another, there was a stack of water bottles.

"No secret password?" Kaylee asked, taking in the clean lines. This was no child's playhouse. "Or marauder's map?"

Jack laughed. "No, not anymore." He handed her a water bottle and a towel from a neat bookshelf. "I'll admit, it looked different when I was younger. There may have been an, um, pirate phase. I flew the skull and crossbones; I even had the most enormous antique padlock you have ever seen on the door. I lost the key and our groundskeeper was not happy about the climb to go about cutting his way back in." He picked up another towel, wiped the sweat from his brow, and unbuttoned his shirt. Beneath the open shirt, Kaylee could see his smooth chest and toned six-pack.

He met her eyes and smiled. "A few years back, I had the roof replaced with glass. Every year, a powerful storm knocks out some panes of glass. I'm kind of surprised it's intact after last weekend's storm."

He slipped off his shoes, setting them in the corner, and Kaylee followed suit. When she had set them next to Jack's, she turned back to him and realized he was inches away.

They had been edging towards this, playing a complicated dance, and now, here they were, high above the ground, deep in a forest, yet minutes away from one of the largest cities in America.

Kaylee's breaths were uneven, more so now that she was this close to him. He reached out one hand, tucked a lock of hair behind her ear, and brushed the side of her face. He trailed his long fingers down her neck as he stepped closer, into her personal space, his eyes never leaving hers.

"I can't stop thinking about you, Kaylee. It's driving me nuts." His gaze dropped, and he reached for her wrist. "Whoever did this to you, I want to..." His teeth ground together, and his hand tightened briefly on her wrist as he visibly fought with his emotions. "I'd finish them if I could."

Kaylee felt the pulse of desire flare, the thrum of her body reacting to his, and she closed the distance, just a few inches, between them and placed her hands on his chest. His cologne, musky and rich, filled her senses. She stood on her tiptoes in order to reach his lips.

Jack leaned down to meet her, his lips gentle, sweet. Their first kiss almost chaste. He encircled her with powerful arms that lifted her up, cupped one hand on the small of her back, the other under her ass, and their kiss deepened in intensity.

Kaylee could feel her desire build, her body responding to his touch. There had been the occasional make-out session, the hurried and self-conscious groping at parties and behind the bleachers, but nothing prepared her for this. His hands roamed over her slowly, taking his time. No half-measures, no fumbling with clothing. Here was experience, and the promise of pleasure that wouldn't end in a few hasty, awkward moments.

He walked backwards, gently guiding him with her, and down to the softly cushioned floor. The sun was already low in the sky, and it warmed one window and set the rest of the inside in a light shadow. The kiss had intensified, transforming from the gentle kiss, to something far more primal, demanding. It promised more, tantalized, and teased. Jack slid one hand to her shirt, pausing at the first button.

"Are you okay with this?"

Was she *okay* with this?

God, yes, I'm okay with it.

The swirl of attraction and desire was in her blood now, flowing through every part of her body. His lips had moved to her neck, and they paused now, waiting for her response.

"Yes," Kaylee breathed out, reaching for him in return, wanting him closer. Her hand danced over his smooth chest. His shirt had vanished, tossed aside, out of sight. She could feel the hard ridges of muscle, the six-pack of abs covered in velvety-smooth skin.

He pulled back, undid the buttons of her shirt, and pulled it off of her before claiming her left earlobe, gently sucking the skin into his mouth.

Kaylee moaned as he nibbled the lobe, his hands busy as he removed her bra. No fumbling, no half measures. He reached up to the base of her skull, weaving his hands into her hair, and gently tugged her backwards down to the cushions as his mouth inched away from her ear, to her neck, and down to one erect nub of breast. He paused again, his hand warm against her hip, a finger notching at the waistband of her shorts.

"And this?"

Was he asking permission? To take what she was so willing to give him?

"Oh," she gasped as his teeth gently nibbled her breast. "Oh yes."

He pulled away from her, sitting up, and met her eyes as the fingers of both of his hands reached out and slid her shorts down and off of her body. Kaylee felt a moment of self-consciousness that vanished as she saw the look in his eyes. The gulf in age between them didn't matter to him, and it certainly didn't matter to her.

"You are beautiful," he said, his voice husky with desire. He reached down, slowly, and lifted the edge of her panties with one finger, slipping it underneath, taking his time as he slid it between her folds, smiling at her damp heat, and rubbing it against her clit.

Kaylee sucked in a gasp of air, her body humming. The waves of pleasure moved over her. It felt so good. Nothing she had ever done had felt that good. She closed her eyes and Jack reached out, stroked her cheek, and said, "Open your eyes. Look at me."

Kaylee obeyed, and he held her gaze, his finger circling and circling, until it was too much for her to bear any longer. Her breath caught, a cry issuing from her lips as she orgasmed, writhing against his hand, reaching for the other, fitting her fingers between it as she came.

"But you..." Kaylee couldn't say more. She shuddered again, and Jack smiled.

"We have time."

He pulled her against him and lay back on the cushions. Kaylee could still feel the pulses of pleasure rolling through her. His left arm was around her, threaded through her hair, and his other hand was now roaming, gently trailing his fingers along her skin, deftly avoiding her healing cuts and bruises and setting her skin alight with desire.

Kaylee realized he was still half-dressed, although from the bulge tenting the fabric of his pants, at least one part of him longed to be free. She moved her hand down his chest, discovering an almost delicate treasure trail of hairs that disappeared into his pants. Kaylee brushed her fingers along his groin and felt his dick strain against the fabric. She rubbed harder, reaching down to cup his balls in her fingers, her mouth on his pecs, kissing, licking. He groaned and shifted. She reached down and tugged on his pants, and Jack sat up, freed himself from the fine linen pants, and turned back towards her, a growl of desire escaping his lips.

He buried his face in her breasts, moving from one to the other, claiming them as his own, licking, nipping, until both were standing at attention and Kaylee ached for more.

"Jack, please, I want..." What she wanted was something she had never had. Part of her was afraid of that, the other desperate for it to happen.

His hand stopped at her groin and he tugged at the piece of fabric, pulling it off with one swift yank, before divesting himself of the last article of clothing on his body, silky black boxers.

He moved between her legs, spreading her wide, and thrust into her.

There was only a little pain. It faded with the next thrust, and the next, the slickness of her arousal, and of his easing the way. It was primal, and intoxicating, and her hips rose to meet his every thrust as she moaned in time. When he stopped, her eyes flew open, confused. He turned her, flipping her onto her knees, his mouth moving over her buttocks, then licking a line up her spine before he entered her again, hard and deep, his cock thrusting into her wet recesses, faster, harder, until there was nothing left to do but explode.

At What Cost?

The sun had slipped behind the horizon, the light fading quickly, and the first stars were peeking out. Sounds of their lovemaking from inside of the treehouse had finally faded, and the squirrels returned to their nests in the tree branches, settling in for the night along with the birds.

Now the creatures of the night emerged. The hoot of a barn owl, followed by a tiny scream of its prey, sounded through the night. Despite their proximity to Los Angeles, the night was reasonably quiet. Kaylee could hear the faint sounds of a guitar and in the very far distance the monotonous grind of traffic. This near a city center, traffic was unceasing, no matter the time of day.

She lay wrapped in a soft, fuzzy blanket, her head on Jack's chest.

"The stars will be out soon," he said, "but I have flashlights for our descent, and the way is lit with solar lights as well for safety."

"I like it right here," Kaylee said, her finger drawing a circle on his belly.

They lay there in silence. She was grateful for it. It allowed her to gather her thoughts. She needed to tell him the truth, about the past week, about her life, about all of it. It felt like he was waiting, patiently, for her to speak.

"My real name is Adrienne. Adrienne Cenac. My family has owned Cenac Shipping for five, no, six generations, if you count me," she began.

Last Friday

165

Rainier had handled purchasing the tickets, and Adrienne had looked at him in confusion when he asked for two first-class tickets to Los Angeles.

"I thought we would fly into San Jose...isn't that the closest airport to Santa Cruz?"

Rainier shook his head. "I've been staying in L.A. for the summer, with my friend Lincoln."

"Oh." Adrienne still felt foggy from the laced tea. "Okay." How little she knew of her brother's life since he had left home two years earlier. It suddenly made her feel sad at the thought. He had made a life for himself, and not only did she know nothing about it, but she didn't even know if he had a girlfriend or where he was living. She stared down at her bare feet and Rainier followed her gaze.

"Let's get you some shoes, Addy." He pointed down the long expanse of hall with stores on both sides. "I know I saw someplace that sells footwear."

Rainier using his pet name for her buoyed her spirits, and she slung her purse over her shoulder after the ticket agent returned her identification. It felt strange for the woman to not question her. The last time she had flown had been three years ago, for a trip to New York with Sydney and her parents. That had been like watching the Inquisition. A minor traveling with people who weren't her parents? It had been a big deal and Sydney's mom had brought along a letter signed in Father's shaky hand, allowing the trip. Now? The ticket agent had simply handed over the tickets. No questions, nothing. Eighteen really was the magic age.

A few minutes later, she had found some horrid slip-on shoes she would never have considered but found ridiculously comfortable. Together, she and Rainier made their way through security and to the gate without incident. Part of her wondered if Julianna would suddenly appear and she looked for her face, scanning the crowds, before Rainier put his hand on her arm.

"I'm keeping an eye out for her too, Sis, but don't worry, even if she found you here, she couldn't stop you from leaving. You are eighteen, an adult, and she does not have any power over either of us any longer." He said it with no small amount of bitterness.

"Did she try to stop you?" she asked, the thought occurring to her he hadn't come back for visits, not once, except for Father's funeral.

"Oh yeah. Well, not so much stop me as to make it really hard for me. She controlled the purse strings until Father died. And from what I learned from the reading of the will, that's still the case. At least until we are both twenty-one." He shook his head and grimaced. "I've got nine months to go, but you, well, yours is a ways away."

Rainier's eyes focused on the display screen for their flight. "We can pre-board now; our tickets are next to each other in Row Two." He stood up and handed her a large satchel he had purchased for her at the same place as the shoes. She had slid her spare outfit, a blue summer dress, into it and joined her brother in the line for first-class ticketholders.

Hours later, they stepped off the plane and out of the terminal into the hot California sun. They hadn't spoken on the plane much. Rainier had tried to ask her questions, but Adrienne had simply shaken her head. She didn't want others to overhear. She was still processing the thought of it herself. It left a sour taste in her mouth and an uneasy knot in her stomach. Julianna had used her family's business, one that was decades old, as a cover for nefarious activities. It sickened her. What was their family legacy in the face of this? She had finally slept a bit, despite having already slept most of the morning away. By the time she had woken as the plane was making its descent, the drugs seemed to have finally left her system. She awoke sharp and focused.

Rainier shouted and waved at a car driving past slowly. It swerved in front of a taxi and halted. The cab driver engaged in a frenzy of shouts and arm-waving as the man inside ignored the driver and waved back at Rainier. Rainier's friend was cute, dark-haired, and tall with warm, brown eyes. As they hustled over to him, the taxi behind honked impatiently and Rainier opened the two passenger doors and ushered Adrienne into the back seat before jumping into the front passenger seat.

Lincoln gunned it. "No-parking zone, sorry about that," he said, a friendly grin on his face, as he turned and flashed Adrienne a quick glance. It was hot outside the car and in, and Adrienne rolled down her window to at least catch a breeze. As it was, she just breathed in more fumes, and traffic moved at a snail's pace. The sun slipped low in the sky, a ball of fire that lit up the smoggy air in a riot of oranges and pinks. By the time Lincoln parked his car in a narrow alley behind a Chinese restaurant, the sun had completely disappeared and night had descended. The smell of garlic and soy sauce hit her as she followed Lincoln and Rainier through a door, up a long flight of steep and narrow stairs, to a dingy apartment above the restaurant.

"This is where you have been staying?" Adrienne looked around. It was small, Spartan as only a bachelor's pad can be, and dimly lit. The canned music from the restaurant below wafted up, along with the tantalizing odors of stir-fry.

Lincoln laughed good-naturedly and patted her on her arm. "I like your sister. She has taste, something you are distinctly lacking, Rainier."

"Don't put this on me, Sorenson, it's your apartment!" Rainier turned to Adrienne. "I'll go get us some dinner and then I want to hear what you overheard, and I'll show you what Lincoln and I have put together." He didn't wait for her to answer, just disappeared through the door and back down the stairs.

"You want a beer?" Lincoln asked. "Or um, let's see, I've got some rum here and cola in the fridge. Would you like a rum and Coke?"

Adrienne blinked at his offer. He was offering her hard alcohol? Perhaps this was how early twenty-somethings lived, on alcohol and takeout. "Um, a rum and Coke would be great, thanks."

He grinned at her and turned away, searching, it seemed, for a clean glass in the small, dirty kitchenette that had a sink filled with dishes. He found one finally and pulled a cold soda can out of the fridge and appeared to pour the rum and soda in equal measures before handing it to her and pointing to one clear spot on the couch.

"Jeez, I uh, sorry about the mess. I've been ass-deep in financial records and more." He grabbed a mass of papers and books and moved them into a larger pile, which threatened to capsize. "I'm investigating a couple of anomalies with a recent election, digging into a recent sudden death in the ranks of the Hollywood elite, and helping Rainier with, well, with your dad and all. I guess I need to do some organizing."

Adrienne sipped the drink, wincing at the amount of rum in it. It was far stronger than what she had tried at the high school parties, which had mainly been composed of cheap beer and the occasional spate of Jell-O shots. She could hear Rainier coming up the steep stairs outside of the apartment seconds before he stepped inside, bags of food held in his hands.

The rum was already spreading its warmth through her body as she dug into the Mu Shu Pork and Chow Mein heaped on her plate. Rainier and Lincoln shoveled the food in, and no one spoke for a few moments, choosing instead to focus on the food in front of them. Rainier finished his meal first and reached for Adrienne's glass, taking a large gulp of it before glaring at Lincoln.

"Jesus, Link, she's eighteen!" he sputtered. "Did you add any soda to that rum?"

Lincoln shrugged and grinned. "Sorry, man. She looked like she needed it." He looked quite unrepentant. He winked at Adrienne.

Rainier frowned at his friend, grabbed the half-empty can of cola, and dumped it into Adrienne's glass.

"Julianna drugged her this morning. If I hadn't gotten there when I did..." He didn't finish his sentence, just stared at Adrienne, the edges of his scowl deepening. "One funeral is enough."

"It isn't as bad as you think, Rain, I just heard something about some illegal dumping and..." Adrienne's voice petered out as all the events of the past ten years, and especially the last year, came together. What she had overheard, all of Rainier's accusations, and the newspaper articles and specs she saw lying on the table when she had entered the apartment. Rainier had been investigating the accident from ten years ago, the one that had nearly killed him and Father. He had suspected Julianna from the very beginning.

"Oh, God."

Lincoln spoke, "Perhaps we should start with what we have learned and give you a chance to see all the evidence we have assembled. Then you can add what you know into it." He stood up, walked over to the table, and gathered the stacks of reports. Rainier cleared a space on the coffee table and took the empty food containers to the tiny kitchenette, pushing stacks of empty takeout boxes over, adding to the heap.

"Let's begin with the accident that nearly killed Rainier and your dad." He dug into the pile of papers and found a folder with several crisp photos inside of it. "The accident investigator took these. He died suddenly, less than one month after the accident."

The photos zeroed in on a cable. Rainier stabbed at it with one finger. "That cable was cut, not torn up in the accident."

"What is it? What does it do?" Adrienne asked and took another sip of the rum and Coke. It was easier to drink now with the addition of the cola.

"It is the line that delivers brake fluid from the reserves to the brakes, keeping them lubricated. Without it, the brakes burn up and stop functioning," Rainier answered, his eyes intense. "Someone cut those lines before Father and I got on the road. We had stopped for breakfast because we had been out of cereal that morning. Do you remember?"

Adrienne thought back to that morning. "Yes! And no eggs, either."

Rainier nodded grimly. "The one morning when we were out of everything, and Julianna had some unexpected appointment and couldn't take me to the doctor. Not just that, but she had scheduled us for the other office location, the one that took Father out of his way on a poorly maintained road that had plenty of twists and turns."

"A perfect storm of coincidences," Adrienne protested half-heartedly.

"Or the perfect storm of planned, intentional murder," Lincoln commented dryly. "Occam's Razor."

"Do you remember they had an argument a few days before?" Rainier asked. "One around some irregularities there at Cenac Shipping?"

"Yes," Adrienne answered with hesitancy, "Sort of."

"Well, I remember it well." Rainier's hand curled into a fist. "Father had questions and Julianna seemed intent on explaining it all away. Father worried about the legalities, concerned there was something being covered up, and then three days later, we both nearly died."

Adrienne took another sip of her drink. Despite the food, it was giving her a warm glow and the same half-numb feeling she had after drinking the tea Julianna had given her. "This accident investigator, how did you find out about him? How do we know he took pictures of Father's car?"

Lincoln tapped his chest. "I'm an investigative reporter. I have connections, and my connections have connections. It took some digging, and an impassioned plea from Rainier to the man's widow, to get these documents. The originals had disappeared from the police files, but he had stored the photos on a memory stick, and she gave it to us. These images, and the notes on the incident report, were all on the memory stick."

"This is evidence that she tried to kill you both. Why haven't you gone to the police with this?" Adrienne asked.

"We have proof that someone cut that brake line, but not the how or the why. Considering the short distance the car would have been able to travel with the brake line cut like that, it would have had to have been done while we were inside the restaurant, not at home," Rainier answered.

"So, you couldn't prove it was her?" she asked.

"Even if we know it was," Rainier answered grimly.

"We also have the quarterly blood draws," added Lincoln, "from the past few years of your father's health records. We just received them. But they aren't for your father, at least not all of them. They can't be."

Adrienne stared at him; her brow furrowed. "How do you know?"

"These reports should show opioids, painkillers," Lincoln explained. "Your father suffered from considerable nerve pain and from everything we know, he should have had high levels of those opiates in his bloodwork." He sifted through the stack of papers and pulled out several sheets, pointing to a circled number. "Here, this is from over a year ago. You can see this is a high reading, that's why it appears in red. Someone got concerned about the high dosages. Maybe Julianna received a call from a doctor expressing that concern." He shifted to the next page. "This was from a month later. No reading at all. As in, no more opioids in his system. At all."

Adrienne frowned and drank a large gulp from the glass, draining it. "And there's no chance she had his medications switched or actually took him off of them?"

Lincoln smiled. "You would make an excellent investigator; you have a questioning mind. And that was the first question I asked, and then I pulled the pharmacy reports. The drug in question is oxycodone. I show a continuing prescription for it over the past three years." He slapped down a readout of dates that occurred monthly and stretched to several pages. "But I also found this record, the same medication, the same dosage, and issued by a Dr. A. Smith and filled at another pharmacy for almost the same time period." He slid the other report towards her and she held it in her hands, staring at the circled data.

"Twice as much medication?" Her voice wobbled a bit, an image clear in her mind of Father seated in his wheelchair facing the large picture window, his gaze clouded, his reactions slow and often nonexistent.

"Yes. And in those doses, enough to kill him. It's likely why she pushed to have him cremated." He snarled, "I knew it was weird, having him cremated and then put into a casket. It made no sense at all."

Rainier met Adrienne's eyes and his voice grew soft, kind. "Julianna kept you distracted. I think she liked the idea of you enough to spend the time, the effort, to keep you in the dark. Especially once I left, and she knew she would need a figurehead to run the company if Father were to die." He sniffed, his lips twisting into a snarl. "Father had put the protections in place, even before he married her. And after, he had amended the will to include a stipend for her, but he locked her out of any power position in the company if either of us stepped forward to run it."

"Why wouldn't she just dissuade me from taking control of it after I returned from college, then?" Adrienne asked, desperate to find a place where Julianna wasn't guilty of murder and more.

"The will stated that if neither of us took control of the company by our twenty-fifth birthday, then it was to be sold," Rainier answered.

"And if I took control of it?" Adrienne asked. "What then?"

"You would have been a figurehead. If you actually paid attention, perhaps noticed the irregularities, well then, maybe you would end up like Father." Rainier shook his head at Adrienne's shocked expression. "She did it once, why not again?"

"Adrienne." Lincoln handed her another glass full of the rum and Coke. "Why don't you tell us what you overheard?"

Adrienne took a sip of the drink. It was less strong this time. She took a deep breath, then told them exactly what she had heard and how she had escaped from the situation.

"I thought I pulled it off," she said, taking another sip, "I thought I fooled them. But maybe they said something to her. And that's why Julianna drugged me with that tea. I mean, we don't know for sure if she drugged the tea. I was awake most of the night, trying to figure out what I overheard, but I've done all-nighters before and never fell asleep like that before."

"Oh, you were drugged, Sis. I was calling your name and trying to shake you awake for damn near five minutes. You don't sleep that deep." Rainier turned towards his friend. "What do you think of all this?"

Lincoln leaned back against the couch. "I think Julianna was going with Plan B. Plan A was to install Adrienne as the figurehead there at Cenac and be the perfect fall guy along with your dead father if the illegal dumping and fire-bombing became known. But Plan B was simply to keep what she had built within the organization protected, and if that meant offing Adrienne, then so be it."

Adrienne shuddered and drained the second glass of rum and Coke. She tried standing up, and the room swam around her.

"Easy there, Sis."

"I gotta pee."

"Yep." Rainier slipped a hand around her waist and walked her towards one of the half-open doors. "Right here." He steadied her until she could turn on the light and then released her so she could close the door. "Christ, Link, you got her drunk."

"She looked like she needed it," Lincoln responded, laughing.

Adrienne closed her eyes as the world tilted and swam. The bathroom was filthy. It was very much a bachelor pad, and a poorly maintained one at that. She finished the roll of toilet paper and levered herself upright, listening to her brother and his friend's voices murmuring. She flushed the toilet and stared into the cracked and smudged mirror. It had been twenty-four hours at most, and they had turned her life upside-down. Had Julianna truly murdered their father? What had her stepmother planned to do with her once she had drugged her? She had so many questions and yet, she feared the answers.

Present Day

Kaylee stopped, her mouth suddenly dry, her stomach churning.

Jack's hands held hers. "The men who were looking for you, they killed them, didn't they?"

Kaylee nodded, wordless, tears falling against his smooth skin. She sat up, reached for a water bottle nearby and took a sip, wiping at the tears, her shoulders shaking.

"It all happened so fast. I was asleep on the couch. I think it was around midnight, maybe later. They shot Lincoln and Rainier. Just a couple of small pops, though, not loud. I would have thought it was a pop gun, not real, but then Rainier was on the ground and there was so much blood.

Before I could scream, before I could do much of anything except try to fight them off, they tied me up, drugged me. Then the big one slung me over his shoulders. I think the other one stayed behind long enough to set the fire." Her tears fell harder. "They were going to kill me too. I'm sure of it, once they were sure that the evidence burned up in the apartment and that I hadn't talked to anyone else."

Jack's hand was on her back, warm, soothing.

"They will kill anyone they think knows anything. I'm sure of that now. If they find me, they will kill you, Malcolm, and even Azule. You aren't safe around me. That's what you need to know, Jack. You aren't safe. No one is."

Survey for Prey

Jack soothed Kaylee as best he could. He held her in his arms and felt more helpless than he had in a long time. There was no way to take the experiences she had suffered from her mind, or go back in time and stop the murder of her brother and her brother's friend. Jack couldn't restore her parents to her, any more than he could his own. He felt as helpless as he had when he held Allie that one last time, knowing that she was gone and that he was powerless to bring her back. Allie, who had her entire life in front of her. Allie, who he had promised to protect and failed utterly at.

Kaylee, or Adrienne, he couldn't help but think of her as Kaylee. She also had her entire life in front of her as well. And Jack swore silently that he would do everything in his power to protect her, to make sure she had that life to live where others had not.

The stars filled the sky, even with the light from Los Angeles masking many of them. Here on this night, he could see so many. It was the planets that caught his eye tonight, however. He pointed to Mars, midway up in the southwest, and Saturn, its yellow hue clear in the south-southwest, only 30 degrees from the orange blob that was the Red Planet. He could just barely make out Mercury west-northwest. The waxing crescent moon hung just above it.

He whispered all of this in Kaylee's ear and gradually her sobs ceased, and she asked after the brightest of Virgo's stars so close to Saturn. "That's Spica, one of the twenty brightest stars in the sky," Jack said, his lips buried in Kaylee's hair. "It is actually two stars so close together that we cannot tell them apart through a telescope." His hand, restless, moved along the length of her, trailing his fingertips over the contours of her body, desiring more of her, but also wanting the simple connection that the feel of her skin against his made.

They lay there, staring at the stars, without words. Jack tried to think of the words to say to her, to reassure her, to encourage her to stay. Not just here, in this moment, but for longer. She was so young, younger than Malcolm, and yet, her presence here felt good and right. As if she had always belonged here with him.

Kaylee turned towards him and he could barely make out her features in the dark.

"Jack, I..." He stopped her from saying anything more with a deep, intense kiss. He didn't want her to tell him she had to leave. He didn't want to hear it, and he didn't want her to remind him of the danger of her presence in his life, or Mal's. Instead, he wanted to make love to her. The whole damn night, if that was what it took to take her fears away, or at least silence them until he could prove to her that she was safe here.

She returned his kiss, matching him in enthusiasm and attraction, her body moving under his in just the right way. Above them, the night sky blinked, the space station passed overhead in a slow, lazy arc, and the other denizens of the enormous tree listened, or slept, as the two made love in the treehouse, repeatedly.

There was no sense of time, up in the branches, far from any clocks. They slept, limbs intertwined, bodies sated, until the birds woke them at dawn.

Jack groaned. Cushioned or not, the treehouse was not half as comfortable as his bed, and his body ached. One arm had gone numb where he had wrapped it around Kaylee. She sat up slowly, stretching, her breasts perky. She covered them, a small blush blooming on her cheeks as she caught his gaze.

Jack protested, pulling her hand away from the left breast and sitting up to capture it in his mouth, feeling himself harden. He pulled her onto his lap, his tongue making its way up her chest to her neck and ear, before capturing her mouth again.

Kaylee groaned and then squirmed away. "There is one thing missing from this treehouse," she said, reaching for her clothes.

"A proper bed?" he asked, wincing as his back reminded him he was no longer ten and able to sleep on whatever surface he chose.

"Okay, two things then. A feather bed and a toilet!"

Jack laughed and turned to find his own clothes. They were mixed with hers, and they bumped heads twice trying to hurry into their discarded outfits.

The way down the tree was difficult in places, but Kaylee stepped confidently. She was a natural and not fearful of heights. If it was possible for him to like her even more than he already did, it was her ease in descending that impressed him the most.

"You aren't afraid of heights at all, are you?" he asked as she took a series of twisting steps in a rope ladder without complaint.

"Oh no, I'm terrified," she answered promptly, "but I'm more worried about peeing my pants right now to care about how high up we are, as long as we get down to the ground now."

Jack threw back his head and laughed. "We're almost there. You could go in the woods if it gets too bad."

"What, and wipe myself with poison ivy? No thanks." The ground grew closer.

"It's more poison oak rather than ivy around here, but I get your point."

The moment her feet were on the ground, Kaylee scampered down the trail and Jack was laughing so hard he couldn't keep up.

Jack watched as Kaylee zipped inside of the house and felt his stomach growl. They hadn't eaten dinner last night. He had been too busy to notice until now. He felt a twinge of guilt at the thought of Malcolm. His baby brother wasn't helpless, though. There were plenty of prepackaged meals downstairs in the second kitchen, and Mal could cook in a pinch. Jack usually gave him some kind of notice, though, instead of just disappearing. He'd have to fix something besides omelets. After four days in a row, he needed to make something else; all he'd done was feed her omelets and takeout. As he climbed the stairs to his own room, he could hear the water pipes. She was showering, and he paused, remembering how he had walked in on her showering. Had it only been two days? Covered in suds, steam billowing up over the clear glass walls of the shower. Eyes closed, her fingers...

"Hey." Jack's eyes flew open and he saw Kaylee standing in there in a fluffy robe, a half-smile on her face. She tilted her head towards the bathroom. "Join me?"

He didn't need coaxing. His shirt was already off, along with his shoes, and she laughed, shedding her robe inside of the door. A wash of wet heat greeted him inside of the bathroom and he stepped out of the last of his clothes and joined her inside.

When Kaylee reached for the shampoo, he reached out his hand. "Here, let me." He poured a generous amount into his hand and turned her so that her back was to him. She shivered as he worked the shampoo into her hair, digging his nails into her scalp slowly. "Are you cold?"

Kaylee sighed. "No, it just...it feels so good."

He pulled her closer to the water, the spray from the multiple jets sending the suds and shampoo spinning away into a vortex. His fingers made sure every bit of suds rinsed out, before his mouth worked its way along her slender neck, eyes closed in the downpour. Kaylee arched her back, fitting herself against him, her hips swaying as if to a silent beat. Jack could feel his cock swelling, his smaller head quite unconcerned with the lack of sleep or a sore back. He turned her around, so that she faced him, and pressed her against the cool tiles that lined the far wall of the shower, ignoring the water, capturing her mouth with his. She gasped as he lifted her up and then thrust inside of her, burying himself to the hilt in her silky depths. He stood like that for a moment, reveling in the warmth, the rush of sensation, and when he couldn't stand it anymore, he thrust in and out, harder, faster. Kaylee clung to him, her fingers digging into his shoulders. Jack's hands cupped her perfect round buttocks, his eyes watched as her mouth formed a perfect 'o' of ecstasy. She moaned with each new thrust and then, as the orgasm approached, her eyes flew open.

"Oh, Jack!" A rush of warmth, her hips bucking, and with one last thrust he came so hard he saw stars.

They stood there for what felt like moments, his heart hammering in his chest, and his face nestled in her shoulder, the water coursing over them. He let her go gently, her body sliding down the tiles until they reached the floor.

When his heart rate had returned to normal, he captured one last kiss from her and then pulled away. "I should see about breakfast."

"I could make us something, if you like," Kaylee said, reaching for her towel as steamy clouds billowed past them both. "Jul... well, my stepmother, she taught me a lot. We would bake something special each weekend." She wrapped the towel around herself and grinned. "It's not a breakfast food, per se, but I can make us some beignets, or even sweet potato ham hash if you prefer a healthier choice."

They settled on beignets, if only because he didn't have any sweet potato in the kitchen. Malcolm had a serious sweet tooth, and Jack figured that would trump his usual avocado omelet request. He headed to his own room, a spare towel wrapped around his waist, and dressed quickly.

Mal was sitting in his usual spot when Jack arrived. He had been waiting for Jack and his magnetic board read:

WOMAN HERE YESTERDAY
ASKED QUESTIONS
LOOKING FOR K
TALK TO A

Jack read the words and stared at his baby brother. "You're sure she was looking for Kaylee?" Mal gave a tiny nod and tapped the last line. "Did Az talk to her?" There was another small nod.

Jack felt a tight knot in his gut form, and it wasn't his hunger. Something felt off about this. He looked around the room.

The entire first floor was an open layout with high ceilings and tall picture windows. If this woman had gotten past the front gate, what would she have seen if she were standing right outside of the house?

Jack's eyes landed on the light jacket Kaylee had been wearing yesterday afternoon. It lay on the back of the couch, a delicate pink and blue.

Shit.

He strode around the kitchen island and reached for his Samsung Galaxy, which sat charging on the counter. He picked it up, tapped a few keys, and found a text from Azule.

> Azule R: A woman was here. Said she was a survey taker. Black hair, lean, muscled. Her smile didn't reach her eyes. Mid 20s at most. Was asking after women between ages of 15-25. Raised my hackles. Looked around a lot. Said gate was open. CALL ME.

Double shit.

Jack turned to see Kaylee's face pale at the words on Mal's board. "Could it be your stepmother? Julie..."

"Julianna?" She frowned. "I can't see her doing something like that, but I didn't suspect her of killing my dad and I'm pretty sure she did." She peered over his shoulder at the text. "Black hair? Lean muscles? No, definitely not."

Jack read the text to her, and Kaylee shook her head again. "No, that's not her."

He pressed the Call button, and the phone rang once before Azule answered. "You left your phone on the damn counter again, didn't you?" She didn't wait for an answer. "I've been thinking about it all night. And I don't like it. She set off my shit detectors."

Jack would have laughed except that right now all of his own alerts were going off. If Azule felt like something was off, then he trusted it. Az was a woman with excellent intuition. He cast an eye around, surveying the open floor plan with the large windows and semi-privacy with a fresh eye. Kaylee was not safe here. None of them were.

"Right. Az, here's what I need for you to do..." Before he could continue, he felt rather than heard the rush of air first and the crack of glass sounded immediately afterwards. The bullet sliced the air between them, shattering the glass tiles of the kitchen behind them. Jack circled a hand around Kaylee's waist and pulled her to the floor, yelling at his brother to take cover as the second, third, and fourth bullets hit the refrigerator, exploded the coffeemaker, and grazed the countertop as Jack pushed Kaylee against the dishwasher, hoping it would protect her even further from the gunfire. He then dove sideways and grabbed Malcolm by the back of his shirt and pulled him close. Malcolm struggled. Even now, faced with danger, his brother could not stand another's touch. He fought to get away from Jack, screaming wordlessly. Jack winced as Mal's free hand formed into a fist and delivered a glancing blow to the side of Jack's head.

Kaylee looked pale, terrified, her eyes wide.

"The basement is a safe room. We have to get to it." His gaze traveled from what little he could see over the kitchen island to the door set in the wall just fifteen feet away. "Mal, stop fighting me! I'll let you go, but you have to go with Kaylee." He released his hold on Malcolm and his brother ceased his struggles, scooting as far from

Jack as possible while remaining down on the floor. He was out of range of the bullets for now. They had stopped, and Jack knew it was only a matter of time before whoever was firing got closer. A few feet away he could hear Azule's voice calling out over the phone, but there was no time, she couldn't help them.

When seconds count, the police are minutes away.

Jack reached into a cabinet, past the rolls of aluminum foil, and his fingers closed on the handle of the Smith & Wesson. He racked the slide back and slipped the safety off. Kaylee's eyes widened even more.

"What are you doing?" she whispered.

"Buying you time. You and Mal need to get to the basement. Get ready to run."

"What about you?"

"I'll be right behind you." He peeked over the kitchen island and saw a lithe figure running towards the house. "Go now."

Kaylee stood up and ran with Malcolm behind her, his binder in his arms. As they ran, Jack shot towards the window at their attacker. The picture window disintegrated in a crash of broken glass, the additional weapons fire overwhelming the expanse already damaged by the intruder's bullets.

The figure dove to one side and he could tell it was a woman now, her dark, long hair neatly braided in a long line down her back. She wouldn't go down for long, and he wasn't ready to hide in the basement below and hope that the police got here in time. The screen on his phone had gone dark, and he knew Azule was already on the phone with the police. He held no hope that they would get here in time to save them. Jack would have to stop her.

He glanced over. Kaylee and Malcolm had made it to the door and slipped inside. Malcolm had pulled it closed until only a sliver of his face was visible. Jack met his brother's eyes and said, "Lock it." He turned away even as he heard Kaylee object and the door snick closed, the bolts sliding into place. No one could get in there. Not without heavy explosives.

She was moving again. He could see her leap through the open wound that was the picture window, firing as she entered his home.

Time to Die

The afternoon before...

Nyra easily climbed over the gate and headed down the long, winding drive towards the house. She plastered her most winning smile on as she approached the main entrance. A voluptuous black woman was standing in the drive, her eyes narrowed in suspicion.

"Hi there! I'm conducting a survey on name-brand makeup choices, and I have free samples for anyone who matches my demographic!" Nyra called out, forcing perkiness into every inch of her voice.

"How did you get in here?" The woman had her hands on her hips and her eyebrows arched.

"I, uh." Nyra looked down at the ground. "Okay, look, I'm new and they assigned me all of this quadrant and *every single driveway* is gated and locked. If I don't come back with something, they'll fire me!" She gave the woman an anguished look. "I know I jumped the fence, but seriously, I'm just trying to keep my job."

The woman gave her a measuring look, and Nyra could see she wasn't convinced. "What age group do you need?"

"Ages fifteen to twenty-five females. Transgender and nonbinary are welcome as well," she reeled off glibly. "I have some lovely MAC eye shadow and blush, full-size samples!"

She had maneuvered her approach so she could see both the woman and as much of the inside of the house as possible. No one was in sight, nothing out of place, except...

"There's no one here in that demographic, miss."

Nyra noticed a spot of color on the white sofa. A pale pink and blue sweater, definitely female. She frowned, pouting a little in mock disappointment. "Are you sure?"

The woman's eyebrows raised even further, and her mouth compressed into a single, disapproving line. "Quite sure. Let me walk you to the gate. You may have better luck if you head to the north."

Nyra had no choice but to walk with the woman back to the gate. It didn't matter. She would scout the rest of the area out in the last two hours of daylight, just to be sure, but she had a strong feeling about this house. No matter, she could sneak back in later to find out more. She gushed her thanks and walked away, down the winding drive. Once she was out of sight of the gate, she pulled out her phone, located the right number, and pressed Call.

"Lucif...I mean, this is Luce..." the girl on the other end stammered.

Nyra grinned. "Lucifer, it's Nyra."

"Oh, hey Nyra, what's up?" The girl's voice on the other end perked up.

"Can you run a license number for me? And also an address?"

"Sure, uh, hang on a sec." There was a brief scrabbling in the background and then Lucifer returned. "Hit me."

Nyra gave her both numbers. "I need ownership on both."

"I'll work on those right now. Hey, how's your sister?" Nyra could hear Lucifer clicking away at her computer, already on task.

"She's doing good. A couple more weeks and she'll get her tat, become one of us."

"That's awesome! I can't wait to meet her!" Nyra smiled at that response; it was classic Lucifer. The girl looked terrifying with her goth makeup, piercings, and tattoos. Nyra knew better. She had met Lucifer when she first joined up, a little over a year ago, still big-eyed and green, a small-town girl in a big city. Nyra had been tasked with showing Lucifer some basic hand-to-hand combat, the standard stuff. None of the advanced "five-finger-death-punch stuff" as Lucifer had called it.

They had struck up a friendship of sorts. At least, as much of one as any of them could have when you worked for the Indalo. Fraternization was not particularly encouraged.

The reality of it was that Lucifer and Zella would likely never meet. Lucifer didn't really understand that yet. She didn't give a single thought to why Nyra needed the information or what she would do with it. And depending on how well she did, she might never know. Lucifer was good, though, very good at hacking, and therefore quite valuable at her job. That she didn't question was even better, because the deeper you went with the Indalo, the less you wanted to question.

"Okay, I've got a hit on the address," Lucifer said. "It belongs to a Jack Benton. Ooh la la! He's rolling in it. I'm getting society pages, a plane crash that killed his parents ten years ago, and, huh, he started Benton Security Services around eight years ago. Looks like they offer protection, high-end bodyguard detail, that kind of thing."

Bingo.

"Thanks, Lucifer, that's all I need."

"Oh well hey, what about the license plate?"

"Unnecessary. I've got what I need. Thanks, Luce."

"Alright, then. But hey, call me back sometime. They keep me in the dark and feed me shit like I'm a mushroom. I think I might get a dog to keep me company. A big one, like a Great Dane...got any good ideas for names?"

"Call her Annabelle," Nyra said, the name popping out of her brain with little thought. It had been the name of her first target, Annabelle Bouchard.

You never forget the name of your first kill.

"I like that."

Nyra didn't say goodbye, just stabbed the End Call button as she reached the end of the drive and turned left towards the north. She'd put on a show, kept the older black woman guessing, and hopefully convinced her she was who she said she was. Once she made her way to two other houses, she would double back and scope out the property.

She handed out samples to two girls, one eleven-year-old who glibly lied and said she was sixteen. Nyra had hidden her amusement and written useless bullshit on the checklist she had created to go with the survey-taker outfit before making the kid's day by giving her the entire bag of makeup. The sun disappeared behind the trees, but Nyra waited for nightfall to once again climb the fence.

There was the main house and then another building that was nearly as large as the main house. She kept to the shadows and investigated it. The door was locked, but that was easy enough to circumvent. Nyra's training hadn't been restricted to combat techniques and inventive ways to murder someone; she'd also learned how to pick most locks. The door to this building had taken nothing more than a credit card to open. It had contained offices, a conference room, and she had enjoyed watching the fish in the arboretum. She cased the house and debated whether to break in and wait inside for this Jack Benton to come back. It was easy enough to find a comfortable spot in the shrubbery that lined the glass house and wait for the billionaire to return from wherever he had gone to.

Nyra positioned herself so that she would be completely invisible to anyone inside of the compound or anyone driving in from the outer road. She crossed her legs, centered her mind, and thought of Zella. Her sister's anger ran deep. For Nyra, the distance of several years away had meant she had time to process the abuse her father had practiced upon her body. Zella had done what Nyra could not—kill him—and Nyra's thoughts flitted to their mother briefly. She had done nothing to stop Jeffery Dean from abusing and raping her daughters. She'd laid in her bed and not lifted a finger, not even acknowledged what was happening in her own house.

And for that, she deserved what she got.

What surprised Nyra was that Zella didn't hate her for leaving. She could have, and rightfully so, but she hadn't. Zella's black hatred of men hadn't faded in the past year, and it was for that reason that Nyra had delayed telling Delta that her sister was ready to join the Indalo. Her anger caused her to act with careless disregard for her safety or others. And while Nyra was sure that Zella could easily kill her marks, she seemed to kill indiscriminately and with no concern for the repercussions. Most of Nyra's assignments had carried with them the expectation of finesse. If Zella couldn't get her emotions under control, she would quickly put a target on her own back, and Nyra's. They were all expendable, after all.

The night was clear for Los Angeles. The smog was absent, and the stars had appeared in the sky, glowing jewels that appeared to wink, even move, across a velvet backdrop.

Her legs ached after several hours of maintaining the same position. Her ankle, the one Zella had hit with such accuracy, felt especially tender.

It was in quiet moments such as these that she wondered what a person had done to get on the Indalo's shit list. This Adrienne Cenac was barely out of high school, and a prestigious one at that. She didn't seem worldly, and Nyra closed her eyes for a moment and visualized the girl's face. They had taken the photo from her school yearbook, from the looks of it. She had a fresh, cheerful smile that reached all the way to her eyes.

Whatever had happened in Adrienne Cenac's life, it couldn't have been too bad. She was rich, pretty, and had her life in front of her. Or at least she had until they handed Nyra her file. Now she was dead, or as good as. Never mind the fact that she had gotten away from Stephan and Rohan. They were cops, after all. In the pockets of the Indalo, for sure, but cops.

As the hours passed, the sliver of moon worked its way across the sky and out of sight, and the horizon glowed as the sun rose behind it. Nyra heard voices coming from behind the house and within seconds, a girl appeared, sprinting for the door. She ran inside and up the stairs.

Honey-blond hair, with only the side of her face visible as she ran by. It had looked like a match to the yearbook photo. But Nyra wanted to be sure. Delta frowned heavily on collateral damage. Besides, she had time, even with the sun up. The black woman was obviously an employee. She had been leaving at five the evening before and would likely return by nine today. Nyra had over three hours to accomplish her mission and disappear into the woods that surrounded the estate. By the time law enforcement processed the scene, she would be back with Zella in their desert hideaway.

She stood, stretched her legs, and fitted the silencer on her pistol. Nyra marveled at the idiocy of the rich. What good was a tall fence without sensor alarms? And to have shrubbery so that they would feel like they were away from prying eyes just gave an intruder somewhere to hide.

Less than a minute after the girl ran inside, a good-lucking guy in his mid-thirties came around the back of the building and walked inside. That was obviously Jack Benton. Lucifer had sent Nyra several photos of him with varying numbers of exclamation points after each picture, apparently showing levels of hotness. And he was good-looking, to be sure. Not Nyra's type. Her interests lay in women. She had enough of her fill of men before she ever left home. Nyra watched as he made his way up the stairs. She could just barely catch a second set of feet before the large window gave way to wall. She watched an interplay of feet and then Jack's following the girl out of sight.

They were lovers, then. Interesting. She had escaped Stephan and Rohan on Saturday night and likely found her way here sometime late Saturday or early Sunday. And was in the man's bed by Wednesday morning? She shook her head.

Men are nothing but walking hard-ons.

The minutes ticked by, and finally she saw Jack's feet head to a room at the far end of the upstairs hallway and disappear for a few minutes before reappearing and walking downstairs. As he did, it surprised Nyra to see a younger copy of Jack Benton sitting at the breakfast bar with a large binder open in front of him. His hair was dark, long, and rather shaggy. Where had this younger man come from? Her surveillance last night had shown only bedrooms on the upper level, and she saw nothing indicating there was a basement or lower level past the main floor. She peered through her monocular. Too old to be Jack's child, possibly a brother? Lucifer's info had included no info on a sibling, but Nyra hadn't asked her for a family history, just the standard property records. No matter. They were talking now, or at least Jack was speaking. The younger man had his back to the window and was as still as a stone. It looked as though Jack was frowning and she watched as he reached for his phone, read something on the screen, and then looked up and out. Nyra felt a thread of anxiety pulse in her.

Perhaps I have less time than I originally thought.

Had the employee she ran into said something to him? Nyra watched as he dialed the phone, put it up to his ear, and waited for an answer. She was so intent on watching his face, on trying to read his lips, that she didn't notice the girl's approach at first. Nyra examined her through the monocular in her hand. Her hair was damp from a shower, but the girl's face was a match. Adrienne Cenac was here. Exposed in this house of glass, she was hiding from the Indalo less than two miles from where the car had been found.

You should have run, Adrienne. Now it's time to die.

Nyra aimed her weapon carefully. Adrienne had moved closer to Jack, a slender hand on his sleeve, her face tight with concern.

Nyra fired and felt a poorly-time breeze at exactly the same moment and the bullet left the chamber. The shot, lined up perfectly accounting for distance, went wide, slamming into the tile between Adrienne and Jack. She fired again as they disappeared from sight. First Adrienne and Jack, and then the younger man, his binder still clutched in his hands as he disappeared from view. Nyra could see his legs kicking to one side, as if he were fighting the older man. She followed the first bullet with three more. They left holes with a starburst pattern around each, but the window held. She had to get closer.

She stood and ran, firing as she did. Nyra saw the small, dark muzzle of a handgun appear and fire, shattering the window entirely. She dodged from side to side, closing the distance, and firing back as she saw the girl and the younger man run for a distance before disappearing into what looked like a wall. Nyra swore silently.

A safe room, possibly. That's where the younger man came from. Damn it!

A bullet whizzed past her ear as she approached what was now an open wound into the house and Nyra dodged to the left at just the wrong moment, another bullet entering her chest, tearing through her like a hot skewer. It took her breath away, and she half slid into the house, gasping for air as she flopped over the edge of the open window and against a white couch.

That the bullet had hit her was shocking. In the past three years, she hadn't been so much as nicked by a knife, much less shot. Nyra lay against the couch, chest on fire, and breath bubbling in her chest. She spit a glob of blood out of her mouth and searched for a solution. None of them were good, none of them ended well. No matter what happened next, whether she was successful in her mission, her future, her life, was something she could measure in seconds and minutes.

Should have worn the body armor. Stupid.

Jack Benton was standing over her now. He reached down and wrenched the gun away from Nyra's hand and then set his own down, his right hand on her neck, checking her pulse.

Nyra whispered the words. It wasn't hard to pretend she was dying, because she knew she was. She gathered her energy as he drew closer. Her knife was in her boot, her leg folded up underneath her on the floor.

Come closer. I'll give you something to remember me by.

He shifted closer, and she struck, slicing with the last of her energy at his belly. It wasn't her mark; he wasn't her mission. But that was okay.

One less rich asshole who can't think past his dick.

And as Jack fell away from her, clutching his side, his blood joining hers, Nyra slipped away into the abyss.

The Price You Pay

Jack struggled to his feet, his left hand pressed hard against the gaping wound, blood leaking everywhere. His head swam. He had to get help. He had to protect Kaylee. These two priorities warred in his mind and worse, the world would not hold still. It kept tilting sideways. He shook his head, which didn't help, not at all.

He could hear a car screech to a halt outside and he turned, his body moving as if through waist-high mud. He couldn't get his feet to work right and he cast about for the gun he had set down on a nearby chair. If it was another like this one, he had seconds, perhaps minutes before the blood loss incapacitated him. He could see a figure running towards the house, but everything was blurry.

"Jack! Jack!" Azule's voice. She was closer now, choosing to cross through into the house the same way the dead woman on the floor had, through the remains of the picture window.

"Oh no, Jack, hold on. The police are right behind me. Ambulance too, by the sound of it."

"Keep her safe, Az." Even his lips felt numb, his tongue heavy. "Don't let the police see her. Don't let them know she's...here."

His feet weren't working, and the ground was moving again. Jack hit the carpet, his eyes closing as he heard Kaylee screaming.

Later, much later, Azule would question her life choices, extensively and with plenty of swearing about rich, white people and their messes. For now, she was hell-bent on doing exactly what Jack had requested. Blood everywhere, as pale as if he had lost half of the blood inside of him, Azule turned her attention to Kaylee, who had burst through the safe room door and was running towards them.

"Girl! If you know what is good for you, which you obviously do not, you will go back there right now. Jack doesn't want you seen, and you will damn well listen."

Kaylee gasped, stopping short of the mess, her mouth agape, her hands clutched to her mouth.

Little girl like this bringing disaster down on us.

"Go back to the safe room. Now. 'Afore the police get here." She gave the girl a stern look. The sirens were close. "I'm putting pressure on the wound. There's nothing for you to do here, 'cept get yourself killed. Jack's already paying the price, now go."

Malcolm appeared at the door as well. He managed a dozen steps into the room before his gaze slid over the blood that stained the couch and floor and two bodies on the floor. He opened his mouth and screamed wordlessly. It was a high, keening wail. He just stood there and screamed as Kaylee ran back towards him and tried to take him by the arm. The sirens were on the private drive; they were running out of time.

"Leave, Mal, I'll take care of him. Go, Kaylee! Now!" Azule bellowed, and Jack groaned as she pressed harder on his wound.

Mal continued his terrible keen as the police arrived, weapons drawn, and Azule did her best to stay calm.

"On the ground, now!"

"If I release pressure, he bleeds out. The screamer over there is his brother, he's autistic, he's non-verbal and harmless. I'm Azule Roberts, Mr. Benton's personal assistant, and I called this in."

The taller cop was a brother, something that gave Azule some hope that they would listen. He was the first to holster his weapon and held up a hand to the other, a nervous, skinny white boy who still had acne. Seconds later, the drive filled with medical personnel as the ambulance and fire department arrived.

Before Azule could stop them, they tranked Mal, and Jack's brother dropped like a stone. The EMTs swarmed the room, and Azule could stand again and stumble to the sink to wash some of Jack's blood off of her. She looked down at her jacket and felt ill. There was so much of it, she didn't know how he could stand to lose so much and be okay.

They were bundling him up on the stretcher, an IV in his arm. "We're taking him to Sinai," one man said. "Should I call an ambulance for psych transport for the brother?" he asked the police officer, who immediately looked over at Azule.

"No, that won't be necessary. Malcolm will be fine here. I'll get this cleaned up before the sedatives wear off."

"We will need to take your statement first, ma'am," the officer said as he watched the ambulance careen back down the drive, its sirens wailing.

"Of course. If I could make a few calls first. It will take just a moment."

She had to call one of the security team and the cleaners. Azule searched her memories. Luke had met Malcolm and been patient, plus he was between assignments. He'd have to do. As the phone rang, she pantomimed to the officer that she was going to step into the bathroom for privacy. There she avoided looking at the bloody mess on the front of her clothes in the mirror and focused instead on explaining to Luke that he needed to come over immediately. The second call was to a crime scene cleaning firm that promised one-hour metro-wide service. She had to get the place cleaned up before Malcolm saw it.

And the third call was to Nia, Marley's ex. "Nia, I know it's your day off, but I need you to do me a solid and bring a clean outfit up to my work. I'll text you the address."

With all of that out of the way, and praying that Kaylee would stay where she was, Azule left the bathroom and returned to the waiting officer. She was on her second repetition of the sequence of events when the driveway filled with vehicles, the crime scene cleanup crew, Luke and Nia, all arriving at the same time.

Nia had Demetrius in the back seat and she didn't want the boy alarmed. "Please," she said, turning to the officer, "could you ask my cousin in that little blue Civic to just come inside and leave her son out in the car for a moment?"

He smiled and nodded. "Sure."

He was good-looking, and Azule watched as he smiled at Nia. The girl was pretty, with her light-cocoa skin and hair perfectly coiffed. He opened the car door for her and she stepped out, giving a long stare at the broken window, before striding into the house, the officer strolling along behind her, getting a magnificent view, no doubt.

"Az, what in the..." Nia stopped in her tracks, her mouth dropping open as she stared at the white couch and chairs speckled with blood and the body lying underneath a sheet. "Is that your boss?" Nia's eyes widened as she took in Azule's blood-soaked clothes. "Oh my God, Az!"

"It's all right, everything will be fine. It's not my blood. And no, that's not my boss." She held her hands out for the large bag Nia was holding. "Please don't say anything to Auntie L., I don't want her getting all in a fuss."

"But, Az..."

Azule pressed a hundred-dollar bill in Nia's hand. "Go on, Nia, go get Demetrius and you somethin' to eat."

Nia shut her mouth, nodded, and with a weak, half-flirtatious smile for the officer, headed for her car. Which was just as well, since Demetrius was pitching a fit, madder than hell that he hadn't been able to follow Nia inside. She watched them drive away, the sounds of the boy's enraged screams floating through the air.

Luke scanned the grounds. His muscle-bound arms looked handsome in a plaid check shirt and jeans. He looked out of place here, as usual. Luke was a man who was at home in a wood cabin, wearing flannel and chopping firewood. Azule was thankful he had left his handgun out of sight. The hunting knife on his hip had already raised the white cop's eyebrows.

"How can I help?"

"Just keep an eye on Malcolm for now. They tranked him. Couldn't handle seeing all the blood."

Luke nodded and pointed a finger upstairs, silently asking permission. When Azule nodded, he hoisted Malcolm over his shoulder and carried his still unconscious body upstairs to Jack's room.

Azule directed the crime scene cleanup team to do what they could about the bloodstains on the couch and carpet and slipped into the bathroom to change. By the time she emerged, the handsome brother of an officer was wrapping up his notes.

"I think that about covers it, ma'am. We have your information if we have any further questions. I just heard from Sinai as well, and they have taken Mr. Benton into surgery. He's had a transfusion and was stable prior to surgery." He flipped his notepad closed. "The rest of our questions will have to wait for him."

He turned to his partner. "Go ahead, I'll be there in a minute." The skinny white cop shrugged and nodded at Azule before heading out the door.

"I live in the neighborhood," the tall brother said, pressing a card into Azule's hand. "I went to school with Nia, feels like a thousand years ago. Ask her to call me, would you?" He smiled then; his teeth white against his dark brown skin.

"Mm-huh, I'll let Nia know." The corner of Azule's mouth twitched.

"Thank you, Ms. Roberts." Another dazzling smile and the door clicked shut behind him.

Azule turned the card over in her hand. Officer Tyrone Hendricks' name was neatly printed next to the LAPD crest. She knew plenty of Hendricks in Compton. There was a whole extended clan of them two streets over. Tyrone. Huh, Janae had a boy named Ty who had joined the force.

She smiled at the thought of Nia hooking up with a cop. Marley wouldn't come skulking around too often if that was the case. He had a rap sheet a mile long. Just seeing a cop made him twitchy and nervous. And Little Demetrius needed a positive male role model in his life.

God knows he ain't getting it with Marley as his daddy.

Azule glanced at the wall that hid the safe room. It wouldn't do to open it while the cleaners were here. Kaylee would just have to wait a little longer.

It felt like forever, but the cleaning team filed out at a few minutes before noon, just as Luke signaled Malcolm was waking up. Azule signed the paperwork and shooed the last one out the door. The groundskeeper covered the gaping hole big enough to drive a car through where the glass window had been. He updated Azule with an estimate on how long it would take until the glass would be replaced and then turned on his heel and power-walked out to the driveway to order the news van off of the property. Azule watched him intimidate the driver until the van sped away, having snapped a couple of pictures of the broken window. She was sure they would camp out outside of Sinai and wait for someone to give them a scoop on the billionaire being treated inside.

Vultures.

Azule waited until the last of them had vanished down the drive, the gates locking behind them, before she turned to the safe room door. The door was unlocked and opened silently; the heavy door perfectly weighted, effortless to open. Two dozen steps down into the suite and Kaylee was waiting, her eyes red, face splotched with red.

White girls look a sorry sight when they been crying.

"Az, do we know anything? Is Mal okay? How did you get him calm? Please tell me Jack is okay. Is he?"

Azule held her hand up. "Girl, you need to stop and just breathe for a moment. Sit down and I'll tell you what I know."

Kaylee gulped, nodded, and sat down on a nearby chair. Around them were bookshelves crammed full of science fiction books.

There was also a small table and chairs along with a kitchenette. A long hallway with several doors stretched away in the opposite direction. Malcolm slept in one room and Azule knew there was at least one other guest bedroom down here, along with a workout room and another that held enough weapons to stop an army of invaders. She shook her head and wondered why in the hell Jack hadn't run inside of the panic suite behind Mal and Kaylee. It was just like him to play the hero and damn near get himself killed.

Azule grabbed another chair and sat down facing Kaylee, opening her mouth to speak just as her cell phone rang.

There was a smile on her face as she ended the call. "He's out of surgery and the doctors expect him to make a full recovery."

Kaylee burst into a set of fresh tears and buried her face in her hands. "This is all my fault."

"Funny, I thought the dead bitch knifed our boy, not you," Azule said dryly. "You order the hit on yourself?" Kaylee looked up at her in surprise. "Girl, he didn't have to tell me you were in trouble, you got the look. It says you got a lot of running left to do if you don't get help."

"Jack tried to help and look where it got him," Kaylee protested.

"Jack slipped up," Azule barked at the girl, her lips flattening in displeasure. "That's the price you pay for thinking a player's out of the game when they aren't. He let his guard down, and that's on him, Kaylee, not you." She examined her left ring finger. She'd chipped the nail in her rush to get here. Azule had been halfway to the house on the 101, nearly two hours early for work, when Jack'd answered. Hearing the shots and the screams, it had her hammering at the keys hard enough to damn near snap it off. "Besides, if that white boy ends up dead, I'll have to go down there and double-kill him. I'll never find a job as good as this one."

She heard something that sounded suspiciously close to a snort from Kaylee and turned to catch the girl's half-smile.

"Do you really think he's going to be okay?"

"Yes, I do," Azule answered steadily, her brown eyes connecting with Kaylee's.

The girl's lower lip quivered, the tears gathering again, and Azule reached out and gave Kaylee's shoulders a small shake. "Get it together, Girl, Malcolm needs you calm. I can already see what a difference you are making. That boy couldn't stand any of the women Jack has brought home, but you? He needs you even-keeled and level-headed."

"Where is he?"

"Upstairs." The voice came from Luke, who was now standing halfway down the stairs and leaning over enough to show his face. "He's asking for a 'K.'"

"That's me, um, Kaylee." She looked back at Azule with a panicked expression, as if suddenly concerned she had said too much.

Azule nodded. "That's Luke. He works for Benton Security Services." She flapped her hand at Kaylee. "Go ask him to play Scrabble. Something, anything, to bring him back to center. I'll go to the hospital. They said he would be awake soon."

She turned to Luke. "I'll be adding extra security, but once you both get Mal back to calm, get them down here. I know that's what

Jack will want. There're meals down here, everything they could need."

Azule took a deep breath as she watched them both disappear upstairs. She had weathered the shit storm. She wasn't sure how, but she had done it.

I'm billing him for my outfit. It was my favorite.

Rabbit Hole

Kaylee nicknamed the basement suite the Rabbit Hole and did her best to stay occupied for the twelve long days it took for Jack to return from the hospital.

The suite held three large bedrooms; one was Malcolm's, the other a spare bedroom intended for guests, and the third had been turned into a workout room. Luke brought a pile of clothes down from the upstairs room where she had been staying and filled the closet with them. He slept on the couch and insisted they bolt themselves in whenever he needed to leave, which was often, as he was apparently overseeing the installation of the new security system.

If Kaylee had been more of the outdoorsy type, she would have fallen for this tall, blond Adonis in flannel. As it was, he was easy on the eyes, and Malcolm apparently enjoyed how Luke cooked steaks because he requested them for dinner each evening as he and Kaylee hunkered over the Scrabble board. Other times she read from *Voyage from Yesteryear* and *Podkayne From Mars*, both science fiction books of Rainier's she remembered him reading. It got to where Scrabble tiles and science fiction had entered her dreams at night, but Kaylee stuck with it. At the beginning and end of each Scrabble game, she convinced Malcolm to practice shaking hands.

"You'll need to know, Mal. It's expected."

In between games, Mal watched the YouTube videos of the World Scrabble Championships obsessively. It had progressed to where even Kaylee had memorized play-by-play the last two annual championship winning games.

The first time she had convinced him to shake her hand, Mal had groaned, as if the touch of another actually hurt him. It had taken him nearly a week to perfect a solid grip and another to manage brief direct eye contact. It lasted for less than two seconds, but Mal was improving, and Kaylee felt a sense of pride flood through her. He might be older than her, older even than Rainier had been, but he felt like a younger brother.

Luke watched the exchange and said nothing, a small smile often flitted across his lips. He had little to say, and Kaylee felt as if she was going stir-crazy. She'd been in the rabbit hole for nearly two weeks and, except for Azule, any conversation she had with Luke or Mal felt one-sided, even with Luke.

When a knock on the door came, Kaylee didn't even look up. She was biting her lip and staring at the Scrabble board, doing her best to figure out how to outsmart Mal's latest move. It was impossible, though. His skills had skyrocketed past hers with his constant study of the championship videos.

"Hey there," Jack's voice intruded on her thoughts.

Kaylee jumped, her eyes focusing on Jack's, and she leaped to her feet. "Oh my God, Jack! I thought they weren't releasing you until tomorrow!" She ran over and hugged him, burying her face in his shoulder.

Jack gave a small "oof" of discomfort and she immediately released him. He smiled down at her. "I got early release for exemplary behavior."

"Don't believe him for a second." Azule's voice floated down the stairs. "He was a terrible patient. If it wasn't for him being rich and good-looking, the nurses would have suffocated him in his sleep rather than spend another day listening to him."

"Now, Az, why do you have to ruin my image?" Jack called over his shoulder.

Azule snorted. "Seems to me the girl needs to know what she's getting into."

Kaylee laughed and, standing this close to him, remembered how he had looked lying there on the floor, his blood staining the carpet. Tears welled up in her eyes.

"Oh, Jack."

"Shh, I'm fine. A little sore, but nothing I won't recover from. I came down to see if you are ready to come out of your rabbit hole."

Kaylee snorted. "Ready? Um, yes, very much so."

Stepping back onto the main floor for the first time in nearly two weeks brought back every searing memory of that day. They had replaced the broken glass windows and the furniture and carpet. She had heard them working away upstairs over the past two weeks, distant thumps and bumps and the whine of machinery. From what Azule had told her, they had amped up security to where, as Azule wryly put it, "A mouse wouldn't be able to fart within a hundred yards without SWAT descending upon the house in under three minutes flat."

Kaylee stared at the large picture window and Jack followed her glance, saying, "They have replaced it with bulletproof glass."

"I'm so sorry, Jack. This is my fault."

"Kaylee, I promised you would be safe here, and I was wrong. This is my fault. I'm in the security and protection business and I never took the proper precautions with my house."

"Especially after that Shane character showed you how poor it was, too," Azule commented dryly.

Kaylee wasn't sure who Shane was, or what incident she was referring to, but the look on Azule's face told her that this had been something Azule had pushed for with Jack for some time now.

Kaylee looked over at Azule, who was wearing a gorgeous blue pantsuit. "That looks beautiful, Az, is it new?"

Azule beamed. "It is. New from Eloquii, courtesy of Jack, who ruined my favorite dress and matching jacket with all that madness the other day. Dry cleaners said I'd never get the blood out."

Jack arched his eyebrows at her and said nothing.

Malcolm slid past the group and sat down in the living room, turning on the television. Kaylee realized it was time for *Jeopardy*. And the creature of habit that Malcolm was, he wasn't about to miss it. The TV was not on its usual station, however, and instead, a news headline flashed across the screen at that very moment.

Kaylee gasped audibly; her eyes glued on the screen.

"What is it?" Jack turned to see, but Mal had already pressed the button and changed the channel. Alex Trebek was on the screen. He turned back to Kaylee. "What's wrong?"

She felt lightheaded, ill. "It's...it was...Julianna." She knew better than to ask Malcolm to change it back; *Jeopardy* had already begun and interfering with his routine caused a negative reaction, no matter how much he seemed to enjoy having her around. She had learned to work within his world, and gently draw him out of his own in increments. Changing the channel would likely cause him to howl in dismay. "I need to see the news, especially out of Louisiana."

A few moments later, after a quick search on Jack's laptop, she gasped and stabbed at the screen with her finger. "There, read that!"

Jack read the article and then glanced up at Kaylee. "That's your stepmother?"

"Yes," she whispered, eyes filling. "I know what Rainier thought of her, but she was kind to me."

"Except for drugging you," Jack pointed out, frowning.

"Well, yes, except for that. But Jack, they think I had something to do with it."

"Yes, I saw that towards the bottom of the article." He pointed to a link. "And it looks as if Rainier and Lincoln's deaths were ruled homicides and..." he clicked on the article, "...you are listed as a person of interest in that as well."

Kaylee's eyes grew wide in shock. "Do they really think I killed my brother and his friend? And my stepmother?"

Jack didn't look up, his lips moving as he read another article link. "Over $100 million in funds were transferred out of Cenac Shipping to an offshore account with your, well, Adrienne Cenac's, name on it." He looked up. "Neatly framed. You would spend years trying to prove your innocence in the courts."

"If she lived that long," Azule spoke up, sitting in front of her own laptop at the kitchen counter, her eyes fixed on the screen.

"Az, mind your bedside manners there," Jack replied, his forehead wrinkling. "It will be alright, Kaylee, I promise."

"No," Kaylee said, her heart plummeting. "It won't." She ran her fingers through her hair, felt them shake. "They, whoever they are, will not let this go. Not until I'm dead. And everyone protecting me is at risk as well."

"We will figure it out, Kaylee," Jack promised her, obviously worried, and yet so certain he could help her.

"No, no, we won't," Kaylee said, equally certain. She looked at him. "I need to disappear. Help me disappear, Jack."

Azule added her opinion to the mix. "She's right, Jack. The girl needs to disappear, not hang out front and center with you."

Kaylee watched as Jack's jaw dropped, and a look of betrayal suffused his face.

Azule persisted. "She can never be safe here. You live in the limelight. What are you going to do, hide out in that there rabbit hole until the bad guys just magically shrug their shoulders and give up? Girl needs an ID, a new look, and then she'll blend in on any college campus. Safe as a bug in a rug."

Kaylee met Jack's eyes and could see an internal war was being waged. He wanted her, and God, she wanted him, but seeing him there on the ground, blood everywhere, nearly dying because of her... She couldn't stand it, not if it meant risking his life and...

"You can't be by my side, Jack. There's Mal to consider. He needs you. You know he does." She looked away, her heart breaking. She had lost everyone she ever loved. Mom, Father, Rainier, and hell, even Julianna. No matter if she was behind most of this or not, Julianna had been kind to her. And now, on top of all of that, all the horror of the past few weeks, she had to say goodbye to both Jack and even Mal, who of whom she loved. Mal, who was well on his way to shaking people's hands and being able to calm himself enough that he could actually take part in a Scrabble championship in the future. She wanted that for him, wanted to be standing there in the audience when he won.

Kaylee didn't dare look at Jack. It was all she could do to not think of him holding her in his arms, making love to her in the shower, or high in his treehouse underneath the stars. She felt safe in his arms; she felt loved and desired. Kaylee uttered the words, quickly, cleanly, before she let the truth stop her and bid her stay.

"I want to leave, Jack, and I need to live my life as Kaylee. I need to be that person inside and out. Somewhere far from here, to college. You know I can't be with you." She met his eyes then. "Help me become someone else and then let me go to live my life."

Her stomach twisted even as she kept her face emotionless. He stared back at her, devastated by her words, before he nodded and turned on his heel, disappearing out the front door, and on out of her sight.

Your New Life

The hotel room had a view of the tallest, sleek downtown skyscrapers in Atlanta, but at the moment, neither of them had any interest. The moment the door had clicked shut, Kaylee had pressed her body against his, on her tiptoes, capturing his mouth in hers. Jack had barely had time to set the bag down. Her lips opened to his, their tongues intertwining. He backed up towards the bed, her body in lockstep with his, until he felt the end of the bed meet the backs of his legs. He fell backward, his feet on the floor, his back sinking into the soft mattress.

They had held off for weeks, Kaylee worried any strenuous activity would injure the stab wound. And he had wanted her, been starved for her, even as they lay spooned in bed together each night.

But today, well, today was different. Today was their last day together.

He had agreed to her wishes, even as every part of him fought the reality. He had gotten a new identity, one that would hold up to just about any scrutiny. She had cut her hair, and Azule had taken her to have it styled, permed, and colored. The colored eye contacts made her eyes a forest green. It was a stunning change, the green eyes and a curly mop of red. She had looked different enough that he had done a double-take, shocked at the transformation. He could still see the girl he had fallen for, especially when she smiled at him, and for a desperate moment hoped that her new look would be enough, even as he knew it wouldn't. He didn't want to lose her, but they were all in danger if she stayed.

She straddled him on the bed, pulling her blouse off in one swift motion and tossing it aside. She leaned down and kissed him again, her fingers busy on the buttons of his shirt, her nails brushing against his now-bare skin as she pushed aside the fabric and skimmed them gently over the scar on his abdomen. It twinged slightly. Another few weeks' recovery and he would be fine, but the scar was still angry and red. It would fade in time. He wasn't so sure if the scar forming on his heart would fade at all.

"Kaylee..."

"Shh, no talking." She unbuckled his belt, and in a few efficient movements had his pants down at his ankles. He kicked them off, along with his linen and leather boat shoes, and groaned as she settled down between his legs and took him in her mouth, her mouth and tongue working up and down his shaft, licking, sucking. Her breath was warm, and it tickled his hairs. He closed his eyes, overwhelmed by the sensation of her touch, awash in a sea of sensation as Kaylee took more of him into her mouth, enveloping him in ecstasy.

When she released him, and wiggled out of her skirt and panties, he was half out of his mind. He tried to sit up, but Kaylee pushed him back on the bed. "Uh uh, you are staying put." Instead, she straddled his waist once more while he rubbed the tip of one nipple until it was hard and tight. She slowly lowered herself onto him and closed her eyes in pleasure as she slid up and down, pulling him deep into her silken depths, then nearly releasing him, before doing it again, and again, and again.

Jack wanted to lose himself in her. He wanted the moment to last for a decade, a century, and for this to not be the last time, but the first. He groaned in pleasure as she slid up and down, the tempo increasing gently, his hands coming to rest on her hips as he drew her up and then back down, burying himself deep inside of her only to come away again, and then return.

He didn't want to be here. Jack wished he could disappear with her. He wanted to take her to Lake Tahoe, to his family's villa in the south of France. He wanted to fuck her in the moonlight high in the treehouse and never think of the people who had tried to kill her, or him, again.

Instead, he let the momentum build. Guiding her hips up and down, his fingers digging into her buttocks as they both drew close, a crescendo of heat, sensation, and light exploded as first Kaylee, and then he exploded into orgasm. They fell together, Jack still inside her, and rolled to their sides as the last shudders racked them both.

Jack wrapped his arms around her. Perhaps if he held her, just like this, she would see how much he needed her to stay, how much she needed him. Their breaths still came fast, and Jack could feel his heart ache in his chest. It wasn't just the lovemaking; it was the dread of having to say goodbye.

She had stayed with him for all of July and most of August. No one had bothered them, no other assassins had attempted to finish what the lone woman had started, and Jack had felt hope. Irrational and hopeless as it was, he had hoped that whoever was trying to kill her had finally given up. That they had a future together.

She was everything he wanted, everything he never knew he needed, and his heart ached at the thought of losing her even as he struggled to convince her to stay.

They had spent the last six weeks working out the details of her new identity. She was an orphan, raised in foster care after her parents died in a car crash when she was fifteen. With no family, she had qualified for a program that would pay for her room, board, and tuition entirely. In reality, the funds had come from Jack, an insignificant amount of funds to him, one that Kaylee had accepted gratefully.

Heir to a multi-million-dollar company. If she showed her face, she risked being arrested, charged, and then held in custody until her trial. The chances of her surviving jail and the murderous reach of the Indalo was small, as Azule had so astutely pointed out.

Which put them here, in this hotel room, the day before Orientation at Georgia Tech.

They lay there in silence, eyes closed, and Jack could hear the sounds of the city in the streets below them.

It was now or never.

"Kaylee," Jack breathed, his heart feeling as if it was breaking apart in his chest, "Please stay."

She sighed, long, sad. "I can't, Jack. I just, I *can't.*" She couldn't look at him, or wouldn't. The end was the same.

He tried again. "Adrienne..."

Tears gathered in her eyes. "No. Adrienne is dead. She died with her mom, with her dad and Rainier and Lincoln. Everything she had, everything she was, she's gone." She looked down at her hands captured in his. "Besides, I'll always be Kaylee to you. I like Kaylee."

She changed the subject. "Mal's ready for his first tournament. I know he can beat some top Scrabble players; he's that good."

Jack wanted to argue with her, tell her that Mal would suffer with her gone, but he couldn't summon the words. They had hashed it out, over and over, in the past five weeks until there had been no more arguments he could use, nothing more he could say.

"Will you promise to sign him up for the tournament in Mendocino? Please?"

Jack nodded, not trusting his voice.

"Good." Kaylee rested her head on his chest, the red curls sprawled along her cheek. It was a good look, to be sure. No one would look twice at her. Well, they'd look twice, she was drop-dead gorgeous, but they wouldn't see Adrienne Cenac. They would see Kaylee. She would be safe, and she would remain that way if he kept his distance. But God, how he hated the idea. She belonged in his arms, in his life, and in his bed.

"Jack?"

"Yes?"

"I'm going to miss you. More than you know."

"You better." She gave a soft laugh in response and nestled closer.

The night before had been nothing but tossing and turning all night. And now, in the warmth of the late morning, with the sun's rays stealing in and warming the bed, Jack felt his eyes slip closed. He had everything he needed in his arms and he fell into a deep, untroubled sleep.

Kaylee's kiss woke him with a start. The light in the room had changed, moved, and he could see that the sun was lower in the sky than it had been. Her curls framed her face and, in the shadows, he could see the glimmer of tears in her eyes.

Jack realized she was dressed. Her blouse done up, her flared short skirt in place, and from the dampness of her curls, he would guess she had showered as well. All while he had slept like a stone, squandering these last precious hours.

"You looked so peaceful," she said, brushing her hand gently along his cheek. "I didn't want to wake you."

He hadn't slept well for days, weeks, really. The thought of her leaving had put everything he had dreamed of doing with her on hold. Barcelona, the apartment in New York, so many things. Instead, they had hunkered down, guards at the gates, and she had practiced shaking hands with Mal each morning, afternoon, and evening among endless games of Scrabble. In between those activities had been the selecting of the perfect college, his calling in a favor through his father's friend, Dean Mahoney, to get her a placement at Georgia Tech when their roster was already at capacity. Kaylee had chosen a major in business management and a minor in architecture.

The change in her appearance had been relatively simple. The haircut, perm, and color had changed the whole look of her face, as had the contacts. She wasn't Adrienne Cenac. Not any longer. And as

Kaylee said, that girl was dead, along with the rest of her family. The birth certificate of a stillborn baby girl by the last name of Stromm and born just three months after Kaylee was, that had been the last piece of her new identity.

It was Azule's and Teeny's connections that had made it happen, the combined efforts of artistry and fraud that would hold up to most inspections, especially once she had her degrees to back her up.

"Come on, get dressed. I found a place that reminds me of home. They have a fusion of Louisiana, Central Mexico, and Belize cuisine. I haven't had red snapper in months." Her smile faltered for a moment, and Jack wondered if she was remembering a meal out with her family or friends. Just a few months ago, her life had been relatively simple, pleasant, and then everything had come apart.

"You want to go out?" He sat up and reached for his shirt and slowly drew it onto his body. "I'd love to eat in."

"It's on the way to the airport. You have that meeting tomorrow. Az mentioned it as we were leaving."

He didn't give a damn about the meeting, not if it meant he had to leave tonight.

I don't want to leave her here. Not for a minute, not for a day, and sure as hell not forever.

He dressed in silence and they stepped out into the fading light of the day. They ate dinner at Lemon Butter Seafood, which sound more like a menu item than the name of a restaurant. It was surprisingly good.

"I'll definitely need to come back here," Kaylee said, devouring her red snapper as Jack picked at his whiting fillet. She kept up a cheery patter of commentary, partly out of nervousness, partly out of an attempt to sound happy. Having spent the last two months in her company, he knew her better than that. She was miserable and anxious, just as much as he was.

The cab waited behind them as they said their goodbyes. The tears pooled in her eyes, then slid down her cheeks. "I'll miss you, Jack, more than I can say."

"If you need anything," he said in return, and she nodded. "And I promise to take Mal to the Scrabble tournament."

She smiled through her tears. "I'll hold you to that, Jack Benton. I expect to see Malcolm Benton in a YouTube video by the end of the year."

They both laughed then, and she stood on her tiptoes to kiss him once more. The softness of her lips against his made his body flutter with desire and ache with loneliness, even with her standing there before him.

She walked away then and did not look back. Jack stood and watched her go, ignoring the pilot until the cab had disappeared into the evening traffic, its headlights one of dozens of sets in the dark evening.

Jack sat down on the plane and reached into his bag for his phone. He had kept it shut off all day. Jack didn't want to talk to anyone, to worry about any problems or issues. He just wanted to spend the little time he had left with Kaylee. He noticed several pages folded neatly sitting next to it in the deep pocket. As he drew it out of the bag, he caught a whiff of Kaylee's perfume. A rich scent of Hermes Jour d'Hermes suffused the papers. He unfolded them and saw that they were from the hotel, the Crowne Plaza emblazoned along the top of each page, covered in Kaylee's looping script.

The pretty flight attendant brought him a scotch on the rocks and the small, private jet took off, pointing back west towards home. He wouldn't arrive home until past midnight. He paused, thought of how her skin had felt in his hands, her soft heat, how he had felt her come seconds before his own orgasm.

I could tell the pilot to turn around right now. I don't want to read this goodbye letter she has written. I don't want this to be a goodbye.

He willed the urge away and read.

Dearest Jack-

You look so peaceful there on the bed, as if all of your cares have slipped away. I've watched you sleep before; you know. Don't tell me I'm creepy, please, because I couldn't help it. You sleep HARD as if it is painful. Perhaps it is. Perhaps, like me, you think of everyone you have lost and they haunt your dreams like they do mine. But today, lying there, you are different, contented, peaceful.

I wish we could have that. But right now, we can't. We honestly cannot.

God, that hurts to even write that. Because, even though we have known each other such a short time, I am in love with you. I dare not say it out loud, or to your face, so instead, I put it here on paper, where you will find it later after we have said our goodbyes.

Thank you for all that you have done for me. I have a chance at a normal life. It isn't one I planned for, and it isn't one I expected or was raised for, but I can see it, just over the horizon, waiting for me. I want to lose myself in a lecture hall, go to parties, maybe join a sorority. I want to be normal, if only for just a little while.

I think you can understand that, or at least accept it.

I think too that you and me, we aren't over. For now, we go our separate ways and I hope that the time will come when it is safe for us to be together again. Jack, I want so much for my life, for yours, even for Mal's. I want to see his name up there in the rolls of champions, and I hope to see us all happy and safe and someday...someday...I want to kiss you again.

I love you, Jack. No matter what comes to pass in the years to come, I hope you remember that.

-K.-

The Situation at Hand

Five years later...

It had been five days of sheer hell since Kaylee's phone call. Whatever he had hoped to accomplish that week, it was derailed by thoughts of Kaylee. Her voice, her face, the memory of her skin against his – it consumed his waking hours and filled his dreams at night.

The updates from Shane had done little to distract him, and the situation had quickly unfolded there in Kansas City—paid assassins with an all too familiar tattoo had raised his hackles. Kaylee had gone radio silent as well, and he couldn't help wondering if she was okay.

It was mid-morning on Friday when he marched into Azule's office.

"Az, I need a flight to Kansas City, please."

Azule lifted one eyebrow and set her coffee down slowly. "I'm guessing you need it for today?"

"Yes."

A smile escaped her then. "Give me a few minutes and I'll get the private jet." She turned away, phone at her ear, long fingernails tapping away at her computer. Jack walked into the atrium, hoping the sounds of the waterfall would ease his angst. He had felt on edge since Kaylee's phone call on Monday, and getting an earful of one of his best employees boning a client, no matter how hot she was, had not helped. Whatever was going on with Shane, Jack was better off dealing with it in person.

He stared at the koi as they moved about, their round mouths sucking at the surface, searching for treats. Every night since her phone call, he had dreamed of her. They had been increasingly upsetting. First her kissing another man as he walked in, another of her telling him they couldn't be together, and the most recent ones had included her running, shot and hurt.

I should have flown out on Monday. I could have dealt with this business with her friend myself, or gotten Jesse involved.

Jesse had been on vacation through Wednesday, though, and Jack had been sure Shane could handle it. Shane had never gotten involved with a client. And Jack was mad as hell at this turn of events. But then again, he'd seen a picture of the young woman, Lila. An attractive girl. But Jack's mind was filled with thoughts of Kaylee. Her soft, Southern drawl, her honey-brown hair, and...

"I have you leaving on a flight at one, Jack." Azule's voice behind him broke his reverie, and he turned to face her. His assistant was grinning smugly at him.

"You look like a cat that just ate the canary, Az," he commented as he took the Post-it note she held out to him.

"I've been waiting all week to book that flight for you, Boss."

"Have you now?" Damn Az and her Cheshire cat smile.

Azule snorted. "Hell, yes. I saw it in your face the minute you heard her voice. Give her a hug from me, will you?" She winked then, a playful smile appearing on her face. "Or bring her back so I can hug her myself."

Jack had been telling himself all morning that he needed to go to Kansas City to deal with the debacle of the shootout at One Kansas City Place and the shortcomings of his employee, but it had been a lie. He could see that now, staring at Azule's smug, pleased look. He was going there for Kaylee. And if he had any sense at all, hell, if she still loved him, then he wouldn't come back until he had her in his arms. He went inside to pack a bag and left a note for Malcolm.

The plane landed after sundown near downtown Kansas City. As it did, his phone vibrated, and he saw he had a message. He read it and then placed a call to Azule as the plane taxied over to the low-slung building next to a busy freeway. "Az, could you please look up a Liam Sorenson? Looks like he might be here in KC." He waited patiently for her response before he thanked her and ended the call. It looked as if he would need to meet this kid while he was here. As the plane stopped and the outer door opened, his fingers flew across the tiny screen and he heard the email swoosh away.

Hours later, however, Jack faced a small army of police officers swarming the house on the hill. His client, Lila, was shivering under a blanket in the back of the ambulance. Ellis was now standing outside with the paramedics as they bandaged his arm.

"We will need to treat this at the hospital," the taller, heavier paramedic stated. "And we should probably get you checked out as well, Miss," he said, looking at Lila. "Your feet really took a beating."

Lila tucked her filthy, scratched feet under the blanket and replied, "I'm fine, really I am, but I'm not leaving Shane."

Shane stared at her and then laughed, startling the paramedic bandaging his arm. "Now you are following The Code?"

"Better late than never." That made him laugh even harder. She laughed too. Jack, however, did not.

Jack shot Shane a look. Between the butt dial that had caught Ellis in a more than compromising position with his client, and a shootout that had ended with a dead body in the basement of his property, Jack was less than pleased.

In the past six years, Shane Ellis had proven himself to be one of Jack's best bodyguards, despite his origins. Jack had worried that his lack of military training would be a problem, but Shane had handled himself well and become a valued member of Benton Security Services. At least, until he met Lila Benoit.

Shane reacted to Jack's look of disapproval, shook his head at the paramedic, and pulled away. "I'm fine, really. The bullet only grazed me."

A police officer walked over. "After they check you out at the hospital, Miss Benoit, we will need to speak to you down at the station."

Shane reached out with his undamaged hand and took hers, glancing at Jack as he did.

Jack interceded, "I understand that Rob Stone is heading the investigation into the shooting at Kurgen Real Estate. I believe the events of tonight are connected to that. I would request that you contact the detective and we will be happy to answer his questions after my employee and client are checked out at the hospital."

The ambulance was crowded, but the paramedics allowed Jack to accompany Shane and Lila to the hospital. The police officer followed behind in a patrol car. When they arrived at the hospital, however, Jack stepped forward and placed a hand on Lila's shoulder.

"Miss Benoit, if you please, they will get Mr. Ellis cleaned up with stitches, and you and I need to speak with the detective when he arrives." The sooner he spoke with the client, the sooner he could track down Kaylee. Jack looked around the large waiting area and found a corner that was empty of others and steered her towards it. The police officer followed, sitting across from them, his eyes watchful as he surveyed the room. His phone rang then, and he stood up and walked away to answer it.

"Can I get you some coffee or tea, Miss Benoit?" Jack asked. Lila was still shivering. The hospital staff had found her a pair of warm hospital socks once they had checked out her feet and pronounced them bruised but otherwise undamaged.

She shook her head. "I'm not cold...it's nerves, I guess."

"Perfectly understandable." He regarded her for a moment, saying nothing.

The silence stretched before them.

Lila finally asked, "So, you know Kaylee?"

"I do."

"How?"

He smiled. "That's not my story to tell, Miss Benoit."

Lila grimaced. "Right."

The police officer returned from his phone call. "Miss Benoit, I'm going to have to ask you to return with me to the station. You will speak with Detective Peisker, and he will take your statement on tonight's events."

"I thought I was going to be speaking to Detective Stone," she said and turned to Jack. "Isn't that the detective who was assigned to the shooting at Kurgen?"

Jack frowned, but before he could speak, the officer answered. "Yes, ma'am, he was, but Detective Peisker is also working that case."

Jack stood up. "Did you say was, Officer, as in, no longer is?"

The officer looked grim. "I'm really not at liberty to say, Mr. Benton, but I must insist that we go to the station directly. If you wish to accompany Miss Benoit, that is fine, but Peisker will question her at the station."

It was a brief ride to the station, and the officer ushered them both into the interrogation room.

Jack had a bad feeling about all of this. Lila Benoit not only needed his protection; she might need his legal services as well. He turned to Lila. "Miss Benoit, would you have a dollar that I might have?"

Lila blinked in surprise, then dug into her purse and handed him the only bill in her wallet, a ten-dollar bill.

"Thank you, Miss Benoit." Jack Benton smiled at her, neatly folded up the bill, and placed it in the breast pocket of his designer jacket just as a tall, heavyset man entered and closed the door.

"Miss Benoit, my apologies for keeping you waiting. I'm Detective Peisker."

Jack asked, "Where is Detective Stone?"

Peisker sighed. "Rob Stone has been murdered."

Lila gasped, her hand going to her mouth. "Oh my God."

Jack asked, "Is it possible it relates to your current case?"

"I do not know, Mr. Benton, but we are exploring all leads." He rubbed his eyes. "Rob and I worked together for nearly a decade. He was a fine man, a good partner, and a devoted father. The KCPD will not rest until we find out what happened to one of our own. Meanwhile, Miss Benoit, I would like to question you about the events that occurred this past Monday and tonight."

"Before I say anything, do you know if Detective Stone found the SD card?" Lila asked, her hands twisting. "The file that I saw, it was on an SD card and it was there in my laptop. I also copied it onto a flash drive for my boss, Mr. Endon."

Max shook his head. "I'm sorry, Miss Benoit, but there wasn't any SD card in your laptop."

"But..."

"And Mr. Endon handed over the flash drive. It was empty."

"That's," Lila said, "that's not possible."

"Mr. Endon stated that the flash drive was blank, and he did not know of any SD card. I'm sorry, Miss Benoit, but we can't find any trace of these suspicious files you believe you may have found."

Detective Peisker stared at Lila. "So, is there anything you aren't telling me? Anyone you might owe money to? Any crime you may have seen committed or," he paused before continuing, "possibly had a part in committing?"

Lila jumped to her feet. "What? You cannot seriously be blaming me for this! I was attacked, not once but three times! They have shot at me! That man I killed tonight; he was the one from the parking garage!" Lila shook, afraid.

Jack reached out and touched her shoulder gently.

Max gave a tired, half smile. "My apologies, Miss Benoit. These are questions I would ask of anyone in your situation. Now, if you could sit down..."

Lila did as the detective asked. Jack watched her as she closed her eyes and took two deep, slow breaths in and out.

Jack spoke up. "Miss Benoit has had some terrifying experiences this past week, Detective."

Max turned to him and frowned. "It is highly irregular to have you here, Mr. Benton. I understand you were communicating with my partner, Detective Stone, but I think it would be advisable for you to wait outside until I have spoken with Miss Benoit for a few minutes alone."

Jack nodded. "I understand how you might feel that way, but I'm afraid that you misunderstand the situation here. Miss Benoit is a client."

Max snapped. "Yes, Mr. Benton, I know she retained Benton Security Services for personal protection, although that worked so well that she had to kill the attacker herself."

Jack smiled. "Actually, Detective, she did not retain my security company's services; I provided those to her at no cost." He reached inside his coat pocket and set down a simple, yet elegant card onto the metal table. "I am an attorney. Lila is my client."

Lila's jaw dropped.

Max Peisker did not look pleased. "I see. Miss Benoit, do you wish for your legal counsel to stay here with you while we talk?"

Lila responded quickly, "Yes, thank you."

The detective grimaced and began his questioning. Jack shot down some of the more outrageous questions Peisker asked, while others he allowed Lila to answer. The hours ticked by as she recounted the incidents of the past week that had led to her shooting the dark-haired assassin that evening. By the second repetition, Lila appeared to be having difficulty stringing her words together. It was past midnight, and she hunched over, holding her head in her hands. Her skin was pale, and she looked exhausted.

"Detective, I must insist that we continue this line of questioning after my client has rested," Jack said, putting his hand once again upon her shoulder. "I am assuming she is free to go?"

"We have no proof of the existence of these suspicious files that Miss Benoit claims to have found, but I think that, until we have discussed this in its entirety, it would be best for her to remain in protective custody. Not in a jail cell," he clarified as he saw the look on Jack's face, "but under police protection."

"Fine," Jack said, "But I would like one of my men to be there as well."

"I'm afraid that won't be possible, Mr. Benton," Peisker said, shaking his head. "No civilians."

"Jesse Bardin is one of your own, Detective, a member of the KCPD who has worked part-time for me for the past two years."

Max gritted his teeth. "Fine, Mr. Benton, have it your way." He stood up. "I'll make the arrangements and we will pick this up again in the morning."

"Afternoon."

"What?"

Jack smiled. "I think that one in the afternoon will be early enough, considering it is already morning."

Detective Peisker glared at him and walked out of the room.

Jack chuckled to himself.

"Thank you, Mr. Benton," Lila said, standing up. "Have you had any word on Shane?"

"Yes, he's fine, and they released him from the hospital. I received a text from him an hour ago. And now, if you will excuse me, I need to contact Jesse and arrange for him to stay with you at the safe house. Frankly, he's the only member of the KCPD I trust with this right now. We will get you someplace safe, Miss Benoit. After you have had some time to rest, we will discuss what happens next. Sound good?"

Lila nodded, and Jack knocked on the door and waited until they opened it. It was late, far too late to see Kaylee now, but he had phone calls to make. Jesse, for one. And Azule, who had insisted on being updated as soon as possible. Despite the late hour, he knew she would wait to hear from him. He pulled out his phone and dialed.

There was no time for sleep. He had some research to do before meeting this Liam Sorenson later in the morning.

Where You Go, I Go

Jack's meeting with Liam, and subsequent discovery of the mistakenly saved file to Lila's personal Dropbox, had been the evidence they needed to hit the Indalo where it hurt. He stepped lighter, knowing that someone would pay for the attempt on Lila's life. With that business behind him, and the FBI taking Lila into witness protection, Jack was free to walk away, knowing that Kaylee's friend was safe.

He parked in front of the house on the narrow street. How often had he looked at this address on Google and thought of walking up and knocking on the door? More times than he cared to count.

There was a nip in the air, the temperature already plunging, the skies gray overhead. A winter storm was on the way, and Jack thought of his home in Lake Tahoe. How long had it been since he visited there? Too long. It had snowed there a few days ago, early for the season. He could picture it in his mind, though. The angular wood and glass house on the hill, framed by pine and aspen trees, the enormous fireplace glowing and warm. Every winter of his youth had been spent there—first frolicking in the snow building snowmen and sledding, then skiing, and finally snowboarding. The plane crash had ended that annual tradition. He wondered what Malcolm would think of the snow. Would he like it or stay curled up indoors playing Scrabble with anyone who was amenable?

She had said she wanted to live her life without fear. An impossibility, given what she knew, what she had learned. But he had honored it. He had paid for the best new identity money could buy.

He had made sure she had a full ride at Georgia Tech, and not called her, not once, just as she had asked.

But was she safe? Really? The Indalo weren't small. If they were, someone at Kurgen, which was clearly Indalo-controlled, would have recognized her as the heir to Cenac Shipping. That didn't mean she was safe here, though, even if Kurgen was shut down. And that file that Lila Benoit had found, and nearly paid for with her life, it had more than just real estate holdings. He would leave it to Liam and Teeny to dig deep into that file and find out more.

The thought of her living here, in this house, with no one to protect her, no one to keep her safe—it was one reason he was here, now. Jack rubbed his hand over his face. But the real reason was far simpler. He hadn't gotten over her. It had been over five years since he found her, soaking wet, half-conscious, on the side of the road. Women had come and gone since, and none of them had held a candle to her. Not a one of them had even come close.

He watched a pickup truck rattle down the road and stop late, nearly getting hit by oncoming traffic. A chorus of honks back and forth between the truck and a small commuter car issued forth.

What am I doing out here, anyway? Go knock on the damn door or drive back to the airport. One choice or the other, Benton.

He cracked the door open and slid out of his seat, his mind finally decided. The house was a unique mix of wood and limestone that was quite prevalent to the area. The yard was stark now, the green fading to brown, but he had seen it full of flowers in the Google photos, carefully tended and full of blooming bushes and flowers. The door was a heavy wood, studded with metal. It had a tiny glass window inset high up. He could imagine her on her tiptoes as she peered out. Below the window was an old-fashioned metal knocker, which he reached for now, letting it hit the strike plate twice before he released it. The house was well-built. He couldn't hear anything from inside, not even a whisper of a footstep, before the door opened.

She smiled up at him, and his heart thudded in his chest.

"Hi, Jack. I was wondering when you would get here." She opened the door further, and he stepped inside, casting a glance around. He had looked up pictures of the house on Trulia when it was first listed for sale. She had made some changes. The furniture, for one. A mix of antique and mid-century pieces that blended in perfectly with the warm hues of paint that she had chosen for the walls. Where the previous owners had painted everything, including the woodwork, a stark white, Kaylee had returned the house to its original wood tones and then combined it with soft greens and blues and blush reds, saving the more vibrant colors for the fabrics on the furniture.

The door closed softly behind him, along with several locks.

He turned to face her. She had cut her hair in a cute pixie cut. It was still red, although she had stopped using a perm and it was now straight. The contacts still made her eyes the same forest green. Other than that, she looked much the same as she had five years before. Just as beautiful as he remembered her.

"I wasn't sure if you would want to see me." The words practically stuck in his throat. What if he had made a mistake coming here? What if she was just being kind?

Her expression changed, softened, and she reached out a hand to touch his face. "I can't think of anyone I would rather see right now."

"Mal misses you."

The corners of her mouth quirked up. "I told you he was a champion. I watched the competition live; his letter combination of prurient was devastating with the triple word score...he was amazing!"

Jack grinned. "He was. The first thing he asked after he won was if you had seen it. I told him I was sure you had." His stomach was doing flips just standing in her house, staring down at her. "I missed you more than I can say."

Two steps. That was all it took. His arms slid around her, lifting her up, his mouth on hers. They didn't bother with words or explanations or questions. It was need, and desire, and love, and a wanting that had waited five years to be acknowledged. He kissed her, deep and hungry. She matched him in urgency. Her fingers busy at the buttons of his shirt, his hand cupping her luscious, toned rear in his hands, her legs wrapping around his waist as they toppled onto a long, velvet-covered tufted couch, his body sinking into the cushions as she straddled him. His shirt gaped open half out of his pants and he slid his hand up underneath her soft sweater to her soft, warm skin underneath.

She pulled her mouth from his and ran kisses along his jaw, to his ear, and then pulled his earlobe in her mouth and nibbled it gently. His hands slipped down, grabbed the bottom edges of her sweater, and slipped it off of her, capturing her lips with his again, his tongue probing, teasing.

He slipped the yoga pants off of her ass and edged them down off one leg, then the other as Kaylee pulled the tails of his shirt out of his pants and undid the last two buttons. Her hands didn't stop there. They glided over his bulging cock and made quick work of his belt and the button and zipper on his pants. He pulled away, stood up, and slipped out of his loafers and pants. Her gaze traveled down to his socks and giggled as he struggled to yank them off. He stared at her lying there, wearing only a silky bra and panties, hair mussed and arrayed on the velvet cushions, waiting for him to return to her. Her eyes had returned to his boxer briefs and the beast that had woken inside. She wasn't an inexperienced teenaged girl any longer, barely eighteen and a virgin. It relieved him. In the months and years after she had left, he had wondered if sleeping with her had been a mistake. If she had regretted having him as her first.

His dick throbbed, almost questioning, as he stood there, watching her, watching him. She smiled then and ran her hands down her sides slowly. One stopped at a breast, the other made its way to between her legs. Her eyes closed for a moment; a delicate tongue licked at the corner of her lips. His dick throbbed again, no longer questioning. He hooked the edges of his briefs, slid them down, and released it.

Kaylee smiled, her eyes half-lidded with pleasure as he bent down and slid the satin and lace aside, settling his mouth on her breast, feeling it harden in his mouth as he sucked, licked, and nibbled it. Each time he did, she gasped in delight. One delicate hand stroked him, keeping him hard as she writhed on the sofa beneath him. He tugged at the panties, pulling them down her legs and tossing them away before he parted her legs and pushed his way into her.

Kaylee moaned his name as he pulled out and thrust in again, his mouth on her left nipple. She felt so good, he was seeing stars. She grabbed his arm, sat up, and twisted her body until he was off balance and collapsed on the couch. Kaylee straddled him then, lifting herself up and onto him, rocking as she worked her way up and down, up and down. The sight of her, her hair falling forward, her bra straps having slid down on her arms and her nipples erect, hard where they had escaped the thin, silky fabric, her mouth open in a round 'o' of ecstasy as he watched her climax. Felt her climax. He bucked his hips, driving deeper into her, and came inside of her, shouting her name.

Her breaths were coming in soft pants, her hands on each side of his face, fingers stroking, and she pulled away long enough to whisper, "I never should have left you."

He answered in a matching whisper, "I never should have let you go."

Later, hours after the sun had slipped out of sight and they had moved up to her bedroom, tastefully decorated with rich colors, he lay in her bed and looked around. It occurred to him only then that she might be involved with someone. Maybe even dating, getting serious, and here he had just waltzed back into her life.

Kaylee caught his gaze. "There's been no one, really. A couple of flings, here and there, guys who wanted to stick around, take it further, but I..." She spread her hands; her eyes focused on his. "I guess it always came back to you."

He gritted his teeth at the thought of any other man getting close, kissing her, maybe even fucking her in this very bed. Without realizing he was doing it, he growled, and she laughed and kissed him.

"Don't be jealous, Jack. You'll get wrinkles if you keep frowning like that."

He kissed her back, harder than he intended, and she responded, her mouth hungry against his. But the nasty business at hand, the reason he was here in the first place, brought him back to the present.

"They call themselves the Indalo," he said, pulling back from her and reaching for his pants pocket, where a card with the image of a stick man with the heavens above was hand-drawn.

"I've had Teeny working on it, and I just hired a kid whose hacking skills are going to get us deep into the heart of this. They are everywhere. They use large firms, like Kurgen Real Estate, to engage in money laundering, or Cenac Shipping for their illegal dumping and government-level bribery schemes."

Kaylee sucked in a breath, her body tensing.

"They are here in Kansas City, Louisiana, Central America, Los Angeles, key locations throughout the world. Nowhere is safe, and that's why we need to stick together." He threaded his fingers through her hair. "You will be safe by my side. One way or the other, we can bring them down, but if you stay here, then so will I. Because the thought of you alone...it would kill me if something happened to you, Kaylee."

He reached into his other pants pocket and pulled out the ragged remains of her note, the one she had written in Atlanta and secreted into his bag to read after they parted ways.

"If you still feel this way about me, Kaylee, then come with me, or let me stay here with you. I've been in love with you since the moment I found you there on the side of the road in the rain and no one, *no one*, has ever come close to possessing my heart the way you do."

Her eyes glistened with unshed tears and she nodded before her mouth met his and she pulled him over her. Kaylee's legs wrapped around him and he slid inside of her, marveling at how her body and his felt so right together. Her hips rose to meet his as he slid in and out of her warm depths, her moans coming quicker while her body writhed beneath his. He wanted all of her, every bit of her body, her heart, her mind. As he came inside of her, her name a shout, he knew he would never leave her side again.

Calling All Hunters

Z ella Dean's phone rang. She stared at the caller ID. She was busy. It could go to voicemail. After four rings it stopped, then began again.

Damn it.

She wiped the blood off of her hands and stabbed the green button. "What?"

"Am I interrupting?" Delta's voice always made her think of velvet wrapped in steel.

"I was just finishing up," Zella answered. She looked around. With this amount of blood, she'd be here for hours cleaning it all up. Her orders were to make him disappear, but the stupid fuck had looked at her tits, and really, that was all it took.

"I wanted you to know that the mark who killed Nyra has resurfaced."

Zella stilled, her skin tightening, her teeth gritting together.

"Would you like for me to send you that information?" Delta asked after a moment of silence. "Or, I could..."

"I'll take it," Zella answered, her words clipped, fury surging through her. Finally, she would learn who had dared to kill her sister.

"Excellent. I'll have it sent to the usual drop site." Delta sounded pleased. "Oh, and Zella? Make them suffer. Your sister was unique, talented, and, well, we miss her. Even now."

Zella ended the call. Triumph at finally being allowed her revenge flowed through her. She smiled, then got back to work on the body on the floor in front of her. She was going to make them pay in ways they couldn't imagine, not in their worst nightmares.

Author Note

Thank you for reading *Smoke and Steel*. I hope you enjoyed every last bit of it! As you may already know, *Smoke and Steel* is the second book in the *Benton Security Services* series. Next up will be *Broken Code*, and it is not to be missed, because Lila and Shane from *Hired Gun* will be coming back for more danger, and hot, hot, sexy time!

If you enjoyed reading *Smoke and Steel*, I would like to ask two things from you:

#1 – Post a review on your favorite bookselling platform and/or Goodreads. Let folks know what you thought of the book. Social proof, reviews, they are the life blood of success for an author. Just as importantly, a great review can really make my day!

#2 – Tell others about it. Tell your gal pals, your archenemies and co-workers, and anyone else you think could use a nice, steamy diversion from daily humdrum life.

I don't make a lot at writing. Honestly, at this point it still doesn't pay for the costs incurred in creating book covers and proofreading services, but I *know* that if enough people read my books and enjoy them, that will change. I hope you will like my work enough to help me with getting the word out.

I write cross-genre, so if you enjoy dystopian, sci-fi, and more, be sure to check out my website at: https://www.christineshuck.com/ and sign up for email notifications and the monthly newsletter. I hope to see you there!

About the Author

Fueled by homemade coffee ice cream, a lifelong love of words, and armed with strong female (and male) characters I cross genres like the Ghostbusters crossed the streams in pursuit of the question.

"What is the question?" you ask.

The question is simple. It asks, "What would you do, if..."

What would you do if you were fifteen years old and the world as you knew it fell apart? Would you run? Would you fight? Would you survive? – Meet Jess and her brother Chris in *War's End*[1].

What would you do if you had a chance to live your life over? Not just once, but twice? – Meet Dean Edmonds in *Fate's Highway*[2].

What would you do if everyone you loved was lost to a terrible virus and you faced the real possibility of the extinction of the human race in the dark void of space? – Meet Daniel Medry in *G581: The Departure*[3]

What would you do if hitmen were after you and you had no idea why? – Meet Lila and Shane in *Hired Gun*[4]

If I don't keep you turning pages late into the night, desperate to know what happens next, then I have failed at my job. I'm a Taurus and born in Missouri. That makes me bull-headed and stubborn to boot. I don't believe in failure or mistakes, only learning

---

1.   https://books2read.com/u/bwYNpY

2.   https://books2read.com/u/bPJG5Y

3.   https://books2read.com/u/4jDgPl

4.   https://books2read.com/u/bP0dOj

opportunities and clever conversation. There's not much I won't do to make you burn the midnight oil reading my words while you suffer sleep-deprivation the following day. It's my secret superpower.

Born in flyover country, I've also lived in Arizona and northern California. I am an eclectic mix of snark and oddball humor. My colorful metaphors would make a fishwife blush. I'm an incompetent gardener, a dreamer and doer, in love with old houses and shooting pool, and chief organizer of all thing's household and financial. Feed me tiramisu and I'm yours forever.

Follow me, find my books, and more by going to:
https://linktr.ee/christinedshuck

All Published Works

Christine writes cross-genre and her books can be found in e-book and in paperback through most book distributors.

<u>Non-Fiction</u>:

Get Organized, Stay Organized

The War on Drugs: An Old Wives Tale

<u>Fiction Series</u>:

<u>WAR'S END</u>

    The Storm

    A Brave New World

    Tales of the Collapse

<u>Gliese 581g</u>

    G581: The Departure

    G581: Mars

    G581: Earth (Late Summer 2021)

    G581: Zarmina's World (Spring 2022)

<u>Chronicles of Liv Rowan</u>

    Fate's Highway a.k.a. Schicksal Turnpike

<u>Benton Security Services</u>

    Hired Gun

    Smoke and Steel

    Broken Code (Fall 2021)

<u>Children of Ruin</u>

    Winter's Child (December 2021)

CPSIA information can be obtained
at www.ICGtesting.com
Printed in the USA
LVHW080022010421
683081LV00002B/241

9 781955 150026